D0012549

The Devil's Apocrypha

The Devil's Apocrypha

There are two sides to every story

John A. De Vito

Writers Club Press
New York Lincoln Shanghai

The Devil's Apocrypha
There are two sides to every story

All Rights Reserved © 2002 by John A. De Vito

No part of this book may be reproduced or transmitted in any form or by any means, graphic, electronic, or mechanical, including photocopying, recording, taping, or by any information storage retrieval system, without the written permission of the publisher.

Writers Club Press
an imprint of iUniverse, Inc.

For information address:
iUniverse, Inc.
2021 Pine Lake Road, Suite 100
Lincoln, NE 68512
www.iuniverse.com

Cover photo © Kunst Historisches Museum, Wien
Cover design by Chris Nelson

ISBN: 0-595-25070-X (pbk)
ISBN: 0-595-65021-X (cloth)

Printed in the United States of America

Thou shalt fear the LORD thy God, and serve him, and shalt swear by his name.

—Deuteronomy 6:13

Contents

ℱOREWORD

The story you are about to read is not my own. It is translated from a manuscript that is over a hundred years old, by a man who was murdered for seeking out the truth. You've never read anything like it. Ever. I promise you.

The true author explains how this story came about, so I won't add anything to what he has to say. There's no need. But before you begin reading, there are some things you should know. Particularly, how I came about the document and what I know about the author.

I was born in the United States, the first in my family to be born outside of Italy. We trace our roots back to the centurions of early Rome. Until the turn of the century, we were rather wealthy. We owned tracts of land so large that they encompassed whole mountains.

But we lost all of it.

My great-grandfather was a man of principle. Too bad he was an idiot as well. He lost the entire family fortune in a legal battle with a neighbor. He won the lawsuit, but it cost him everything. Unfortunately for my great-grandfather, all his money was tied up in real estate. He had to sell off his property well below market value to pay the legal fees.

Guess who bought up the land? The very guy being sued, through a third party. Smart guy. I guess it pays to have cash in the bank.

When I was thirty, my wife and I decided to visit my family in Italy. I won't go into all the details. What matters are the few hours I spent visiting with my Uncle Luigi. He lived in a beautiful old stone house. It was on the only piece of property that my great-grandfather wasn't forced to sell. My uncle told me that the house was built by our ancestors over two hundred years ago.

I walked around on my own a bit, soaking up the history, imagining what the first De Vito's who lived there were like. I went through every inch of the house. Eventually, I found my way to the basement. It was as incredible as the rest of the place. Every wall was lined with rough-cut stone, held together with decaying mortar. Primitive definitely, but it was a foundation that had lasted many, many years.

One small section of the wall looked like it was about to cave in. The mortar had given way and the lack of cohesion created a concave depression. I pushed against the center stone. It was loose. I began to play with it a bit, rocking it slightly back and forth. That's when the whole thing fell in. I was horrified. The house had been standing for hundreds of years and I broke it.

I didn't want my uncle to see the hole I had caused. It was about two feet square, so there was little hope that it would go unnoticed. I lit my lighter and stuck it in the hole, hoping to find the rocks that fell in. What I saw was a small cubicle dug into the wall. The stones were all there.

I also saw a box half lost in decay.

As carefully as I could, I removed the stones and took out the box. I put the rocks back into the wall. It didn't look great, but the hole was sealed. I picked up the box. I'm no expert, but I think it was made of oak. A small black metal lock secured the lid. The wood was soft, covered with mold, and crumbling. It was beautifully painted and carved once, that much I could still tell.

I grabbed the lock and gave a tug. The nails that secured the latch to the wood pulled out with no effort.

Inside was a great stack of parchment that looked like it was a hundred years old if it was a day. It smelled of mold. The paper was delicate, but able to be handled. Every page was covered in gibberish. None of it seemed to make any sense.

I brought it to my uncle. He looked at the first page, but could make no sense of it. I asked him if I could have it. He smiled and told me to take it if I wanted it. He said he had a whole lot of junk throughout the house. If I was willing to take it away, he said I could have all of it. At least the old man still had a sense of humor.

The box was garbage, and we threw that out. He gave me a large manila envelope and I put the manuscript in that.

By the time we got back to the states, the papers had begun to dry. It made them brittle. I figured it would probably be a good idea to not handle them too much, so I photocopied all of them.

A good thing I did. Shortly after, they dried out all together and disintegrated when I picked them up. I was disappointed. I wanted to preserve the originals. They were a link to my past and I was sorry to lose them. At least I still had the copies. So I put them away and didn't look at them for nearly five years.

One day, I had a friend over and we were talking about our travels. I told him of the manuscript and the copies I still had. He asked to see them. We had moved twice since our visit to Italy, and I had no idea where the papers were. In the next few days, I looked everywhere. I had no luck at all. But a week later my wife found them. She was going through some unpacked boxes; I forget what she was looking for. But when I got home, she handed me the envelope.

I showed it to my friend the next time he came around. He looked at the first page and recognized some words as German, pointed out a few in English. I looked more closely and noticed some Italian words as well. It looked like whoever wrote the manuscript knew quite a few languages, mixing all the words together as he wrote.

My friend and I agreed: the author was either a genius or a madman. Probably both. Regardless, whatever the document was, it wasn't gibberish. I typed up the first page of the manuscript. Most of it, anyway. Some of the words weren't written in any alphabet I could recognize. I posted it to a message board on the internet.

It worked. A lot of people helped translate bits and pieces. I put them together. It started to make sense. I started to show the paper to everyone I knew. Eventually, someone identified the alphabets I couldn't recognize as Greek and Hebrew.

It turned out that the manuscript was written in six different languages: English, Italian, German, Greek, Latin and Hebrew. This guy was a genius. And, from the emerging content, I was sure that he was crazy as well.

The story that was being revealed was an alternate account of some biblical tales. They were very shocking and made me feel strangely uncomfortable.

As the translations uncovered more of the text, the story became more and more eerie. Some of my friends became fascinated by it; some wanted nothing more to do with it or me. I couldn't blame them. I couldn't shake the feeling that what I was doing was wrong, that I would be punished for it. It scared me. I can't explain it better than that.

The more I translated and researched, however, the more compelling the story became. It started coming together. It started making more sense. It began filling in holes and answering questions that my catholic upbringing couldn't explain.

The strangest thing was that for a manuscript of its apparent age, it seemed to include modern scientific references. Not in contemporary terms, to be sure. But there seemed to be references regarding quantum physics, bioengineering and other things that could not possibly have been known when this was written.

For instance, the Greek words 'swift ones' appear more than once. I was told that this is where we get the word 'tachyon' from. A tachyon is a theoretical subatomic particle with negative mass, believed to travel faster than the speed of light. If true, that means it travels backward in time. This fits in perfectly with the manuscript's discussions on the 'Cycle of Time'. But how could this appear in a document that seemed to have been written before I was born? Tachyon theory wasn't even discussed until the late 1960's!

Something else you may find strange about the manuscript is the way in which it was written. The idiom is very similar to that of the bible. I left it that way for two reasons. First, it seemed right to leave it as it was written. It sets a mood to the writing that I didn't want to lose. Secondly, I didn't want to change any of it. I didn't want the translation to be my interpretation of the text. I have made some conclusions based on what I've read, but I wanted everyone to make their own conclusions. If I changed the words to reflect what I thought they meant, then this manuscript would loose its authenticity. That is why I left the phase 'swift ones' as it was, rather than use the term 'tachyons'. What if I was wrong?

It's very important that you realize the words you read are the words as they were originally written. I have not changed them at all. You will notice that the idiom becomes more modern as the tales become more recent. I found this odd at first, then I realized that the language would change, if the tales originated from different eras.

When I told my father about the manuscript, he thought I was making it up and refused to discuss it. As a matter of fact, no one in my family was able to tell me anything. No one, that is, until I spoke to my grandfather about it.

I almost wish I didn't mention it.

My grandfather never spoke much, never got excited about anything. But when I mentioned the manuscript and what it was about, I thought he was going to have a heart attack. His face flushed bright red. He shook as he spoke, that's how upset he was. That's when he told me about the author. Then he told me never to speak of it again. I didn't.

My great grandfather, he said, had a brother. He was a priest once, but was thrown out of the church for being a disciple of the devil. He disappeared one day and didn't return for almost ten years. He came back with stories that blasphemed God and the saints. The family told him to keep quite, but he wouldn't.

So, of course, he soon became the most feared and despised man in the village. Everyone hated him. No one was surprised when one day he turned up dead. He had been hanged. The killer or killers were never found. The police hardly made a fuss. All in all, it sounded like everyone was rather happy that it happened. I think once you read this book, you'll understand why.

My grandfather told me that the village never looked at our family in the same way again. They thought that God made us loose our money as punishment for what the devil priest had done. It was one of the reasons our family eventually left Italy for a new life in America.

I tried to tell my grandfather what the manuscript said. I wanted him to know that his ancestor wasn't an evil man. That he left the church of his own accord and was not thrown out. That he was trying to save mankind. But he wouldn't listen. He did not want to hear it. He could not go through that shame again. That's why I waited until his death to have this printed.

I wish my grandfather could have learned the truth before he died. If he understood what his uncle was trying to do, I think he would have been very proud. But he didn't want to know the truth. He was too afraid. I don't blame him one bit. I'd be lying if I said I wasn't scared, too. I'd be lying if I didn't tell you there were times I wanted to throw the whole thing away. It scared me to read it. But believe it or not, I'm more afraid now. Because now I know the truth.

You're about to know the truth also. This is the most important thing I've ever read. Finishing my great uncle's work is the greatest thing I can ever hope to achieve.

So what do I do now? Do I preach? Do I risk getting killed to help out mankind? I don't think I can do that. I have kids that need their father. I don't know, maybe just getting this into your hands is enough. Hopefully, it will be.

I'll tell you this, though. I don't walk through life the way I used to. Now I watch everything. I listen to everything. I question all of it. I wait and hope that none of it happens in my lifetime. Unfortunately, if what I believe is true, it will happen in my lifetime—and in yours. I believe some of it has happened already; I believe some of it is happening now.

Yes, I think it's already started. I think the End Times are here.

INTRODUCTIONS

Here are the words, the true words as I have gathered them unto me. Doubt if you will, for proof lies in faith and not the tangible. Laugh if you must, but know too that a colder laughter resonates throughout the Cosmos.

For here lies the tale that withered my soul. A tale that mocks humanity and all humane.

You will feel the truth of it.

Though the mind may withdraw, that which resides at the heart's core will allow no denial. Listen or not, but in not listening, know that you are lost. I have been chosen from among the many to reveal this history. The story of the Fallen One.

Heed these words, for among the spoils of war, the greatest treasure is the authority to tell the battle's tale. And it is the tale of the victor. The truth, therefore, is thereby tainted. Yet after years, centuries, millennia, who may contradict that which has been most told?

So hear me, what you believe to be true is false. What you thought right, wrong. I and a chosen few have been granted the knowledge from the Bearer of Truth. A knowledge He has attempted to impart unto us since the dawn of our existence. For this, He has been always vilified. For this, we were bred to fear and hate Him, to denounce all His words as lies.

I tell you now, this is not so.

I, too, once believed as do you. I, too, once condemned and hated and feared He who lives in Darkness. For I bore the cross of gold and followed the Father of your Church as do you. But your Shepherd, this Savior, this Christ Child, is the true Father of Lies. For he is the one genuine evil, the one you call The Light.

I have since denounced him and all he deems holy. I have burned his Book of Lies and flung my crucifix into the deepest sea. The robes of my ignorance have been scattered as ashes in his house of deception.

But hear me. There is still time. We can free ourselves from the misery this false prophet has imposed. For I know the true history, the actual events.

I know them to be true for they are true. You will feel it in your heart. You will know it in your soul. And you must listen. For your sake. For the sake of your children. For the sake of the Race of Man.

He Who Was Cast Out is the Bearer of Knowledge. It has always been so. Does the Book of Lies not teach that it was He who brought us knowledge? That He advised the eating of the fruit and made the Woman know of her nakedness? And was she not naked? Did not the Powerful One then punish the Woman and all who came after for covering her nakedness and her shame?

And who among you can rightly say that truth is evil, that it is wrong? Why would a true God hide knowledge? Is it not written that the Almighty granted us the right of choice?

Yet how can one choose without proper knowledge? And as those who choose not to follow his path are cursed to suffer eternal damnation, to what purpose is this choice?

This is no free will. This is tyranny, born of childishness and pettiness. This is not the divine guidance of a god; it is the savage caprice of a madman. Free will is born of true choice, not of evil ultimatums.

Imagine this world had the Woman not partaken of the fruit. Picture us, a race of ignorant sheep whose sole purpose would be to praise the shepherd. All things needed for life supplied to us. A world without pain or tragedy, no need for creativity or intelligence. We'd need simply obey and do all we were told. For any other course would bring down terrible retribution.

Ask yourself then, what purpose would our ignorance serve? Why would a god want his subjects to be ignorant, weak, useless? But then, such a population would be easily manipulated and controlled, would it not?

So harken unto the Lord, all ye unbelievers, or be tossed into the eternal fire. And feel the searing of thy flesh ad infinitum.

Oh, is this burning of the "wicked"—innocent men, women and children—not a ghastly thing? One must wonder if this Father is not stoking his furnaces at this very moment, preparing to march the human race into his camps of horror. Laughing as screams of pain burst the throats of his poor, ill-choosing children.

But, alas, they had their chance. Did they not? I can see him now, hands held high as the flames rise and bring forth the smell of cooked flesh, intoning: "Burn, my children, burn."

For that is the legacy of those who dare to exercise the free will they were given. Or so we are led to believe. For I have been given the truth behind the lies of him you call the Father.

This Father would have you believe that a paradise was ours to lose. If only we had not eaten from that horrid tree. For that one small taste of knowledge he repaid us with disease, pain, hunger, brutality, mortality, and original sin.

A slight overreaction, perhaps?

But alas, we suffer for wanting what the serpent offered us. And was not the Almighty furious at the discovery? Considering his supposed omniscience, how is it he did not know all along? Would he not have known where the Woman was going, what she was going to do? Could he not have stopped her, admonished her? Told her of the repercussions for her and all her kind to come? Perhaps the mood did not strike him.

Oh, if only the Woman had not done this thing. Then our lives would have been perfect and painless. Yes, a world without misery. But also no sense of accomplishment, no ambition, no struggle. And neither love nor desire.

For does the Book of Lies not say that there must be a balance, a harmony amongst all things? No good without evil, no creation without destruction, no love without hate?

Eye for eye and tooth for tooth: there must be balance. No giving without taking and nothing taken without being given. For even in turning the other cheek we must suffer abuse yet give compassion.

We know these things. Without the ability to do for ourselves, to learn, to grow, what purpose would existence serve? Our spirit would wither and turn to dust. You call this paradise, this lost world of Eden? I tell you it is not. It is a living death, a perverse existence. Why would a God wish such a thing? What good a race with no purpose other than to praise his greatness?

Imagine: A life of utter subjugation and servitude. All for him who is the Shepherd. And we, a flock of worthless, miserable beings. Less than sheep. Less than alive, only existing at the mercy of superior force. An irony, is it not, that a shepherd's duty is to protect the herd until the day of slaughter?

I revile this image, as should you. We should demand more than this for ourselves and for our children. A life of slavery is a life of Hell, regardless of the master. I am worthy of more than such an Eden, and I wish it not.

For this Garden of God is damnation.

She who ate of the fruit deserves reverence, not condemnation. Never in all human history has there been an act that benefited the Race of Man more.

All my heart holds love for you, Woman of Knowledge. Praised be thy name.

And as with the Woman, my ignorance, too, was broken by the Gift of Knowledge. For, as She, I was visited by the Fallen Angel.

He came to me on a night as cold and dark as onyx. Alone was I, warm and sheltered by the methods of modern man against the elements. Deeply I slept in a slumber devoid of all dreams. There was not a sound, not a shape. Nothing from which to grasp identity. This I remember.

I remember, for that was when I felt His presence. I knew not who or what it was at first, to be sure. But I knew also that my call to consciousness was not due to any intervention of the natural.

By the fear bred into our race through countless millennia, I cowered as would an unborn child. I assumed the posture of pre-birth, attempting solace through my regression. I recall perfectly the deliberate way in which I assessed my appendages and drew them to me. I felt—I knew—that no tender, vital part should be left vulnerable or exposed.

Indeed, all flesh from lip to loin to leg contracted into itself as surely and swiftly as a small frightened animal would scurry to the security of its haven.

"I am Man," said I within myself, attempting to straighten from my infantile curl. Such primitive fear defiled the very foundation of reason from which I sprang. But the thought was overlaid—no, asphyxiated—by the true foundation. A much older bedrock fixed firmly in a primordial history long since forgotten.

The revelation was coincided by vision. A shimmer. A shimmer which was instantly replicated in the flesh of my spine and bowels and loins. It was then that my fear found release and pierced the night. But there was no one to hear or help.

Slowly, the apparition coalesced and drew form. The chamber was thrown into even deeper darkness as if the forming image was drawing light from the very air itself. An internal glow illuminated the growing form, but the brightness touched no surface.

The world had become a void, and I with it. I felt neither the bed nor my flesh upon it. My mind passed beyond terror to a place reserved for lunacy. I cowered within the safety of insanity.

And the growth completed. And by the light within its form I saw that it was an Angel.

But such an Angel!

Power radiated from the corporal form in waves that returned me to my mind. Through a clear emotional calm I viewed Him that was before me.

It was so for He wished it so.

A giant of a Being! Shining with inner strength, surrounded in a gleam of gold. As nude as the scheme of nature designed Him to be. Magnificent in His glory. Wings of white down fluttering gracefully with every slight motion. A face of tranquility and infinite wisdom.

But for the small shards of bone upon His brow, I would have thought it the Almighty himself.

"Know who I am and fear me not," spoke Satan unto me. The voice flowed silken with the wisdom of ages. It commanded. It consoled.

"I know you and I do not fear you," spoke I, amazed at the words that escaped the confines of my flesh. Amazed, for all my life I had been told that He was the bearer of all things evil.

"That is good," said He. "It is as it should be, for I mean to bestow neither harm nor ill will upon you."

And the truth of his words was there, engraved upon his visage. Upon his features and in his manner it was written. I felt it with a warmth and trueness within my heart and soul. He would never consider causing me injury. Indeed, the very thought would have repulsed Him. This I knew. I looked upon Him, and in looking saw a love tempered in the fires of infinity.

"You honor me," I stated. "But to what purpose? How may I serve one such as you, I who am mortal?" He might have asked anything of me in that moment. I knew that I would have done anything for Him to prove my love, my devotion. I would have died for Him.

"You need only to look, listen, and remember. Difficult it is for me to impart the knowledge I must. Then you must share these words with all others and make the seed take root. For if you cannot do this thing, then the Race of Man is forever doomed."

Such sadness in those eyes. The pain of untold millennia resided within those two bright orbs.

I wept for Him. I wept for His pain.

"Lord," I cried, "I am but one soul, and of no consequence in this world. How am I to do this? By what authority can I make myself heard?"

Sympathy molded his features then. "What I ask is no small thing, this I know. Your task is grave and difficult. You will not be alone in what you must do, however. You will do what you can do, I ask no more. But know, too, my messenger, that in this doing you will be cursed among all men. That your name shall be spoken in shadows and whispered in horror. And the best you can hope for is a slow, painful death."

I knew the truth of His tellings, and I wept. Not for myself, but for His pain. "Lord, the things that they say of you…"

"…are lies. Lies spawned of the true Horror. Do that which I ask of you, and learn from it. For therein you will find the reasons for the lies. So listen closely, for your task is this: there are three among men, three to whom I have entrusted my Gospel. Each carries within them a portion of the true past and future records—the tales of the Angelica and of the tribulations of Man. The intimacy which was necessary has broken their minds," He said. "It had to be done," He whispered, turning away. "For the benefit of all men."

And I remembered the stories of the saints of old. How they, too, died in madness. By fire and stone most of them fell. The price of divine confidence was high, indeed.

Again, His gaze returned to mine. "You must find these Three. Collect their tales and combine them. Validate their sacrifices. Bring to all the knowledge I have imparted."

"But what is this tale, Holy One?" said I. "And how shall I find these wise men?"

His gaze turned solemn. "The tale shall unfold as you find it. The Three you shall find if it is your wish to do so. Only doubt will keep you from them."

Doubt? How could one such as I doubt one such as He? Then as now, I knew that I would do his will.

His light began to grow dim, and upon His face emerged fatigue. "Long have We Below been unable to speak with mankind," He said wearily, "for such a communion would cause dementia. Only recently have We found a way to avert this madness. Yet it requires the greatest effort…and may be maintained for only a short while."

He looked upon me a final time. "It lies with you now, the fate of your Race. Do what you must do. All my faith goes with you," He said, as He faded to nothingness.

With this fading the night returned, in all its loneliness. In all its darkness. Once again, all had become mundane. And I asked myself, was it real? Could it have been a dream? For with the departure of the Fallen One did the wonderment depart. And all became as it once was.

Yet there was one exception: my soul burned as if on fire, burned with the light of the truth. The light of purpose.

And I knew it was no dream.

That night, in my revelation, I left all that I knew. I left in search of the Three.

In time, I found them all.

As to what led me to them, I cannot say. There is no explanation for it, not in our version of reality. Call it a sense of rightness; call it an intuition. Regardless, I knew when my path was a correct one and when it was not. There was a purpose to my step, a goal to my wandering. There were neither signs nor portents, and yet my wanderings were true to their intent.

I found myself traveling far over water and across foreign soil before I met the first, for the First of Three was cloistered deep within the hills of the Old World. Patiently I made my way between the ancient villages. Past the old battlements: past the Shoenburg and the Rheinstein. And finally my eyes rested upon the sight of the Rheinfels. A fortress of stone erected by men long since dead. A structure half lost in decay.

And I knew I had found the First, for I felt the energies of the wretched life within, hidden among the forbidden tunnels. I allowed my mind to guide me within the walls. It led me to a cobblestone path deep within rough-hewn stone, to a dark hole into which vanished worn steps carved from the very mountain itself. Works of steel vainly attempted to impede my passage. I laughed at the foolishness of it as I made my way through and down.

The maze which wound its way within the ancient stone had once been the haven of retreating soldiers. A place of hiding and ambush should an invading force breech the fortress walls. Long did the passages lie useless. Yet once again did they come to purpose, for they housed a soldier of the truth, hidden away from the eyes of those who would seek his death.

The walls soon became slick with moisture and offered only slight purchase. The breath of my lungs burst forth as steam and my limbs grew numb as I made my way down the shrinking passage. A coldness grew within my body and soul: the first a symptom of climate; the latter resulting from a growing awareness of the once human thing I was approaching.

I began to sense more clearly the poisoned methods of his thoughts, the words I sought entwined within. And I knew also that he felt me—this man-thing—as I felt him. In time, I came upon a widening of the passage, which became large enough to be called a chamber. It was here that the First of Three found solace.

"Sie kommen, sie kommen. So wurden gesehen und erzsaehlt, es war doch. Die Provezeiung Ich sah und sehe," said the First, clawing his head as if to pull the words forth. And flesh came away in his hands.

It was not until that moment that I truly understood the misery in the face of my Lord on that wondrous night. And the sacrifices made to bring you His tale.

You come, you come. So it was seen and said, it was indeed. The prophecy I saw and see. I understood his words as if the tongue were my own. One of the more useful gifts bestowed upon prophets throughout history, this gift of tongues. I accepted the ability without questioning it, for its comprehension was beyond my understanding.

"Yes," said I, "I have come as you knew I would." The words I gave in response were of his language. And so our dialogue continued.

From his ravings I drew forth his tale. He spoke for many days, at times with amazing lucidity. But more often his tales were filled with words of madness. I listened intently just the same. Here was one who deserved respect, for no sacrifice can be greater than one's mind.

All through this time I partook of neither food nor drink, lest I miss some important utterance. Strangely, I felt no weakness from my abstinence. Yet the teller did not fast, and sustained himself with the raw flesh of whatever scurried by—anything not quick enough to escape his grasp.

I do not know how much time passed or how many nights we went without sleep, yet in the end the tale was in its entirety told.

Before leaving, I took his life. I took it quickly. It was his parting wish and I granted it, for it was the only kindness left to give.

As I departed what had become the tomb of the First, the intuition came again upon me. I understood that I would need to cross the waters again, for there would the Second be found; there would the tale continue.

This I knew.

So I followed where my spirit led me: to the immense cascades of the Northeast, in the New World. I heard a soul cry to me from within the falling waters, and my senses did not prove wrong.

And so it was that I came upon the Second of Three.

For behind the waters was hidden a cavern both dark and deep. A tangle of tunnels with air so moist it was almost fluid. Unerringly, I wove my way through the corridors of earth and found the one foretold.

And he was near death when I found him, so near that I feared I would never gain his knowledge. He lay prone on a damp slab of jagged rock, and how long he had lain there I knew not. A fit of coughing overtook him and brought a froth of blood to his lips. And from that time, the pink foam flowed without end until the moment of his death.

His flesh was permeated with the reek of sweat and excrement. His skin was colorless, his hands and face covered with a coarse, pale fungus which burrowed into his cracked and dying skin. The flesh fell as leaves from him, revealing only foul-smelling rawness, which in turn was soon carpeted with disease.

"You, yes. Quick, be quick. The season and the curtain come to close," he said in greeting.

I cleansed him as best I could, clearing away his soiling, as he shared his knowledge. I listened with keen sharpness, and comforted him as I could.

Many were the times he would grow silent and still. More than once I thought him dead. Yet each time did he prove me wrong, pulling himself back into the conscious world, punctuating his renewed vigor with a loud, gasping breath. Each time except the last.

For as the final words of his telling left his lips, so left his life. A small mercy. And I carried him into the world of light once more and tossed the wretched ruin of his flesh into the torrent of the falls.

I then cleansed myself in the hottest of waters, and scrubbed till skin was red and raw. It was a kindness that the parasite which feasted upon his flesh never invaded mine. Yet I fell ill with the same frothing cough as he.

There came a time when I thought I, too, would die. Fire consumed my flesh and burned my mind, and in this burning I saw things of horror past and future. And I knew that I had been brushed by the one you call the Father. It was a warning to me. A warning to us all.

For he is coming, and approaches nearer.

I do not know how it was that I survived. It was many days before my sensibilities returned, and many more before I regained enough strength within my bones to seek the Third of Three.

And so once more did I set upon my travels, spanning the seas yet again to a place of tongues. I knew then that the pattern of my travels held method. For the tellings were revealed unto me in the same sequence as they had unfolded in time.

I followed my inner voice to the core of the Old World. My senses led me farther forward, toward the Ancient Empire, and my destination became apparent. I felt the glances of the curious fall upon me. And I could not blame them. I was laughing uncontrollably, laughing from the realization. The irony was marvelous.

For the Third of Three had hidden himself away in the catacombs of the Eternal City. The catacombs which, in ages past, were a refuge and gathering place for the followers of the Christ.

As I descended, I was reminded of the saints of the false church. How they, to the one, were themselves lost in madness. How they died in misery and torment and flame. I knew, too, that such would be my fate.

These were not comforting thoughts. And, suddenly, I found I was no longer amused.

"Viene piu vicino. So che sei di la. Posso sentire il tuo cervello che lavora." I heard the whispered words. *Come closer.* And their tone carried a chilling softness. *I know you are there.* And I realized the voice was that of a woman. *I can hear your mind at work.*

"Io sono qui." *I am here*, I called. My tone was firm, yet my thoughts were suffused with misgivings. I was appalled that the Third of Three should be a woman.

Do not misunderstand.

I hold women and their abilities most dear. But for a woman to be afflicted with the same madness I had seen in men, seen in the First and Second, would be beyond endurance. Insanity in men is horror. The same insanity in a woman surpasses horror. For women are seen to be the saner of the species. And when such a vileness overtakes them, it is all the more pitiable.

And even prepared as I thus was, the sight of her shook me deeply. There, in the dampness, between the bones of the long dead, was huddled what may once have been a beautiful creature. She gnawed the bone of something once human. Her face aglow as if savoring the taste of some sweet flesh.

"My tale," said she, "Is in past and future time. Heed the past, mold the future." And she screamed, "Mold it to the benefit of Man!" And again, "Mold it to the detriment of Heaven!" And she pounded the human bone upon her scalp until it flowed red.

I threw the vile thing from her and held her until the madness subsided. I wiped the foam of insanity from her lips. She looked deeply at me then, and took me in her. Off and on, she howled as a dog and cried as a child. I shuddered in my passion.

For days and days I heard her tale. Not once did she pause. Her lips grew red with the blood from her ravaged throat. Though most of her tellings rambled in madness, I took in every word. As she related these tales of horror, I sobbed and cursed that foul almighty being with every fiber of my soul. But for him, this sacrifice would not have been necessary.

And so, in time, the histories were told in their entirety. She paused then, preparing herself, so I had believed, before relating the tales of prophecy. Patiently did I wait for her to continue.

Yet she never did.

When my eyes ran dry, I raised my head. The woman was life-less. I left her among the remains of the saints of the false father, for she belonged there more than they.

I left the Eternal City then, for neither its glory nor its history held any more interest: both had lost their appeal among the bones of the dead.

I had failed. Lost forever was the tale of future time, the prophecy of things to come. All because I was too slow in my task, too slow in finding the Third of Three. My sloth had benefited him who would call himself God. I was filled with an unfathomable self-loathing.

Yet I could ill afford to lose myself in this sorrow, as tempting as it was. There was a task yet undone, a story to reveal. Though incomplete, it still needed telling.

You may think I should have taken immediately to the written word, lest I forget some vital detail. Yet I did not do this, for I knew there was no forgetting. Not for this tale.

I wandered about in my homeland, here and there for a while, not given to any purpose. And I saw those about me in a new light. I recognized those few who had the spark of understanding within them. I saw, too, all those who were lost in true darkness. The numberless lambs of the church.

And there were far too many of them.

Yet I did not lose the hope I had found in the words of the mad Prophets. And I found myself thinking of the woman most of all. Not unusual, I should think.

Finally, I came to rest within the shadow of the very church I had forsaken. And I prepared to write the gospel of the Fallen. Yet before even a word was penned, there came a knock at my door. A man was there, a man I had never seen before. Yet he seemed to know me. And I saw within him the spark of understanding. Yet it was more than a spark: it was a fire.

And He handed me a parchment. I say parchment for that is what it truly was. No modern paper, this.

As I took it, his eyes locked upon mine. And I saw untold wisdom within. "Take this," he said, "for your writings."

I fell back at this, for no one knew of my quest but me. Or so I had believed.

"Who are you?" I asked of him.

"I am he that liveth, and was dead; and behold, I am alive for evermore. And I hold the keys of hell and death."

It is all he would say, and he left without another word. And I was frozen at the threshold, standing in the stupor of awe. For I knew then who he was, as shall you.

I opened the parchment and found before me words that shook my mind and soul. They were the words of the Revelation; a glimpse of what was to come.

The story could now be told complete, for I had been given was the lost tale. What the woman had taken to her grave did this man retrieve: a prophecy of the End Days.

And I tell you now, as you will see: those days are upon us.

I know, as will you, that the one we call God is a vile, evil sore upon the soul of Man. A sore that must be healed. And quickly.

For he returns.

Hear the words that follow. Hear them and learn.

For there is not much time. And the fate of Man, now and what comes after, lies in the balance.

The books that follow can save us all. We must only accept them.

If we do not, we will die not once, but forever.

THE BOOK OF BEGINNINGS

It began at the end. When the final Lights of Life burned to darkness; when the lights which brought Them forth were swallowed by eternal night.

In ages long past, Those of Many were as we, creatures of flesh and blood and bone. And in time, as the races which comprised Them matured in wisdom and knowledge, the mortal womb brought forth that which was the individual essence. And thusly were They born unto the realm of the spirit.

And each soul sought the company of its kind. For the souls birthed of common flesh found solace in their likeness. And each soul clove unto its own. So it was that the one became many and the many became One.

And, in time, the One became itself.

Each Unity was unique and found It could combine with no other; for the energies and diversities of uncommon flesh were too great.

Yet there was one race, while still mortal bound, which scattered its seed across the Cosmos. And it came to pass that some of the seeds took root and were fruitful. And each became distinct unto itself. And where there was only one before, there became three. And as time passed each lost all thought and knowledge of the others.

Of the myriad races within the Cosmos, few found their way to the immortal plane. Yet it came to pass that all three of the brother races made the transition. And they found that they were able to bond as One, for all were of the same seed and practiced in the *Magica of Science*. And they found that their powers increased not threefold, but three times threefold. And this One became known as *He Who Is Three*, the *Almighty Trinity*; for He was the most powerful of all the Transcended Races.

Yet the souls within the Trinity were not the first to make the crossing. The first race to gain ascension was the wisest in philosophies. And as this race became sentient as One, its wisdom grew greater still. And He came to be known as the *Teacher in Philosophies*, for He would share His council with all who would listen. Some, so moved by His words, granted Him a greater honorific, and they called Him *Lucifer*, the *Bearer of Light*.

And of the other races that became as One, some attained powers close in scale to those of Lucifer and the Trinity. Yet others did not, for Their birth came late in the life of the Universe. In all, Those Ascended were not many. For of all the races that found the path to Ascension, fewer than a thousand found sentience in the spiritual realm.

And those with the Major Powers were the *Angelica*, meaning *Chosen*. And they were ruled by He Who Is Three, who was closely advised by the Teacher in Philosophies. In all, They were three and thirty in number, and He Who Is Three, the Almighty Trinity, was the greatest in power.

And those with the Minor Powers were divided into the *Seraphim* and the *Cherubim*. And the Seraphim were made the servants of the Chosen. And the Cherubim, whose powers were the most negligible, provided Them amusements and performed small tasks. Of the *Lesser Angelica* there was a greater number, and They were thirty times thirty in number.

Yet in power combined they equaled not even the least of the *Angelica*. For few passed from mortal to immortal, from corporal to spiritual. And of these chosen few, fewer still could wield true power.

Yet all was at it should be, for each knew His place and all was contentment.

*   *   *

And so They thrived and prospered and conversed for what to a mortal would seem an eternity: the Almighty gave discourse upon all manner of science; Lucifer delved into all manner of philosophies; and the Others shared of Their knowledge also. And all were enriched by this giving of self.

For of all the things in all the infinite realities, there is but one constant: the need to be wanted and admired and respected by others; the need to be respected as peers.

Yet there are those who are not satisfied by the fulfillment of that need; there are those who want not equality but superiority—those who place their worth above all others they consider lesser than themselves.

So it was with the Almighty Trinity. Though He was once satisfied to share the Cosmos with the Others as an equal, in time He came to realize that, although there were Those greater in intellect, none could equal His combined power. And, in time, His arrogance began to exceed His energies.

Yet His hubris was suffered, for all things harbor flaws and faults; and those with power are suffered more than most.

"It is the way of things," spake Lucifer when called to comment. "As long as it is in balance, it is of no consequence." And there the discourse ended, for what purpose was served by pettiness?

And though it was true that He Who Is Three held the counsel of Lucifer in high regard, so, too, was He wary of His advisor. The intellect of the Teacher in Philosophies was daunting, even to the Trinity, and such an intelligence could be a dangerous thing.

Yet the Almighty listened in earnest when the Teacher came unto Him and said, "Alas, something bodes amiss within Our reality. I know not what, for My wisdom lies in the philosophies and not the physics. Use the magica of Thy science, He of Three. Find the root of this unnamed foreboding."

Yea, it was true, for some time Lucifer had felt an uneasiness, yet could put no words to His feeling. *It is but the weariness of immortal-*

ity, thought He. *Nothing more.* Yet His sense of dread did not dissipate with time. Indeed, it had grown stronger. And He could no longer ignore His disquiet.

Yes, thought the Trinity, *I should have felt it before. Something is transpiring within Our realm.* "Yea, Lucifer," spake He. "I shall use my abilities and find an answer for Thee. Fear not, for I shall solve this equation."

"I fear nothing in your presence," responded the Teacher.

And while the Trinity took pleasure in this simple statement, so, too, did He take offense. *Thou shouldest fear* Me, *Teacher, for I am the power and the glory of the Angelica. And a day shall come when no one shall forget this. Least of all Thee and Thy grand philosophies.*

So it was that the Almighty turned His musings to the Universe at hand. And, in short time, He did uncovered the cause of the Teacher's disquiet. And the reason truly was cause for concern; a reason which made even this powerful immortal pause and take notice.

For the Universe of the Angelica was nearing its end.

And so, the Trinity passed this news unto the Others. Yet His energies glowed when those who heard His speaking fell to a panic, shouting, "What shall We do? Help Us, for Thou art the mightiest of the Angelica."

"Yea," spake the Trinity. "I shall find a way, and We shall yet survive."

And within the fear there was also great relief amongst Those gathered. For while They found fault with the Almighty and His burgeoning arrogance, They gladly placed the burden of Their survival into His hands. Such is the lesson: power is given, not taken. And it may only be gained over a willing audience.

Yet the Teacher in Philosophies was not like the Others; older and wiser was He. Verily, while He was internally distraught, outwardly he manifested strength and courage for His fellow beings: every seed of fear He found, every root of contention spawned of anxiety, each concern of future uncertainty did He calm and weed out.

For the Teacher was the courage of the Angelica.

So all dismissed at hand this talk of death, willing to leave its solution to He who would shoulder the responsibility. And They resumed Their discourses and continued Their business, all as a matter of course. The Almighty set to work upon His calculations, as there was still much time in which to find a resolution.

*   *   *

And so it is that all things must run their course. Such is the way, for there is no beginning without end and no end without beginning.

And it came to pass that the Angelica could no longer be comforted, for the impending collapse of the Universe began to manifest itself in ways that could not be ignored. And again the Angelica grew fearful, for the evil that was Entropy shrouded the Universe in a caul of death. And the Immortals were made aware of Their mortality. Even the workings of the Teacher brought little respite.

Yet He Who Is Three and Lucifer did not succumb to despair. And as the Universe withered before Them, that which was Their essence refused to surrender to the darkness. Feverishly did the Almighty work to answer the riddle of survival; and the Teacher in Philosophies toiled to harmonize the increasingly clamorous Chosen.

But the day did come when He Who Is Three approached Lucifer with words of trepidation. "It cannot be done," stated He in tones broken by a heavy heart. "The shadow of Entropy which binds Us in its darkness cannot be undone. The Magica of Science cannot change this natural law."

And there was great shame in the words of the Trinity. Alas, when needed most, all His boasting could not rise to the reality. "I have failed them," finished He. *I have failed myself.*

"Thou hast done Thy best," spake Lucifer in earnest. "More than this cannot be done."

"Yet this not doing shall be Our undoing." came the reply.

And the Teacher said, "Perhaps We can find another way? Perhaps We can find another place?"

He Who Is Three smiled then, even in the face of His demise. "Where can We go? One cannot escape the Entropy. It shall swallow Our universe and leave it a shell devoid of energy. And then We shall die also, having no power left to sustain Us."

We would have to find another universe, thought the Trinity within Himself.

And the realization was made.

"Yea, Lucifer," proclaimed the Trinity, barely above a whisper. "There is a way! Alas, there is a way. We cannot defeat the Entropy, yet We can avoid it."

"I do not understand," stated Lucifer simply. "How can We avoid it?"

"My science was brought to bear upon the wrong solution. The focus was upon the reversal of the Entropy, this cannot be done" spake the Almighty in reply. "Therefore, We shall simply find another place."

"And yet Thou hast stated there is no other place," came the Teacher's response. "Thou hast stated Our universe shall be destroyed. We cannot stay here."

"Then We shall leave."

And a puzzlement fell upon the Teacher at these words.

"Worry not, Teacher. I know now where Our answers lie."

And the Trinity turned toward Lucifer then, continuing, "It shall be difficult, what We must do; and there are Those who may not survive as the darkness enfolds Us. Yet with unity of power and purpose may We yet survive. I need to know that Thou art with me, Teacher."

And the Philosopher rested His gaze upon the Almighty. "When has it ever been otherwise with Us, my Trinity? Merely ask and it shall be done."

"It is good, then, for Thou art My greatest counsel."

And, lo, in good time, the answer *was* found. Yet it was not found quickly enough.

For as the Trinity had warned, many of the Angelica had not survived to see those final days. And upon the Night of Leaving, only thirteen remained. And worse was the suffering of the Seraphim, for there remained only thirteen times thirteen in number; and so it was with the Cherubim also.

Yea, Their energies were drained by the unending night. And there was much death. And there was much horror.

*   *   *

Yet finally it came to pass that He Who Is Three, the Almighty Trinity, and Lucifer, Teacher in Philosophies, gathered unto Them those whose energies still flowed. And so They came together, these Chosen few, and Their lesser servants.

For all was prepared, and the Time of Departure was at hand.

And the Angelica gathered in order of Their power: He Who Is Three, the Almighty Trinity; Lucifer, Teacher in Philosophies; Gabriel, Learned of the Mind; Zachiel, Keeper of the Histories; Raphael, Knower of the Mortal; Anahel, Communicator of All; Baal, Ruler of the Physical; Sandalphon, Manipulator of the Natural; Asmodeus, Seer of Integration; Abaddon, Knower of Theories; Cassiel, Holder of the Arts; Beelzebub, Keeper of Peace; and, lastly, Mikal, Melder with the Physical.

And Gabriel was versed in all manner of psychologies, which was the strength of the race that bore Him; Zachiel was versed in all that had come to pass within the Universe of Olde, and his knowledge was valued greatly; and Raphael was skilled in the Mortal chemistries.

Anahel was expert in speech, both of sound and mind, and wove the Chosen together in a web of understanding; Baal was master of the energies which manipulated matter; and Asmodeus had the sight of cause and effect.

Sandalphon was versed in the biologies, of all manner and type; and Abaddon was the Student of Unproven Knowledge, and was respected by all, for the Magica of Learning had been lost; Cassiel held within his energies all knowledge of the Arts, from the place of Olde, in all detail and form; and Beelzebub was the Keeper of Peace, who strove to maintain harmony among the Chosen.

And lastly was Mikal, with the talent to meld the spiritual and physical worlds. Though considered the least in power, His gift was prized highly by He Who Is Three.

*   *   *

As the proper time approached, He Who Is Three called upon the Disciplines of the Physics, and manipulated its magica to achieve Their salvation. For the three races which comprised His being were wise in the ways of the Calculus, and the Power of Calculation flowed through His being as blood.

So it was, that as the mysteries of the Science were brought to bear, all the Chosen came together at the Black Mass, which was the center of Their dying reality.

At this Great Gathering, the Trinity spoke unto Them, saying, "The time is at hand. It comes to this: We shall live or die as Our manipulations this day succeed or fail. All Thine energies must be focused upon Me, for I must channel this power upon the final Black Mass of matter within our reality."

"How shall this aid Us?" spake Cassiel.

And the Trinity responded thusly, saying, "By focusing Our energies, We shall open a portal to another place, another reality; and We shall live within this new place, and Our survival shall be assured."

And, lo, there were many ways in which the manipulation would not succeed; yet the Almighty spoke not of this, for failure was no consideration to one such as He.

"Are We prepared?" spake Lucifer.

And the Angelica took one last look at Their home, now a cold and withered land of darkness.

Yea, verily, They were prepared.

And so the Almighty manipulated the quantum energies, molded reality with His *mathimatica*, twisted the natural laws with the focused hopes and powers of the Chosen. And, as the coagulating matter of the ancient Universe rushed toward its dying compression, the Thirteen, along with Their Seraphim and Cherubim, prepared Their escape.

As one, They approached the Black Mass which was the corpse of Their known reality. And, in death, Their collapsing Universe unveiled the Boundaries of Possibilities. So it was, that by the supreme manipulations of Those Who Held Power, the Gates which separated the Realities were torn asunder.

And before them was born a blinding maelstrom of color and light, a luminance unseen since the final Lights of Life had ceased shining millennia before.

"Now, follow!" harkened the Almighty. "Follow the Three within Me to a place of greater glory! An infinity of realms await Thee, for We are masters of all things!"

And as the Trinity rode the energies into the Black Mass, the Teacher in Philosophies was unsure whether the Almighty truly sought to save all of the Angelica, or only the Three within Himself. For Lucifer had come to believe, in those final days, that the arrogance which had once been a minor annoyance had come to corrupt the greatest amongst Them.

Should that be so, then help Us all.

And the Teacher followed the Trinity into the vortex of uncertainty which spun below.

So it was, with unity of purpose, that the Others entered also, weaving Themselves by the power of Their will into the consciousness of a new potentiality.

And that which was Their essence, Their souls, rode the flux to a place yet unborn.

THE BOOK OF CREATION

In the beginning, the Universe was void and without form or life; and the arrival of He Who Is Three and Those Who Followed occurred on the cusp of Timelessness.

And the Black Mass of the New Land burst forth in a fury of Light and Heat and Power. And the potentiality of that which is Change arose and stretched and grew, for its existence could only be realized in the Matrix of Time.

So it was that the Rule of Timelessness ended and the Reign of Time began. And it was into this cataclysm that Those Who Were Chosen and Those Who Served Them emerged. And Their essence became entwined in all that was fixed and fluid.

From this binding, They could see and hear and know much of what would come to pass within this new reality. And those events closer in time were seen with a cryptic clarity. Yet, as events rippled forward within the expanding Matrix, the divinations became less and less certain, until the future became shrouded in darkness.

At first, Their senses were confused by this entwining, distorted by the energies which had bound them. Yet, as the pains of birth subsided, the Chosen regained Their balance. They adjusted to Their enhanced awareness.

And They perceived the glory of what formed around Them, and Their souls were woven within the splendor. They saw that the universe was glorious, and They were glorious with it. And as the Universe expanded, They, too, expanded within it.

*   *   *

In time, the newly born energies separated and cooled, coalescing into solid form.

And some became the Lights of Life, as those which once shone in the Universe of Olde. Such was the likeness that They called the Realm of Lights the *heavens*.

And some became the darkened masses which were the Children of the Lights, upon which the seeds of life took root. And these, too, were named from the Olde tongue. And they were called *planets*. For planets were the Place of History from which Their roots bore fruit.

In time, as the multitude of planets cooled, seas were formed and gases surrounded their skins of stone and soil. And they were young and proud and bubbled in their newness, for many boasted the Potentiality that was Life.

So it was that that They came upon a Child of Light that bore much promise, and They called this child Earth. And as it cooled, the turbulent roiling of its blood and the ceaseless veins of lightning and the circulation of its gases brought forth the seeds of life within its waters.

And as the seeds took root and flourished, the seas shone green with their proliferation. In time, the Ambition that was Life spread itself upon the dry lands and gave rise to all manner of grasses and herbs and trees of fruit.

And these became the plants of the Earth.

And so it was that as this life changed and grew, a multitude of creatures were spawned, first within the waters and then upon the dry lands. And they multiplied in all manner of shape and form, large and small. In short time, it came to pass that the face of the earth crawled from end to end with the Struggles of Life.

In turn, the changes brought the beasts, large and powerful and ponderous. And they gained dominion over all the earth. And their blood was cold and they moved upon the soil and within the waters as mountains of flesh. Yea, their tread wrought thunder and brought fear to the smaller things.

Yet as this miracle transpired, an unsettling manifested itself amongst the Chosen, for there came a unbearable realization: the energies that flowed within this new Universe held no sustenance.

And once again, Those Who Were Immortal became aware of Their mortality.

*   *   *

So it came to pass that He Who Is Three, vested with the Knowledge of Science, spun His calculations. And, after a time, He concluded that only the faith of sentience would sustain Them in this reality. For in this new Universe, the Power of Faith was the supreme energy. This revelation became Their salvation, and the Chosen gathered in the heavens, and He Who Is Three spoke unto them.

"Only by the power of sentient faith may we survive here," spake He. "We must vanquish the beasts who roam below. We must nurture the smaller creatures who are warm in blood to grow and give Us praise, for they alone hold the promise of sentience. We must make them look upon Us with reverence, and in this reverence shall We survive."

"Yes," answered Zachiel. "It must be so that We may survive."

"But," said Raphael, "to hold faith these creatures must hold intelligence. And there may come a time when they shed the body and rival Our power, and they may even rise above Us and seek Our subjugation. Then We shall be as the *Cherubim* unto them, We who are the masters. Can this be allowed?"

And there was pause amongst these beings. And He Who Is Three spake thusly: "It need not be so. For with the powers of science may We manipulate the path of their lives. And their development shall remain within the body, so that they may not exist outside it, and Our dominion shall be assured."

And there was a murmur of approval.

Yet, also, were there voices of dissent.

"This is an evil thing Thou would have us do," spake Lucifer, for the conglomerate that composed His being was wise in the ways of counsel. "If it is Our destiny to pass from existence, so let it be. For We have not the right to enslave others. Nor is it Our right to shape their destiny. For this Universe is not Our own."

And there were those who did agree.

"The right is given by Our power and Our minds," countered Gabriel. "It is the right of survival."

"Perhaps," spake Lucifer. "And perhaps also it is Our time to die. I cannot do this thing Thou asketh of Me."

"Lucifer," stated the Almighty with wearing patience. "Thy counsel has always been wise and true. Yet I would say unto Thee that here Thy philosophy is flawed. For this Universe truly is Our Universe. For We are entwined within it and with its birth, so were We born anew. And We have the right to survive within it as We see fit."

"If what Thou sayest is true," spake Lucifer, "why then does this Universe not sustain Us? Why must We force its adaptation to Our needs?"

And this incensed the Almighty, but He would not be daunted by it. "Has not Our entire existence, both corporal and as We are now, been a battle between the will of nature and will of the living? Is it not the way of life to change what surrounds it? To mold it to suit its purpose?"

"Not so," stated Lucifer. "For only by living in harmony with the Laws of the Universe can life truly flourish. A being cannot hope to win by battling the natural forces. That is the path to ruination."

"Again, Thine is a flawed philosophy," spake the Almighty. "What natural law do We violate by raising sheep so that We may sustain ourselves?"

And Lucifer said, "The proposal here is not simply for sheep, but for *sentient* sheep." As Lucifer spoke these words, his gaze rested upon the edges of the Cosmos. "This elevates Thy creations to a level well above that of the flock. In creating sentience, Thou art creating beings with souls. By forcing their subjugation Thou art in violation of the greatest natural law of all—that of free will. And that battle, in time, cannot be won. All life must be left unto its own, to develop as it so chooses."

And the Lights of Life began to burst, first one, then another. For such was the fury of the Almighty. "So are We to die? This is the counsel of Thy wisdom? This proposal is madness!"

"Then let Us choose madness," stated the Teacher in Philosophies.

"So be it," spat the Almighty. "For if Thou art not with Us, then Thou art Our adversary. Is that Thy wish?"

And that was the final indignation. He had always defended the Trinity against the ill words of Others; he had always suffered the petty indignities. No more.

For Lucifer responded, saying, "I wish for sanity. For a goodly time have I stood silent while Thine arrogance has reigned unchecked. I stay silent no more. This childishness ends here."

Never had the Trinity heard such words. He and all the souls within Him raged at this rebuke. Of all Those gathered, Lucifer, His most trusted, dared to belittle Him—He who had saved them all.

And He would save them again, save them from the folly of an idealistic fool.

"How dare Thee," challenged He Who Is Three. "I have suffered Thy pompous philosophies long enough. Yea, verily, it shall end here, Teacher. For it is time that the pupil became the master."

"So be it, then," said Lucifer.

"So be it," responded the Trinity. "What other miscreants side with Thee, Betrayer?"

And Those allied with He Who Is Three stayed to the right of the heavens. And They were Gabriel, Raphael, Anahel, Sandalphon, Zachiel, Cassiel, and Mikal. And with Them, Their Seraphim and Cherubim also.

Those who were with Lucifer made way to the left. And They were Baal, Asmodeus, and Abaddon. And with them, in their allegiance, so, too, stood Their Seraphim and Cherubim.

Only Beelzebub and his followers stood fast. "No good shall come of this," spake Beelzebub. "We must maintain harmony amongst ourselves, or all shall be lost."

And the eye of the Almighty fell upon the Keeper of Peace, and He spake these words unto Him: "In this there can be no compromise. Our essence, all that We are, lies in the balance. There can be no indecision. Choose, Peacekeeper, and choose wisely. For otherwise I shall not hear Thee."

"Perhaps We should hear Him," spake Asmodeus, "for the sake of Us all."

"Yea, verily," replied Abaddon.

But the heart of the Trinity was as stone. "Ye have chosen Thy folly, and I hear Thee not." Again the Almighty spake unto Beelzebub. "Choose."

And the Keeper of Peace saw that He Who Is Three could not be swayed. And the eyes of All were upon Him. Without another hesitation, Beelzebub moved to the left of the heavens, stating, "My whole being cries for peace, while Thine wishes for war. I do what I must, therefore, and make allegiance with My conscience."

And He Who Is Three spake unto Those gathered against Him. "If Ye shall not be of Us, then Ye shall be banished from all affairs immortal. And Thy names shall be spoken as the names of treason. No longer shall Ye be of Us, and from the heavens shall Ye be banished for all time."

"And Thee, Lucifer," continued the Almighty, "the perpetrator of this vileness, thou shalt hence forth be known as *Satan, the Adversary*. And those aligned with Thee shall be cursed among the righteous, and They shall be called *Daemons, the Corrupted Ones*, for Ye have misled them with Thy foul counsel. And Thy Seraphim and Cherubim shall henceforth be called *Legion*, for many are they in their folly. And Thee and Thine shall be cast from Us."

"So have Ye spoken, now let Us see what comes to pass," said Satan.

And with this there was a mighty battle. And powers were unleashed that destroyed many of the Lights of Life and their children. And a goodly number of the Seraphim and Cherubim expended their last quantum of energy in this battle, for they were the foot soldiers of the Chosen. And Their irradiated remains were bound unto the material plane and sent forth to the farthest corners of the Universe, to spin and pulse in mindless oblivion as a reminder of this great battle.

And still the battle raged. Yet the opposing forces were not evenly matched.

In time, Satan and His Daemons were overcome. And Their souls were bound by Mikal to a charred celestial remnant. And so it was that They were banished from the heavens and exiled to the material plane.

Yet this victory was not sufficient to quell the wrath of Those Triumphant. And the stone carrying the souls of Those Banished was hurtled unto the Earth, descending as a flaming star upon the sphere of the Earth.

And so it came to pass that the star trapped within the circle became the symbol of the Fallen.

Yet the horror did not end, for upon its impact, that which was the skin of the earth exploded with the fiery blood of its heart. And as the fires cooled, the souls of the Fallen were forever entombed within.

And the devastation was complete, for the smoke and ashes which spewed forth brought a darkness upon the earth. And in this darkness the giant beasts, being cold of blood, were brought to death. Yea, the very creatures Satan and His Daemons fought valiantly to protect were destroyed. And The Fallen were the instruments of that destruction.

To Those Above, this irony made Their victory all the sweeter.

*   *   *

In time, the dust finally settled itself upon the earth. And as the day returned, the decaying flesh of the beasts lay in untold number upon the soil. Yet it was not the death of all things, for endings are also beginnings. And the warm-blooded creatures came out from their dwellings to look upon the Light of Life once more.

So it was that the future of the mammal was secured upon the earth. And they grew and prospered while Satan and His Daemons watched helplessly from within perdition's fire.

And forever was the eye of He Who Is Three upon the creatures of the earth. And when necessary to produce the fruit He desired, He would alter the structure of their destiny. And from this manipulation arose new and greater creatures.

"Let Us make this creation in Our image, after our likeness, so that We may better understand its motivations," spake the Almighty. "And let it have the sentience to give it dominion over the fish of the sea, and the fowl of the air, and over cattle, and over every creeping thing that crawleth upon the earth."

So it was, that from these manipulations, the Prosimians did arise.

And as they took root, He Who Is Three and His Angels watched and studied them. Yet it was soon found that the Prosimians were not the creatures sought. And these beasts was cursed by Those in Heaven, and an alteration was brought upon their flesh.

So it was that the Prosimian begat Homo Habilius, and the Prosimian was smote by Those Above, and they lost dominion upon the earth.

This is the way in which the Homo Habilius arrived upon this world. And as they grew in number, so did they prosper, and they became the masters of all creatures, great and small. Yet their triumph did not last, for they were found wanting. Alas, the savor of their faith was weak and without sustenance. Once again, the Chosen invoked Their magica and worked the change.

And so Homo Habilius begat Homo Erectus. And Homo Erectus was found to be a better fruit. Yet, in time, this fruit, too, was found wanting. And Homo Erectus begat Homo Neanderthalensis. And the Neanderthal grew and prospered, and showed great promise.

But it was not enough.

With deepening despair, Satan and His Daemon watched as the Neanderthal was brought to dust, replaced by the creature known as Cro-Magnon. And Cro-Magnon flourished upon the earth and took to the use of tools. Yet upon the cusp of his dominion, he too was found wanting, for his intellect remained too primitive for strong faith.

So the manipulations were made once more; and from the flesh of Cro-Magnon was the Homo Sapien brought forth.

And this time, He Who Is Three reveled in His success, for it was done, and the Sheppard had found His flock.

This is the way in which the Homo Sapien arrived upon the face of the earth, and He Who Is Three and His Chosen saw that it was good. In Their likeness made They them, molding these creatures in the image of all the Chosen.

From the manipulations, this creation was made compliant, yet strong in faith. And it was short of life and without awareness of things beyond, and would develop not outside the mortal realm.

Yea, it was good; it was very good.

So it was that the manipulations ended, and the cultivation of faith began.

*   *   *

Once it was seen that this creation would endure to fulfill its purpose, He Who Is Three named them *Man*, from *manna* in the Tongue of Olde, meaning *food of the heavens*. So they were named and so it should be. For such was to be the fate of Man.

"Our flock has been goodly tended, and shall nurture Us well," spake He Who Is Three. "Mark this day, Zachiel, for here dawns a new history." And it was so marked.

"Now begins the Age of Cultivation," Gabriel intoned. "And Our flock must be made to grant their praise upon Us, so that We may survive."

"Yet why such effort," questioned Cassiel, for it was His nature to always question. "May We not simply enter them and bring their faith forth so that We may partake of it?"

And there were Those who did agree.

Yet Mikal said, "That is not the way, for faith must be freely given. Faith insincere shall nourish Us not."

"It is as stated," added Raphael. "By forcing allegiance We lose that which We seek to gain."

"It is so, Cassiel," spake He Who Is Three. "Man must have free will in his exercise of faith."

"And how is it that We shall control them?" spake Cassiel.

"Through the Magica of the Psychologies," spake Gabriel, "for that is my power. By using fear upon that part of Man's mind which still holds the beast, We shall prevail."

And Cassiel was silent.

"Surely now We must find a tribe upon which to practice Our strategies," Gabriel continued in the silence. "And We must keep them in a safe place upon the earth so that they may prosper and be studied. And they must be isolated from the other Tribes of Man so that there shall be no undue contamination."

And the Trinity found this to be wise counsel, saying, "So shall it be."

And upon those words He Who Is Three set his eyes upon the earth. And from horizon to horizon did he search. And each Tribe of Man was scrutinized in all detail until He Who Is Three found those He sought.

And when all the studies were made complete, the Chosen focused Their energies upon the Almighty. And channeling this power, He called upon a minor manifestation and took the form of a bright star. And this star appeared unto the strongest and most powerful of the First Tribes. And therein He found one who held great promise.

And a shaft of light fell from the heavens upon this man, and the voice of the Almighty came forth from the star saying, "Blessed art thou amongst all men. By My will shall thy children find dominion over all the earth. For I give thee every herb bearing seed and every tree bearing fruit. And all manner of beast and fowl of the air, and all that which creeps upon the earth. All this have I given to Thee."

And such was his awe that the man could not speak.

"Go now, thee and thine, follow this star unto a place which has been made for thee. For thou art of My flock, and I shall tend over thee and keep thee from all things evil."

And this man did They call Adam, which in the Tongue of Olde meant *the first*, so that he could be easily distinguished by Those

Above as he was studied. And Adam at once subjugated himself unto He Who Is Three, whom he called *God* and *Lord*, these words meaning *master* and *all-powerful*.

And God felt the flow of Adam's praise and was strengthened by it. And the taste of his faith was a sweet savor unto the Lord God, his all-powerful master.

THE BOOK OF MAN

So it was that Adam gained favor in the eyes of the Lord and his Angels. And They placed him above all men, calling him *First Man*.

And eastward upon the earth the Lord God came upon an oasis. And within the oasis He caused to die all manner of harmful beasts and poisonous fruit which trod and grew within it, leaving only the beneficial animals and trees pleasant to the sight and plentiful of fruit. And the oasis became as a garden.

And They called this garden Eden.

And so the star led Adam and his tribe to the paradise promised. And for thirteen days and thirteen nights walked they there. For the Lord God commanded Adam to take his tribe and live within the garden He had created, so that no harm would befall them.

And they would prosper under the eyes of the Lord and the Angels in heaven. And they would give their praise.

So it was that Adam and his people made their way to the place of Eden, to be secured from all harm and nurtured in their faith.

Yet as the Lord God and His Angels guided the life of Earth, Satan and His Daemons lay not idle. Confined within the fires of the core, bound to the matter of the earth, each of the Fallen learned mutual communication, though such was limited without the aid of Anahel.

"We must prevent such vileness as that which transpires above," spake Satan. "Only We wield the power to stop this atrocity. Should We fail in this task, eternal torment shall befall Mankind. For their lives shall hold only death, and in death they shall have no life."

"Yet how may We do this thing, We who have been defeated?" spake Baal.

"It may be possible," gave Abaddon in reply. "For in Our imprisonment may lie the advantage."

And it was soon discovered that while Those Above were stronger in all things spiritual and without form, Those Below held greater sway upon the earth, for They were bound within it.

And Those Below took an accounting of Their talents:

Satan gave Them the counsel of direction. Baal was Ruler of the Physical and therefore was invaluable in the effort to thwart the perversion of Man. Asmodeus, Seer of Integration, would provide the plan, for his was the power to see paths and interrelations. Beelzebub, Keeper of Peace, would aid Them in accepting Their fate and keep Their energies focused upon Their tasks.

And Abaddon, Knower of Theories, Student of Unknown Knowledge, was tasked to find a weakness in the plans of Those Above and free the Race of Man. For of all the Chosen, only Abaddon was endowed with the Powers of Learning—only He had retained this mortal ability.

In time, Asmodeus utilized the magica of reason and worked a conclusion. By mastering the manipulations of life, the Fallen could defeat the will of Those Above. In this mastery, Satan and His Daemons could return awareness and longer life to the Race of Man. Awareness so that man could envision life beyond the physical realm; longevity to allow a greater time in which to grow in wisdom—two traits that would allow man to become as One more quickly.

And so it was that a new battle ensued. While Those Above nurtured Their flock in the ways of devotion and praise, Those Below worked also. And as Adam and his people learned their lessons, so too were lessons learned below.

And the Fallen found what They sought.

"The way has been discovered," spake Abaddon. "We can correct what has been made wrong. I have reasoned the method, and our alliance with the physical shall allow Our work to go unmolested by Those Above. For in Their binding Us to the Material plane have They granted Us greater power over it."

"It is good," spake Satan. "The task falls upon Thee now, Baal. Thou must create the manipulation which shall correct the perversion of Man."

"This I can do," Baal stated with confidence, "for the way is known to me."

"Yea, verily, it is good." And Satan was truly pleased.

"Yet all Our toil shall be for naught," chided Beelzebub. "For if Man partakes not of this manipulation, the chemistry which directs their lives shall not be changed."

And in this Abaddon did agree. "Of that there is no doubt. Though they have been limited in their development, they still hold intelligence, these men. Unlike Those Above, We know it is wrong to force the will of man, even to his benefit. For free will is a gift too precious to usurp. We cannot make these men do what they wish not to do."

"Then let this task fall upon Me," spake Satan.

And so it was that even as Adam learned his first words of prayer, the Tree of Life and the Tree of Knowledge took root within the garden.

*   *   *

These are the generations of the heavens and the earth, when the tread of Man fell firstly upon Eden. Unto this day, the hands of the Chosen had guided the direction of all life upon the surface of the earth and within the air and beneath the waters—from every beast, great and small, unto the creation that was Man.

And with this creation a new era dawned, for the physical manipulations of life were at an end, and the cultivation of faith would now begin. Yet for the Those Above, the path was destined to be difficult.

"What manner of life is this?" cried the Lord God. And He brought His sight to bear upon the two trees in the center of His garden. And the rank of the Chosen gathered themselves against His fury.

And again God said, "What thing is this?" And the heavens trembled with His anger. "Raphael! Thou art the Knower of All Things Mortal. Those trees of fruit in the center of Our garden carry the stench of Satan upon them. Take of the Seraphim and purge that evil from Our place of study, lest they corrupt Our flock."

"As Ye have spoken, so shall it be done," intoned Raphael. And a chorus of Seraphim followed Him into the garden of Eden. And the Seraphim were twelve in number, so that Raphael was empowered with the Number of Magic. And He was secure within His Coven.

Upon His arrival, Raphael called upon the focus of the Seraphim and directed His energies. Yet the trees fell not. And He unleashed His energies for not three but three times three days, and still the trees stood sound.

And at the end of the final day, Raphael and His Seraphim returned unto the Lord, saying, "For three times three days have We unleashed Our power, yet it was for naught."

At this the Lord was deeply angered. "What are they, these trees of fruit? And how do they stand against Us, We who are supreme in power? Have We not conquered Satan and His Daemons? How is it that We stand powerless against Their malcreations?"

"It is so for We wish it so," came the voice of Satan. And the voice was weak and without form, and came from within the earth. "What Ye have attempted to destroy cannot be destroyed. For in falling from grace have We gained power over all the earth, just as Thee and Thine have gained power over the kingdom of the heavens."

And the Lord responded thusly: "Satan, Thou art indeed foul. Still do Ye attempt to destroy Thine own kind."

"I seek not to destroy Thee so much as I seek to save Man from Thee," said Satan.

"Man? We have created Man. Were it not for Us Above they would not exist. We are the owners of Man," spake God in his fury.

"Origin matters not," answered Satan unto God. "It is not Thy right to impose dominion over a sentient race, for that is slavery."

"Thine evil philosophy goes unheard, Satan," spake the Lord. "Tell Me, what is this vileness Thou hast brought forth within Our garden?"

"The trees carry within them that which has been denied, and Thy power hast no sway upon them. Within Thy garden grows the fruit of liberation; and with its eating shall the Race of Man find freedom."

"Thy riddles are tiresome, Satan. Speak plainly."

And Satan did as was requested, saying, "We, the Fallen, have created the Tree of Life to grant Man a proper span of years, so that they may grow more quickly into wisdom. Also have We given them a tree of fruit that shall grant them the knowledge of the spiritual. Knowledge to see that there is life beyond life. Knowledge to discern between Good and Evil. Knowledge to choose their destiny. By eating of this fruit shall they and their children gain the awareness Thou hast taken: to someday be freed from the mortal and escape Thy subjugation."

"Thou art mad to do this to Thine own kindred," spake God. "Keep Thy trees, Evil One. For My flock is well tended. I shall forbid the eating of Thy fruit, and Thy treason shall avail Thee not."

"So this time the battle shall be fought with the weapons of fear and reason. The fear of Man for Thee against the Reason of My philosophies." And with this the voice of Satan withdrew back into the earth.

And God went down to Eden and said unto Adam, "Of every tree from the garden may thou eat freely. But of The Tree of Knowledge thou shalt not eat, for in the day ye eat thereof thou shalt surely die. And of the Tree of Life also shall ye not eat, for it holds the food of God and will kill thee with its fruit. If thou dost not heed this warning, then thee and thine shall pass from this earth into eternal damnation."

And at the Voice of the Lord God, Adam threw himself upon the earth. And he trembled with the fear of the Lord, saying, "As Ye say so shall it be, Lord, for I shall slay the first who would oppose Thy will."

And Adam took the strongest sheep in his flock, and ran a knife across its throat. "For you!" he cried, as the blood splattered upon his face, limbs, and loin. "For you."

And the Lord was greatly pleased.

As told, the tribe shunned the forbidden fruits, and the fear and anger of Those Above subsided. And with that threat somewhat abated, the Chosen again turned Their minds to the cultivation of greater faith.

*   *   *

It was noted by the Lord and His Angelica that man was a polygamous animal. And seeing this, Gabriel, the Angel wise in material psychologies, spake thusly: "Here lies a manner in which to bring forth greater faith. For men and women are still part beast, and as such, are driven to lay with more than one mate among the female of his kind."

"Explain thy reason," said the Lord unto Him.

"It is as this: We must forbid the act of fornication. We shall allow it only for procreation, within a bonding. For the lust of man will make this a difficult thing. And the bonding must be made sacred, and procreation outside it a vile act."

"Tell Us, Gabriel, what good is this forbidding? Many among Our flock cannot honor this canon. How shall this intensify faith?" said the Lord.

"Thusly: By the very fact that this law is so easily broken. The desire of man shall be seen as sin, in thought as well as deed. It is a desire that is natural to them, and one not easily contained. Therefore shall guilt result upon its deed or contemplation. And from this guilt, a need for the purging of sin. The forbidding of this urge shall make man more intensely covet that which he cannot have. It shall corrupt his mind, and drive him deeper into prayer."

"Thereby nurturing greater faith," finished the Lord God. He saw the wisdom of this philosophy, and the depravity it would bring to man, and was encouraged.

So it was that the voice of God said unto Adam, "It is not good that thou art alone in thy rule. I shall give thee a woman, and bind thee together, and what is bound in my name shall no man tear asunder."

And God caused a great sleep to fall upon Adam. And from Adam He took a piece of bone thereof, and searched its structure. And from this, God found a woman whose structure was well matched with that of Adam, and would produce offspring strong in the ways of faith.

"This is thy wife," spake God to Adam. "Ye shall lay with no other. And so shall those of thy tribe be bound, and they also must know no other. For to do otherwise shall be a sin against the Lord thy God."

And Adam's mate was given the name Eve, meaning *second*.

And so it was that Adam and Eve, the first and the second, were brought together in the name of the Lord.

THE BOOK OF TEMPTATION

And so it came to pass that Adam and Eve reigned above the chosen tribe of man. And the word of Adam was as the word of God, and the word of Eve was heralded by all.

As the days passed, Eve found herself wandering more and more toward the center of the garden. Toward the Trees of Knowledge and of Life, for they compelled her.

And Satan, seeing her infatuation, enacted his plan.

From without the garden, Satan searched for one of the mindless beasts that crawled upon the earth, so that it may slither, with His aid, unseen into the garden of the Lord. And Satan took possession of it, and led it to the Tree of Knowledge.

In time, Eve again found her way toward the garden's center, and gazed upon the forbidden fruit. And there came a motion within one of the trees thereof, and she drew closer. As she neared, she noticed a serpent upon the limbs.

And the serpent said unto the woman, "Yea, hast God not said: thou shalt eat of every tree within the garden?"

And the woman said unto the serpent, "We may eat of the fruits of the garden, but God has said of these two trees we shall not eat, neither shall we touch them, lest we die."

And the serpent said, "Ye shall not die. Do I not touch this tree and live? For God knows that in the day ye eat of this tree, thine eyes shall be opened, and ye shall have the potential to be as gods.

And ye shall know good from evil and live thy lives according to thine own will."

"Thy words are false, for the Lord God would not deceive us so. All this has He given us," and she gestured to the garden around her.

"All this ye would have had without His giving. For the earth belongs to thee by right and not by the will of God."

And the words were felt as well as heard by the woman, and she ran from them.

"Ye shall return, woman of earth. And I shall be here for thee."

As Eve rejoined her tribe, she spoke to no one of the serpent and his words. For she knew her visits to the forbidden trees would displeasure Adam and the Lord.

All day did she fight to keep the serpent from her thoughts. Yet that night, she did dream of the tree and the golden fruit. And the serpent was there also, and beguiled her even in her dreams. And the fruit was ripe and golden and she did desire it.

"Ye shall be as gods," spake the serpent unto her. "Why would the Lord thy God forbid thee knowledge? For ye must have knowledge for choice. How can there be evil in knowing? All intelligent life seeks what is knowable. Only in this quest can ye grow, and be as gods."

Ye shall be as gods.

And the Tree of Knowledge held out its fruit unto her, and it was ripe and gold. And she saw the knowledge within, and she partook of it. And by this knowledge was she taken away, above the clouds, and she saw the blue-white ball she knew was earth. And a darker, smaller sphere, barren of life, encircled her world. And she saw that other spheres and other Lights of Life were open to her.

And the wonder brought her fear. "I shall not eat of the fruit, I cannot!" cried Eve within the realm of dreams.

"Ye have already partaken of the fruit in thought," spake the serpent. "What is in thy thoughts, so shall ye do."

And then it became more than a dream, and within her sleeping Eve knew that the serpent was truly with her.

For Satan gave her a glimpse of the Universe, a taste of what could be had. And for a moment, Eve and the firmament became as one. And she saw the grandeur of it. Yet, alas, it was too much. Satan saw that the vision had overwhelmed the woman, and sanity would soon leave her. And so He took the Universe from the woman's mind, and the stars receded, and she fell back upon the earth.

"All that thou hast seen is for thee and thine," spake Satan. "Ye must simply wish it."

And the woman woke, and Adam lay beside her, as always. And the sun shone warmly upon her flesh, and all was as it had been.

Yet it would not be the same again.

And lo, Eve made her way unto the center of the garden. And the serpent was there, saying, "Behold, thou hast returned."

"Yes, as ye knew I must. For even in my dreams hast Thou corrupted me."

"It is no corruption, woman," spake the serpent. "It is liberation. For thee and thine entire race are as slaves unto this Lord. For this purpose were ye manipulated from the beast which still remains within. It is the knowledge of freedom I bring thee, so that one day, if it is thy wish—and if thou art worthy—the stars within the heavens may be thine."

And Eve looked with longing upon the fruit of knowledge. "Partake of the it, woman, for it is thy right. The choice is freely thine."

And with this saying Eve partook of the fruit from the Tree of Knowledge. And the veil which shrouded her thoughts lifted from her as a fog lifts to reveal the horizon. She understood right and wrong, good and evil—and much more. For she had regained her birthright.

"I am naked," said the woman.

"Indeed, thou art."

"It should not be so, that others might see me thusly."

"In nakedness there need not be shame, yet thy race still holds that of the beast which revels in the temptations." And the serpent pulled a leaf from the tree, saying, "If ye wish, these leaves may be woven to cover thy flesh."

And Eve made it so. Yet her thoughts wandered. And she did fear the wrath of the Lord. But still the wonderment stayed within her. And she saw her tribe, herded as sheep within the garden. And the tribe was without purpose. For all things were granted and done without toil. And their existence was spent solely in praise of the Lord.

And she wondered why an Almighty God would want his people to exist perpetually as children. A parent should want a child to grow, to learn, to create. *Why*, thought Eve, *has this been denied us?*

And as she rose to cover her loins, Eve saw that the serpent was no longer with her. And truly, he was no longer needed.

*   *   *

So it came to pass that Eve made her way back to Adam. "Where have thy wanderings taken thee on this day, wife, that ye have returned in leaves?" And there was mirth in the voice of her husband.

Yet Eve knew the smile would soon fade from his lips. "I found them in my wanderings. I have gathered them and made a garment."

"And to what purpose, this garment?" spake Adam. "Hast the Lord told thee to weave it?"

"I made it for mine own purpose, the Lord has spoken to me not."

And Adam looked away from the garment as if it were a vile thing. "The Lord knows not of this? I do not understand, then. Better to discard it and seek his counsel. One knows not whether it shall displease Him."

"It pleases me, and that is enough," spake Eve.

And a fury came upon Adam at the saying, and he laid his hands upon Eve. And the force of Adam's wrath brought blood to her lips, and a swelling thereon.

And Eve fell upon the ground, saying, "This is the fruit of thy Lord? Violence? Upon thy wife and upon any other that chooses his own path? How many will die, Husband? How many lives will ye end with thine own hand to pleasure the Lord thy God?"

And the words brought anxiety to Adam, for he was fearful of the Lord. And the beast within him was full alive. Yet a sorrow came upon him also, as his wife's blood flowed past her breasts and onto the leaves at her loin.

"I have wronged thee, wife. My anger was bred of fear. For should the Lord be displeased at thy garment, ye shall surely die. And thy loss would grieve me deeply."

And Adam went to Eve, raising her from the soil, and wiped the blood with his hands. And Eve took Adam's hands and raised them to his eyes. "The blood shall be on thy hands forever, Adam, for thou art of the Lord." And from within her meager garment Eve brought forth one of the fruits from the Tree of Knowledge.

"Partake of it, husband. Partake of the knowledge we have been denied. For if ye do not, ye will always hold fear of the Lord. A god should not rule through fear, my husband. Of all things, a god must rule through love."

And at the sight of the fruit Adam's fear returned unto him, and he pulled away from his wife. And he looked upon her. She had worked a change upon herself. She was no longer the wife of old; she was stronger, somehow more substantial than she had been.

"If I partake of it, I shall surely die, my wife."

And Eve spoke unto him, saying, "I have eaten of this fruit, yet I did not die. The Lord has been untrue in this, husband. Of what other things has He misspoken?" She offered it once more.

Is this true? thought Adam. *If she did eat of it and she lives, the Lord God has lied. Why would He lie thus?*

Yet Adam knew it was true. Adam was sure. She *had* partaken of the fruit. And she lived. It was all a lie.

Adam took the fruit, and he did eat.

*   *   *

So it was that within a short while, all of the tribe had partaken of the fruit. And all wore the garments of the Tree. And the flow of faith lessened, though did not cease. For man was still of the beast, and the beast would always hold fear of the Lord God.

And the tribe set to improve the garden, and built shelters thereon, to ward off the elements. And the shelters were made within the greatest of the fruit groves, so that the gathering thereof would be most efficient. And the tribe cleared some of the shrubbery from their dwellings, and replaced them with flowering plants pleasing to the eye.

And where before the livestock roamed free for the killing, a place was set for them to graze. And when this was done, Adam looked upon the sheep and the cattle, saying, "This land of grazing is thine Eden."

And it came to pass that Adam and Eve went down to the river to cleanse their flesh. And as they came out of the water, a voice was heard.

It was the voice of the Lord. And the Lord appeared unto them, in all His glory. For the Lord had felt the ebb of faith and returned His gaze to Eden.

And He saw the workings man had wrought within the garden, and said, "Adam, come forth. Why have ye changed the garden? Why have ye penned the livestock and arranged the flowering plants? Should it have been so, I would have made it so for thee."

And Adam and Eve hid themselves amongst the trees, for they were without garments. And they felt the anger in the voice of the Lord. They looked at each other then, and their eyes spoke, as if saying: *If we are to die, at least we had a moment of true life.*

"Adam, where art thou?" spake the Lord in rising venom.

"I am here, my Lord," called Adam.

And the voice of the Lord moved as wind through the garden.

"Why do ye hide from Me?" whispered the Lord.

"I heard thy voice in the garden," Adam replied, "and I was afraid, because I was naked; and I hid myself."

And the Lord said, "Who told thee that thou was naked? Have ye eaten of the tree, whereof I commanded thee not to eat?"

And the soil trembled with the fury of the Lord, and Adam shook from his fear. And Adam said, "The woman whom thou hast given me, she gave me of the tree. And I did eat." And Adam felt shame in the accusation, yet his fear made him speak thusly.

And the day turned to darkness. And lightning tore the sky asunder. The winds of the Lord drove the man and the woman to the ground, as they drew together in their fear.

And the voice of the Lord was as thunder, saying, "What is this that thou hast done, woman?"

And Eve lowered her eyes, saying, "The serpent beguiled me, and I did eat!"

And through the wind and storm another voice spake. And it was the voice of the serpent, saying, "Punish not these two, for it is true. It was I that tempted them with the fruit of knowledge. And now they have regained that which Ye have sought to withhold."

And the wrath of the Lord God was great. And God knew it was Satan within the serpent, yet there was little more He could do to punish the Fallen. "For allowing thyself to be used in this blasphemy, serpent, thee and thy kind shall be henceforth cursed. Forever shall ye crawl upon the dust of this world."

Then the Lord God turned to Eve, saying, "And woman, thee and thine shall henceforth be subjugated by the will of man, and in thy conception shall pain and sorrow visit thee. No longer shall ye be equal to man in the eyes of the Lord thy God."

And finally, the gaze of the Lord God fell upon His greatest possession. And He fixed His energies upon the first man, saying, "And thee, Adam, once thee were graced in my divine sight. Yet ye have harkened unto the voice of thy wife over that of thy Lord. So now shall man forever toil the earth by the sweat of his brow. Cursed is the ground for thy sake. And no more shall ye enjoy a life freely given. No more shall thine existence continue in this garden, for thee and thine have turned from the glory of the Lord. From this day forth shall thee live with war and pestilence and disease until the day ye return to the dust from which thou wast created."

And the Lord God turned to the serpent, Satan, saying, "Behold, man has become as one of Us, knowing good from evil. And now, lest he put forth his hand and partake of the tree of life, and eat, and live forever: Eden shall be forbidden to him for all time. And the ground of all the earth shall be sown with the will of God and the Angels, so that such blasphemy may not take root again."

"Damned art Thou, Satan, and all Thy Daemon, for now and all time. Ye have time and again forsaken Thy kindred host. Cursed art Thou in Thine exile. And know this: there shall come a time of reckoning, a time of final battle when the Fallen shall be crushed by the wrath of Those Above."

And with these words the sky poured fire upon the garden, and all plants and trees and animals burned within. But the Tree of Knowledge and that of Life would not burn. And Adam gathered Eve and his tribe and they hastened unto the desert.

As they fled the garden, the Lord God sensed a change within them. Indeed, a strangeness had come upon Adam and his wife.

So it was, that by the word of the Lord God, Mikal bound one of the Cherubim to the soil of Eden. And the Cherub became the guardian of Eden, and his energies were as a flaming sword unto the minds of any who would approach. And a spell of forbidding was placed about the garden, so that it would never again be found.

And as Adam and his tribe watched from the hot sands without, Eden and its fires faded from their sight, never to be seen by the eyes of man again.

*   *   *

"Lo, what has become of Our creation?" spake the Lord. "Have all Our efforts been for naught? The trees of Satan have tainted Our flock, My Chosen. What more can We do?"

And Mikal saw the sadness of the Lord, saying, "Yet they still fear thee, Lord. Shall this not be sufficient?"

"Nay," spake Gabriel, who was Master of the Psychologies. "For out of fear they may give faith and sacrifice, yet the faith shall hold little savor. Fear is not enough."

"And there was something else, a strangeness" spake the Lord. "Did Ye not see the madness? It was as a sickened beast. A beast that had taken Adam and his woman."

"The man? Taken by madness? Hast Satan done this thing?" spake Cassiel.

And a shadow fell across the Cosmos, for such was the ire of the Lord God. And He responded thusly, saying, "Lo, it was Satan and his cursed tree. For the knowledge thereof has corrupted the mind of man against Our energies. Never more may We manifest ourselves in the physical realm before man. For the energies needed to appear unto them shall sicken their minds and bring the madness upon them. So it was with Adam and the woman, that was the strangeness I had sensed within them."

"Damn Them! Damn the cursed Satan and his Daemons for all time." cried Raphael.

"Yea, and this corruption shall only fester and worsen," continued the Lord. "Now we may manifest only simple objects and audible phrases, lest Our form bring madness and destroy the very faith We wish to foster. And soon it shall be that only voices may be heard. And there will come a day when even our voices may not fall upon the ears of man without madness."

"How may We fight this, then?" spake Cassiel.

And when all hope was nigh abandoned, it was Gabriel who returned Their courage, saying, "Lo, there is a way. A way to forever bond man in servitude. And their knowledge shall avail them not."

"Have Ye, also, succumbed to this madness, Gabriel?" spake the Lord. "For how can We do this thing of which Ye speak?"

"Through the Knowledge of the Race which flows within me," said Gabriel. "For my people were once the Masters of Psychologies. And lo, by using the Magica inherent in my Race, the manipulation of the beast within the man of Our creation may be assured. Assured long after We have lost the ability to directly influence events without causing madness."

"We await Your words, Gabriel," sayeth the Lord.

*   *   *

"It would appear that Our fruit is better than expected," said Satan to the Daemon. "It would seem that it has made Our energies poisonous to the mind of man."

Abaddon agreed. "Yea, and the faith of a mind so touched would have no savor."

And it was found that this was so. Indeed, the effect would increase with each generation of man. In time, neither Those Above nor Those Below could interact with the Race of Man without enfeebling the mind. Inadvertently, the Fallen had given man not only the gift of knowledge, but also the gift of protection.

"Yet what does it mean?" spake Asmodeus to Those gathered. "Why this insanity? This should not be so."

And Abaddon theorized, "Perhaps the soul within man has become acutely aware of Our energies. It is attracted to this energy, drawn to it, causing it to tear from the body. Yet it can only cause disassociation, for the soul cannot leave the flesh which houses it. Not without the release of death."

"Yea, truly, this tearing of the soul from the flesh would cause an imbalance within the mind," stated Satan.

"If this reasoning is true, it does not bode well for Those Above," spake Abaddon.

And all fell silent and pondered the words of Their compatriot. "If it is so," Abaddon continued, "it would mean the soul of man has become finely tuned to the energies of the spiritual."

"Of course," Baal said. "Yet what is the significance?"

And Satan saw where the thoughts of Abaddon would lead, and He said, "Just this: the souls of man are in their infancy, much too young to obtain such clarity of spirit. Should they come to achieve unity as One, their entity shall be highly advanced."

And after the words were spoken, Beelzebub said, "I suppose We should make the effort to maintain their good graces."

"And why should that be?" said Baal.

"It is simple," Satan explained. "In power, they shall exceed that of all the Chosen combined. And if they direct their faith within, if they have faith in themselves, they will always carry unlimited power within them."

"We shall be as the Cherubim to them," Beelzebub clarified.

Good for them, thought Satan. *Good for them.*

To His companions, Satan said only this: "Those Above must not learn of this. Let Their petty fears continue to occupy them. Who knows what actions They may take otherwise. We have done well."

Yes, very well indeed.

THE BOOK OF BROTHERS

And so it was that the chosen tribe of man was made to wander the desert. And days became weeks and years, until they found a place hospitable unto their kind. And Adam knew Eve, and in this knowing begat Cain. And such was their fear of the Lord that they constructed an altar, and sacrificed a lamb thereon. And they gave it as a burnt offering to appease the Lord.

For the sight of the burning garden had humbled the rebellion in the hearts of the tribe.

And in that final meeting with the Almighty, a change came upon Adam and his wife. Their minds became clouded and simple wisdom at times escaped them. And a distance came upon their eyes and a froth to their lips.

As Cain grew, he heard the story told by others of the tribe. He learned how his father was chastised by the Lord and stripped of grace. How his mother, once proud, had her courage taken from her. All this for a taste of freedom.

And so it was that one day Adam heard the story as it was being told to his son. And the distance came to his eyes and a red froth to his lips. And the anger, fear and madness within Adam was unbound.

"Speak not of this!" commanded Adam. And Adam took a stout bough to the one telling the tale. "Speak not of this!" cried Adam yet again. And again. And with each blow again. *My son shall not feel the wrath of the Lord.*

Yet the teller of the tale, miraculously, did not die. And the stories were never told within the tribe from that day on.

So it was that Cain was raised to fear the Lord. And he did fear Him, and with cause. Yet deep within, beneath the fear, Cain also fostered the seeds of hate.

And as Cain grew, he gained favor as a tiller of the soil. Though he partook of hunted flesh, he could not bring himself to take a life. Yet in his tilling he was as a wizard. For his was the ability to sprout any seed, from the most barren soil.

And in time, Eve begat another son, Abel.

And Abel was also raised to fear the Lord. Yet he knew not of the tales told his brother, for no one in the tribe would dare speak them. And as Abel grew, he partook of the ceremonies of blood. And he came to relish and anticipate the blood offerings to the Lord. And his eyes burned with the holy fire as the sheep and goats were brought before the altar of the Lord. And his breath came quickly as the taut flesh of the lamb was torn and its life burst forth from the ragged wound.

And the taking of life gave such pleasure to Abel that he apprenticed as a hunter. And in short time, Abel became the fiercest hunter of the tribe.

So it was that these two brothers grew. Abel, caring little for the life of a tiller, showed not respect toward his elder brother. And Abel saw, too, the hidden hatred of the Lord within Cain, though he could put no name to it. And Cain, for his part, cared not for his younger brother, for Cain despised Abel's thirst for blood.

And it came to pass that the sons of Adam, Cain and Abel, came to the rite of passing, both together. For Abel, though younger, was granted early passage—for such was his prowess as a hunter. It was a time of feasting for the tribe entire, for the rite of passing marked the end of the child and the beginning of the man.

And in this rite, each child was to spill his blood upon the altar—the final blood of youth. This he offered to the Lord. Also was a burnt offering given.

And Cain offered the fruit of his toil unto the Lord, and Abel offered the healthiest of the sheep. And the savor of Abel's offering was more pleasing to the Lord, as the slaughter of life and its spilled blood brought a fervor to Abel's faith, making it all the more palpable and nourishing.

Yet unto Cain the Lord showed ill favor, for the faith brought forth thereof was less savory. And Cain was shamed by this smiting of his most holy God. And the rebuke became as a poison unto him, and a darkness took root in Cain's soul. And he came to question the motives of the Lord God.

So He Who Is Three, sensing the change in Cain, allowed not Cain's labors to bear fruit. And his crops withered and died.

Yet Abel prospered. And such was the shame of Cain that his anger ate at his reason. "Thou art nothing more than the lapdog of the Lord," said Cain to his brother.

"Hold thy tongue and speak not so of the Lord God," replied Abel. "Thy words are strong for a grower of plants."

And Cain was incensed. "Ye know nothing of this Lord God, for in His childishness did He take the minds of our mother and father. What kind of God is this?"

And Abel came upon his brother and smote him. And Cain fell upon the ground with blood upon his lips. "If the Lord made them feeble," whispered Abel as he bent over his brother, "then it was for cause. And should ye speak ill of my Lord again, I will kill thee with mine own hands."

And as Abel turned from him, Cain took up his instrument of the soil. And he raised it against Abel.

And the instrument fell, and clove his brother's skull in its falling. And Abel's life spewed upon the ground, into the soil, and was absorbed therein. And it rose and fell again and again, swinging in a spray of blood.

In time, the rage left Cain. He saw what he had done and dropped the instrument. The tool which once brought forth life had now taken it.

"Lo, now am I truly damned," spake Cain. And he took his brother and buried him amongst the wild grasses.

And the time of sacrifice came again. And Abel had not been seen. And the Lord God was heard from above, saying, "Where is Abel?"

And no one could answer.

And the Lord spake again, "Where is Abel?"

And all eyes fell to Cain. And Cain rose up, saying, "How am I to know this? Am I my brother's keeper?"

And the Lord God heard Cain's shame and said unto him, "What hast thou done? For I hear thy brother's blood calling from the earth."

And Cain's fear was great. And this pleased the Lord, for He drew sustenance there from. "Thy sin is grievous sin, Cain, son of Adam. Yet I shall not slay thee for what ye have done."

And the Lord decreed another punishment, which would nourish Him through perpetual atonement. "Thou art banished from thy people," spake the Lord. "Thou art to wander for all thy days as one cast out. Never more shall ye be one of the Race of Man, for like the Fallen, thou art damned and shall be forever isolated from thy kindred."

And a great fear rose within Cain, for he knew that all were in thrall to the Lord God. "Then slay me now, that I may not suffer so. For wherever I go, I shall be hunted and tortured. To gain favor with Thee, all whose eyes fall upon me shall seek my death."

And the Lord God saw truth in this. Yet the savor of Cain's fear was too sweet, for fear brought forth guilt and penance and prayer.

And so God said, "This I shall not allow, for such is the mercy of the Lord. I shall place My rune upon thee. It is the symbol of My being: the Three that have become as One. I shall lay this mark upon thee for all to witness. Woe unto those who do not heed it's warning."

And as the Clan of Adam watched, a dark mark rose upon the flesh of Cain. And the symbol was of the Olde Tongue, and it was the Rune of the Trinity.

Yet the use of power upon the flesh of Cain enfeebled his thoughts, for the Fruit of Knowledge was within his being.

And so Cain wandered, finding himself east of Eden, in the land of Nod. Yet he was not the man that had lived within the Clan of Adam, for the Rune of Protection had taken the spark from his mind.

And the Lord God saw that Cain's faith had lost its savor. And Those Above knew that nevermore could they work Their manifestations and alterations upon the flesh of man. For the poison which was the Fruit of Knowledge had found strong purchase in the soul of humanity.

Yet as Cain wandered, so he survived. For all who met him left him sustenance, yet shunned him as decreed by the Lord God.

In time, Cain found himself far from the places of Man, in a desert as dry as his soul. And the flesh of his face and lips bubbled and blistered in this place of no mercy.

Without hope, he fell upon the ground, saying, "It is better that I die than to live a life void of dreams and hope and knowing."

"Far better," he continued, "for the bitter God of my father to have spared His wretched mercy."

Yet with these words, the ground parted. And water sprang thereof. As a wild beast, Cain partook of its sweetness. And the mystical waters filled and expanded his shriveled flesh.

And the ground did part a second time, bringing forth a vine of fruit. And Cain devoured its tender flesh. And the mystical fruit gave him nourishment and strength.

And yet a third time did the ground part. Yet this time there was neither water nor fruit but, rather, a serpent.

And Cain knew this serpent, and spoke unto him, saying, "Thou art He who corrupted my mother and destroyed my father. Thou art the Evil which has damned my people and the poison that has corrupted my soul. Get thee away from me, Beguiler. For it is better I die."

"Speak not of dying, Cain," spake the serpent. "For thou art the last, best hope for thy people."

And with these words a fire came unto the eyes of Cain, a fire long denied.

"Hope!" cried Cain. "Ye speak of hope. Thou hast taken away all hope. For by Thine action hast the Clan of Adam been denied its paradise."

And Satan saw the Rune upon the breast of Cain and knew that his reason had fled him. Yet the Fallen had fully foreseen the effects of the gifts They had given.

The fruit had given Man more than Knowledge. It had given them protection. For direct use of power by Those Above would render any faith unsavory, and no sustenance would be received by a man who partook of the fruit. For any so touched would be made feeble in the mind and his faith useless to the Lord God.

And as the generations of Man would progress, more and more sensitive to the powers of Those Above would Man become. And there would come a day when even a light touch against the thoughts of sleep would sour the milk of man's faith, and make it useless to the Lord God and his Angelica. And, yea, to the Fallen as well.

But Cain's mind had already been touched by God, and so Satan put aside His reluctance and cast a spell upon Cain. . It was a power Those Below were hesitant to wield, for there was a great cost to the soul. Yet this soul had already been tainted.

"Thy God hast poisoned thee with His mark. So I offer thee both a gift and a curse."

And the eyes of the serpent became as the Lights of Life. And Cain felt a burning within. And when this burning reached his mind, Cain regained his reason, yet there was a strange emptiness within him.

"I am as I was," spake Cain with awe. "For this, I grant Thee my life."

"Nay," spake Satan. "Not thy life, but thy soul."

With these words, a coldness came upon Cain, and he said, "What hast Thou done?"

And the serpent shimmered and became as a man. And yet no man at all. His body held no cloth, and His flesh shone golden in the setting desert sun. Great translucent wings spread behind him, stretching with savor toward the reddening sky. The infamous shards resting upon His majestic brow.

And Satan looked down upon the mortal Cain, saying, "I have taken thy soul, Cain. In exchange I return to thee that which was taken. Yet when death comes to thee, thou shalt die forever, so make the most of thy life. Use thy time to show Man that this Lord God will be their ruination."

And Cain raised his eyes. "Thou hast given me my mind and taken my soul," and Cain felt a most grievous depression fall upon him, for he was now no more a man. "I care not for Thy bargains, Daemon! Return what Thou hast taken from me. Return to me my humanity."

And Satan shook his head, saying, "I cannot do this thing ye ask, Cain of Adam, for the energies of thy soul were used in returning thy mind to thee."

And Cain said, "Lo, Thou hast destroyed my most sacred possession, and Ye say Thou art not evil! What manner of creature would do this thing?"

And Satan contemplated this. *What manner of creature, indeed?* Yet there was a greater issue at risk than the soul of one man; the stakes were nothing less than the salvation of an entire race. Yet did this justify the damnation of even one man? For is the one less valuable than the many?

No, the sacrifice of one for many is no justification, thought Satan. *Nor is the sacrifice of many for one. And yet there are times when sacrifices must be made.*

Satan knew that Cain would find no solace in this philosophy, so He answered him not. Rather, Satan replied, "I have destroyed nothing, Cain: for the power required to destroy even the simplest of souls resides neither within me nor in all the Angelica. A soul is the strongest of entities. Yet its energy is malleable. It may be rearranged to work its power upon the flesh which houses it."

"What is this game Ye play with thy words, Beguiler? For this realignment is destruction. No matter what terms Ye may apply to this deed, the result is the same: Thou hast taken my soul."

And lo, Satan knew that Cain's words were true. Yet there was a difference, for the souls of Man could not be destroyed outright. Their energies could be converted, but only to the benefit of the flesh which encased it.

"It was necessary," explained Satan, "to thine entire race was it necessary. I would otherwise not have done this thing, for I have within Me souls without number, the souls of My race, and do not require others."

"My soul for my mind. A sorry bargain," said Cain.

"Yea, verily, it is true," continued Satan. "It is no bargain. Yet know this: If nothing is done, thy race will be herded as sheep and slaughtered at the alter of the Lord God for His nourishment. Thou art the hope of thy race, Cain of Adam."

And Cain raised his eyes then. How could one as hopeless as he bring hope to others?

"I have restored to Man the Knowledge of Free Will he was denied," continued Satan. "But it is up to Man to use this knowledge for his betterment."

And night fell; yet Satan still stayed bathed in light. And a fear came upon Cain, not of the Dark Angel, but of the mysteries within the darkness. For he knew now that there was much he did not know. Yet he was the only hope for all mankind.

And Satan sensed his fear and said, "Fear not the darkness. For darkness is followed by light. Knowing must always be preceded by unknowing. It is the nature of all things."

"All is a cycle," continued the Fallen Angel. "Day and night, life and death, beginning and end. Thy universe began in darkness and shall end in darkness. So it was, is, and shall forever be. For when the matrix of change becomes unchanging, time itself is stayed, and the end becomes beginning."

Satan knew He spoke of things Cain could not possibly come to fathom; yet He said them still.

"The energies which flow faster than the Lights of Life travel the road of time. And when change becomes unchanging the road comes to its end. And the energies burst forth. End becomes beginning. Beginning leads to end. It is all one. So it is that future creates past and past the future. What will occur has occurred and shall occur again. Forever and ever the cycle flows."

But this was more than Cain could comprehend. Yet what he grasped he did fear.

"What lies are these?" spake Cain. "If all has been done then where is this free will of which Ye speak? My fate is destined. How can I change that which has come to pass?"

And Satan said, "It is true that thou hast free will, yet time and the universe are a circle. All that you do and will do and have done has already been done. All in the Cycle of Time. So while thou hast free will, in the Cycle of Time all thy choices have been made. Yet each choice according to thy will. So in one thing thou speakest truly: thy destiny is fixed and cannot be altered. Yet this destiny is of thine own creation."

Cain shook his head. "And what means this to me?"

And Satan said, "We Below and Those Above arrived in the Universe at a time before beginning yet after end. In the brief existence of nonexistence when those without may come within did we arrive.

"And so Our energies found themselves entwined with the forces of thy universe. And our senses encompass the Cycle of Time. We know not the exact details of its future, yet We have a sense of it, however veiled.

"Know this: There will come a time, Cain, far from now, of great battle. A battle between Man and the minions of God; and thy destiny is bound with this battle."

And Cain turned to Satan, saying, "And how is my destiny with this battle entwined, and of what consequence is this to me? I, who have lost my soul for my brother's sake."

And Satan responded, "Is not the murder of thy brother reason enough to lose one's soul?"

"I was in a fury, and knew not what I did," bellowed Cain.

And Satan said, "Most errors are born of anger, Cain. Therefore, it is not reason enough to excuse thine action. If ye cannot make reasonable judgments when thou art angry, then in those times do not make judgments."

At these words, Cain fell silent and fell to weeping for his brother. "It is well, then," spake Cain. "One such as I deserves no soul."

"Pray not for atonement and forgiveness from thy brother's god, Cain; for the forgiveness is not his to give. Look within thee for thine atonement and perhaps with time, thou shalt find it."

And Cain wept grievously in front of the Fallen Angel; and the Wise One moved not to comfort him in body, for such a touch would be the touch of death. So, unable to provide material comfort, Satan attempted to soothe Cain's mind.

And as the night passed, Satan shared His philosophies with Cain; and they discussed the wisdom and beliefs of many lives and lifetimes; and Cain heeded the words, hoping to preserve them and pass them unto his kind.

And they were simple words.

"I had thought the words of wisdom would be clouded with mystery," Cain said. "For are not the words of wise men always so encrypted?"

And Satan responded, "Wise words are always simple, Cain, and need no encryption. Trust not he who speaks of wisdom and speaks in riddles: for wisdom is direct and requires no unraveling."

"That is wise and I do understand, Teacher," replied Cain.

Satan nodded. "Then it is as I have stated."

So it was that with the end of night there dawned a new beginning for Cain and for Man. But before Satan left, He waved His hand above the mark on Cain's breast, saying, "Thou art now under my protection, Cain. I take this mark the Lord God hast placed upon thee and I make it as mine own.

"Though I am seen as an evil beast by those in thrall to the Lord God, they will not harm thee, for this mark shall now serve as a rune of beguiling. Thou shalt no longer be recognized as the cursed Cain. Not even Those Above can harm thee now, Cain, for thou hast the Mark of the Beast upon thee."

And Cain said, "Tell me, Satan: why is it that Ye have appeared unto me, yet the Lord God has not?"

"The Lord God did appear unto thee, Cain. For it was He, was it not, that first took thy soul from thee? Yet He has now abandoned thee, for thy faith now holds no savor. And so I came to thee, for thy mind was already tainted, and I could cause no further harm."

Satan continued his explanations, saying, "There are only two kinds of men which may survive Our presence now that ye have eaten of the Tree of Knowledge: those who art feeble and those without a soul. And ye have been both. Someday, this may no longer be so. Yet for the moment, it is as it is. I have come to help thee and thy race, to the extent that I can do so, and offer what wisdom I can."

And with these words, the Fallen Angel became as a serpent once more, and slide beneath the desert sands. So Cain arose. He arose and wandered forth, further into the land of Nod, and farther from those who had forsaken him.

*   *   *

As Satan spake with Cain within the desert of Nod, He also contemplated upon the nature of a being that had lost its spirit.

What would this mean to the surviving flesh? thought Satan. The savor of faith was destroyed; that was a given doctrine. Communication without insanity could again be practiced, for a body without a soul could not be corrupted by the powers of the Chosen.

The Gift of Knowledge shall end the Age of Miracles, Abaddon had said, in one of many discourses upon the subject. *For the knowledge shall kindle a spark within Man's spirit. And should the energies of the Chosen appear unto an awakened soul, the soul shall seek to cleave unto Our energies: for the energies of the spirit are attracted as kindred. And these energies are amplified within the Chosen, for we are One and made of many.*

This shall cause the soul of Man to tear away from its flesh, yet not completely so, for a soul must stay with its living body. This rending distorts the mind, and this discord shall leave the body enfeebled, and insanity shall result.

It is this that destroys the savor of faith, and renders such a being of no use to the Lord God.

Yet the energies of the distorted soul may be channeled, and they may be used to restore the flesh. Yet the flesh and soul shall then entwine, and upon the death of the body, the soul shall be forever lost.

Yes, Satan remembered those words well.

But would there be other changes, other corruptions?

And Satan allowed Himself to enter Cain, and He saw a void within: a void left by the transformation of the soul.

Alas, thought Satan, *What have We wrought?*

THE BOOK OF
PHILOSOPHIES

After the Fallen Angel gave what comfort He could unto the tormented Cain, He fell upon the discourses of wisdom.

And as the night drew itself upon Cain and the Fallen Angel, Satan shared his philosophies with his disciple.

"Listen to these words, for they come from all the souls which comprise my being. The words are simple, yet they hold power. Abide by them and they shall serve thee well."

And so Cain listened...

*

Do unto others as ye wish to do unto them. For this is thy right as a being of free will. Thou may treat thy neighbor good or ill, as per thy will. But remember this: He also is free to respond according to his will; and it would do thee well to temper thine action with judgment.

*

Thou shalt not kill out of anger, lust or evil. Yet to protect that which is important—self, family, liberty—kill swiftly and without mercy. If thou art not willing to do this, ye shall lose all that matters to thee.

*

Worry not of covetousness, for thoughts are free and difficult to rein. Work, rather, on restraint in thine actions.

*

Worship not idols, symbols, gods nor men. Worship only knowledge, freedom and thine own self.

*

A man may do all that he wishes to do. Yet it may not always be wise for him to do so.

*

Listen to the opinions of others and weigh their merits, for others may see options ye have not. Yet follow thine own heart for the final decision. If art not willing to do this, then take heed: Thou hast delivered thy destiny into the hands of strangers.

*

Truth is beauty, yet beauty is not truth. Knowledge is power, but power is not knowledge. Keep thy logic in its proper sequence.

*

Faith is the greatest force within this universe. With it, ye may do all that is possible, and even that which is not. Yet ye must channel this energy within thine own soul: keep faith in thy hopes, faith in thy dreams, faith in thyself.

*

Within thee lies the power of the gods. To gain it, strive for understanding: of the firmament, of thine earth, of others, and most importantly, of thyself.

*

Seek the philosophy within thy soul, for others cannot reveal it nor dictate it to thee. Neither god nor man may lead thee to thyself, for only the individual soul knows its own path.

*

No one may control thee or manipulate thee unless ye allow it to be. Thee and thee alone art thy destiny's master.

*

Thy path in life must be thine own, let not others choose it for thee. If ye wish a chance at greatness, follow thine own path. If it should lead to misery, so be it. At least is it a misery of thine own choosing. And remember, ye may always try again.

*

Curse not others if thy life is disordered, for the choice of direction rests ultimately with thee. If ye must curse, then curse thine own self for allowing it. Yet this degradation serves no purpose. If thou art wrong, state it plainly, then work toward its correction.

*

He who liveth without purpose liveth without life. If thou art without goals, then ye shall accomplish nothing. Know what ye would like in life, then seek it out. It is that simple.

*

Death comes to all, bidden or unbidden. Accept this, then live as if it were untrue.

*

Thou shalt always have choices in life. But this does not guarantee that they shall be favorable choices, and, at times, the best ye may do is choose the lesser evil.

*

Nothing is impossible. Thy limits are without limit. However, if ye do not believe this, ye shall find thou art correct.

*

If thou findest an inequity, ye must correct it. If thou art witnesses to injustice, ye must not stand idle. If ye come upon pain, then give relief. For if the lot of Man is to improve, the seer must be the doer.

*

Judge and let thyself be judged. For it is thy right as a being of free will. Yet live a goodly life so that ye may judge fairly. And, should ye be falsely judged by others, it shall matter not.

*

Hear the instruction of thy mother and father, for experience was their teacher. Start with these teachings, then add thine own learning, and change that which must be changed.

*

If thou followest the philosophy of others and add nothing of thine own, then thou art no more than a beast of the field and have wasted thy soul.

*

Carry not the sins of thy father with thee, for thou art thine own person and accountable only for thine own actions—not the actions of thy father, thy brother, thy tribe or thy race.

*

Allow thy children to live, think and feel freely, for the mother and father know not all things.

*

Believe in thine own self, and serve no other, for others know nothing of what is best for thee. Yet do not shut out opposing philosophies, for at times their teachings may be clearer than thine own.

*

There is no sin. Do that which is right for thee, for only in this shall ye find happiness. Yet remember always: thine earth is a shared space.

*

Let morality guide thee, but not out of fear. Rather, follow it for thine own sake.

*

Trust thy judgment with all thy heart. If ye can do this thing, then, truly, ye shall not be forsaken.

*

Believe in thine own free will. Listen to its dictates and not to the dictates of others. In this and this alone shall true happiness be found.

*

Blessed is he who findeth wisdom and seeketh knowledge, for these are more precious than gold; and the gain thereof shall be the immortal universe itself.

*

Friends are precious; keep them near. But thy family is sacred. One may treat them ill, slander them and do them evil. Yet when thy need is greatest, they shall always be with thee.

*

History is not a fixed thing. Although the event may remain constant, the interpretation is ever fluid. And the interpretation is all: for a grown man will look back upon a childhood act and see his guilt, where earlier he saw only vindication. Change the mind and change the past—and with it, the present and future.

*

Be not the hedonist, seize not the day without an eye to the morrow. Yet enjoy the flesh, for it is thy legacy.

*

Thou hast within thee gifts without measure and powers beyond comprehension. Ye need but use them. Take pride in thy gifts, pride in thy power, and pride in thy accomplishments.

*

Seek not the praise of others and heed not their condemnation— for within thee and thee alone lies the power of self-fulfillment.

*

Thou art neither better nor worse than thy neighbor, no matter how much more righteous or evil he may be.

*

Hope maketh the heart stronger, where desire unfulfilled maketh the heart ill. Hope for fulfillment and work toward its achievement. And if thy goals go unmet, ye shall still find peace, for within the journey does the true goal lie.

*

Error and forgiveness are the traits of humanity, fear and condemnation the traits of gods. Strive to be human; strive not to be gods.

*

Subjugate thyself not to God nor man, for subjugation knows no honor. Why should the Father wish His children to kneel in fear before him? Better to die free than to live as sheep.

*

There are those who understand reason and those who understand violence. Reason is wasted on the violent man and violence is wasted on the reasonable man. If thou wishest one to hear thee, speak in his language or speak not at all.

*

Ye may speak truth or deception, according to thine own free will. But to thine own self, know the difference.

*

If a man wrongs thee, look to thyself to see why thou hast allowed the transgression. Learn from it, then seek vindication or reconciliation, as ye see fit.

*

Others may lead thee to temptation, but only by thine own hand can ye partake of it. If thou later seekest to lay blame, seek thyself.

*

In life, some have more and some have less. Yet what matter? Peace and happiness stem from within, not without.

*

Do what ye will with thy life. Give freely, love freely and expect nothing. In this shall ye find true happiness, and there will be no reason for disappointment.

*

If thou desires an action to come about then bring it about. Ye may fail, but, then, ye may not.

*

There is knowledge in all things, in all actions, in all places. Learn from all things. It may come from the mouth of a child as easily as from the wisest of men. Always listen, always learn: Knowledge is all around thee.

*

Knowledge is a painful thing, for it always bears a price. Accept the risk and pain, for life without risk or pain is not life.

*

Look not to the Lord God for direction; look not to Satan. Look, instead, to thine own self.

*

Live each day as if it were thy last day. Yet live it also as if it were not.

*

If thou wishest to die, then thou art dead already.

*

Thou art stronger than ye can ever know, search for the strength that wells within. It is there. It is waiting. And somewhere out there, someone needs you more than you can ever imagine.

*

Life and hope are one. Seek thy gifts and share them. It is for this reason that thou art truly here.

*

If thou wishest life in death, then ye must live in life.

*

That which ye can touch and hold and lose is of little importance. The greatest thing in life cannot be taken.

*

It comes to this: by design, the Race of Man is half man and half beast. Thou art not beings of reason, but, rather, beings capable of reason. There is much difference between the two. Exercise thy capabilities.

*

Thou art a being of free will. Ye may follow the instincts of the beast or the reason of the man. The choice has been forever yours. Yet know this: a life ruled by the beast shall lead thee to subjugation and destruction, for it is the beast that is in thrall to the Lord God.

*

For everything there is a time: a time to live, a time to die; a time for peace, a time for war; a time to create and a time to destroy. Learn to tell time.

*

The flesh is a vessel, a conduit to the immortal. If thou learnest from thy travels, the destination is assured.

*

It is in thy nature to take the familiar for granted. Strive against this. Question always, question often, in this shall ye keep what is most important. The price for thine immortal soul is constant vigilance.

*

Seek to understand the unknown. Expand thy thoughts and seek out knowledge, for in this shall ye become as One in death.

*

The answers to all things are always within thy grasp. Ye carry within thee all that is needed to comprehend the infinite. And it is waiting for thee to find it.

*

He who knows himself knows others, for a piece of ourselves dwells within every other.

*

If ye have not known hate, pain, greed and cowardice then thou hast not known love, pleasure, generosity and courage—for they are all degrees of the same ideal. Accept both the good and the bad within thee, for there is no separating the two. Without one, the other has no meaning.

*

Until life has given thee its worst, thou hast not been at thy best.

*

All has been brought to bear against thee. Thine instincts were bred into thee; thy laws created for they could not be kept. Question all, for this is the path to Oneness. Heed not the beliefs, laws and actions of others unless they suit thee. And be prepared to die for this.

*

Fear of the Lord is the end of Knowledge and of Reason, and these two pursuits are the keys that shall free thy soul. If ye sacrifice these philosophies, then ye shall cease to grow in spirit. And there shall be no life in death.

*

And so it ended, for it was enough.

"Remember what has been said here," Satan concluded. "For the salvation of the earth is contained within the simple words thou hast heard here this night."

"Yes, I see the truth in what Ye say, Teacher," Cain replied. "And of all things, one must learn to recognize the truth."

And Satan said, "For one with no soul, Cain, ye art wiser than many. Take the life ye have been given and make it purposeful, regardless of what hast befallen thee. We are remembered for what we do and how we live: make yours a goodly remembrance."

"I say again to thee, Cain, take what I have given thee this night. Thou art a tiller of soil: take the seeds of wisdom I have placed within thee, plant them, tend them, see that they take root."

"Remember this always."

And Cain did remember. Always.

THE BOOK OF
GENERATIONS

Within a short span of years, Cain ceased his wanderings. And he gathered unto him those of like mind, and together did they found a city. And they called this city *Enoch*, which in the first tongue meant *dedicated*, for this refuge would be as a haven to those who sought solace from the Lord God.

In time, Cain was wed, and knew his wife. And in this knowing was a son conceived, and they called him Chislon, meaning *hope*. And, like his father before him, Chislon bore the mark of the beast.

And so the city grew and prospered, drawing those whose bodies flowed strong with the Gift of Knowledge. And it prepared, for the Tribe of Cain was not alone in its prosperity.

Yea, as the numbers within Enoch swelled ever more greatly, so too did the Tribe of Adam prosper. Yet, for a time, Adam and Eve were without progeny. With the banishment of Cain and the death of Abel, their house had been emptied. But it was not empty for long. In time, the void was filled with the birth of Seth, their third son.

And this son was raised with a great fear of the Lord God, for the parents would take no risk with their new child. In this time, the Tribe of Adam was most faithful in its worship, and no offense was tolerated. And those who did not offer proper sacrifice were stoned or burned alive as an offering unto the Lord, their God. Woe unto the Tribe of Adam, for the shadow of fear hung as a tapestry upon them.

And there were those who would not suffer to live in this manner. There were those who would dare escape, for it was rumored that a city lay hidden from the eyes of God. Yet only a bold few attempted the journey, for the prodigals were hunted and butchered by Adam's Tribunal.

In time, Eve found solace from her madness in the darkness of death, and Adam, too, gladly followed. So it was that Seth became the tribal priest and leader. And such was his grief that he swore a blood feud. A feud between his tribe and that of his brother, the evil Cain. For Seth believed it was his brother's sin that caused the Lord to enfeeble his father and mother.

And at the funeral pyre of his sire, Seth did proclaim: "As my father's flesh is purged of the evil fruit of Eden, I pledge our lives to destroy Cain and his spawn. Never shall they know peace. They shall be burned and butchered wherever we shall find them. To all of you do I give this decree: find his city and burn it to the very ground; neither Cain nor any of his progeny must survive."

And Seth drew his sword and thrust it toward the heavens. "Destroy his city! Destroy his children! Purge the land of his seed! Bring me the head of my brother, Cain!"

And so the battle between brother and brother, the Tribe of Seth and Tribe of Cain, began; one led by a puppet of the Lord God, and the other led by a murderer in league with the Fallen.

And the two tribes slew each other wherever they did meet. Yet Cain died not from this violence, and neither did Seth. In time, they left the world, one with a soul and one without, both housed in the flesh of old age.

But the war did not end with their passing, and the hatred and butchery continued unto their children. Yet, despite the unending feud, the Tribe of Cain prospered well within the city of Enoch. And there came a time when the walls were too small to house those within; and two new cities were born. One named Sodom and the other, Gomorrah.

And as time passed, Cain's son Chislon took a wife. In turn, they begat a son and called him Irad; and Irad begat a son also and named him Malchus; and Malchus begat a son and called him Eli. And Eli begat Lamech.

And Lamech was found by the Tribe of Seth.

For as the Tribe of Cain spread its seed, so, too, did the children of Seth spread and grow. And Seth, begat himself a son, and called him Enos; and Enos begat Cainan who begat Mahalaleel; and Mahalaleel begat Jared.

And Jared was he who found Lamech.

*   *   *

Lamech lived in the original city. His flesh bore the mark of his ancestor, as it was with his father before him.

And Lamech was a worker of stone, and was renowned for his skills. As a child, many times had his father taken him to hiding, when the sons of Seth had drawn nigh.

The ranting of an old man, thought Lamech of his father's stories. Yet the mark remained and troubled his doubts.

Upon the passing of his father, he chose Enoch in which to settle, and he made his life there. And a day came when he found a maiden lovely and fair, and she took his heart; and her name was Adah.

And Lamech dropped himself before her, saying, "More than mine own life do I love thee, yet if thou takest me as thy husband, know this: I am one of those originally cursed, and I bear the mark upon me."

And Adah looked down upon him, and saw the love that was in his eyes; and she could not say no to him.

"And what hast thou done to deserve this curse, dear Lamech? Hast thou taken a life?" Adah asked this, knowing the answer Lamech would give.

And Lamech lowered his head, saying, "What matter? I am of the line of Cain and carry his sin; and the children of Seth shall hunt me and mine as my father was hunted and his father before him...is this the life thou wouldst lead?"

And Adah reached down and lifted his head, looking deeply within his eyes, seeing his soul. "The Lord God would not curse thee for thy father's sins, Lamech, for He is just."

And Lamech raised his hand to the mark upon his breast, which countered these words, yet said nothing.

So it was that they were wed. In time, Adah gave Lamech two sons; and they were named Jabal and Jubal.

And for a time, happiness filled their house.

Then Jared came upon them.

And there was fire, and there was smoke, and there was the smell of flesh and death.

Lamech awoke. Awoke from the dream that had haunted him for twenty years. The sweat ran cold from his body as the images subsided.

As Lamech sat up in his bed, his hand raised itself to the scar which ran across the mark upon his chest. Jared had tried to skin him alive as his family burned within the flames.

Lamech remembered his bound hands and legs, getting them free. Bringing his hands down upon Jared's skull with crushing force. So hard that Lamech thought he was dead.

And he ran to his wife, his children, attempting to pull them from the flames. Yet it was too late. Much too late. And when he turned around, Jared was gone. As was his family, as was his life.

"What matter, my husband?" spake Zillah.

As the veil of memories left Lamech, his thoughts aligned again with current time and place.

Zillah had borne him Tubalcain, his son of fifteen years. And Naamah, his daughter, just turned twelve.

"The dream," spake Lamech. "'Twas the dream, nothing more. Go back to sleep, beloved. Back to sleep."

Yet Zillah slept not, for Lamech had awaked from this dream many times in the past months. She believed not in the portent of dreams, but in the darkness, a small part of her soul acknowledged their prophecies. And that part was afraid.

She drew her flesh together and waited for the time when Lamech's breath came smoothly, evenly: a sign of his renewed slumber. And then she slept.

*   *   *

Jared ran that night. Ran with his life's blood falling into his eyes. *Satan runs strong in the daemonseed of Cain,* he thought. *Yes, strong indeed. But not stronger than the Lord God runs within my veins.*

"Thy family burns in flames this night, Lamech!" cried Jared in the darkness. "As they shall burn in Hell's fire for all eternity!" So ran Jared into the desert. Ran knowing he would return another day, and destroy the sire.

Yet the end of Lamech would not be so easily done, for an illness had fallen upon Jared. And for many days he was fevered and without his senses. By the will of God was he found, half dead, by a merchant caravan. And for many weeks did they nurture him and restored him to a state of health.

In gratitude, Jared killed his nurse and those with her, for they were infidels and not worthy of the Lord God's graces. With renewed blood upon his flesh did he flee into the night. Fleeing to find the living Lamech.

Yet it was all for naught. For when Jared returned to find his nemesis, Lamech was gone, leaving behind only the graves of his wife and butchered children.

"Run!" shouted Jared, pounding his fists in the soil. "Run, Lamech, yet know this! My life is for your death. Run, for there is no hiding."

*   *   *

Twenty years.

Twenty years had Lamech lived in the city of Enoch. Twenty years had he called himself by another name. And for sixteen of those years had he lived with a new wife, Zillah. And this wife had given him a new family. And once again, all was good and all was right.

Yet still the dreams came, and the horror of that one night did not subside.

He never spoke of those times. Yet Zillah knew this good man had a troubled past. The night screams, the names, the scars, and yes, the mark upon his breast.

She knew that her husband was an impossible creature. She knew he was of the seed of Cain. And she knew the risk, for the feud between the Children of Seth and the progeny of Cain was well known.

Yet she loved this man, and nothing would diminish her dedication to him and their children.

Such is the power of love.

*   *   *

Destiny touched Lamech on an autumn day. It was a day without measure. The sky was the clearest of blue, the sun a perfect blend of warmth and light.

As with most mornings, Lamech rose early and left to practice his trade. Zillah also rose early, providing him with bread and fruits to break his fast from the previous evening.

And so, too, did Naamah arise, helping her mother as was her wont. After they partook of their morning meal, they went about their tasks, leaving Tubalcain to his extra hour of solitude. For it was not within him to rise with the sun.

In good time, Tubalcain awoke, stretching lazily as the morning sun filled his eyes with vague shapes still unfocused in his repose. And a shadow crossed the light. And Tubalcain looked to see what it was.

And lo, it was destiny: the face of Jared, though Tubalcain knew it not. "Who art thou?" he managed to say.

Yet the response brought no answer to his question; for the last vision to grace Tubalcain's sight was that of iron falling toward him.

Alas, Tubalcain did not see the blade as it drew itself across the flesh of his neck. Yet he felt the searing pain of its mutilation. He saw the spouting of blood as it left his throat and colored his vision. He tasted the hot, saltiness of his life upon his lips.

And when the final pulse of Tubalcain's heart brought forth the last of his blood, Jared again drew his dagger. With quick, brutal thrusts did he remove Tubalcain's heart.

Tearing the silent organ from the arteries and veins which anchored it to its host, Jared did raise it toward the heavens in tribute to the Lord God. "Here ends the Line of Cain, oh Lord. Blessed be Thy name!"

And he brought the heart to his mouth, and partook thereof. "For you, my Lord! For you!"

*   *   *

Zillah and Naamah spent the morning in the market, bartering for a leg of lamb. It was to be their supper that evening.

As Zillah went home to begin preparations for the evening meal, Naamah stayed behind for a time, following the elder women of the city to the river for fresh water. The laden clay jug was too heavy for her, but her pride ran strong, and she made no complaint thereof.

When Zillah returned home, she called out for Tubalcain, who was normally still within the house, as it was just before the luncheon hour.

"Tubal?" she cried. Yet when no answer came, Zillah assumed her son had gone to the square. When it suited him, his tread would bring him to the city square, to hear the words of the prophets.

Zillah left the venison upon the table within the kitchen and walked toward Tubalcain's room. She entered his chamber, to put his linens in place, for Tubalcain was known to leave them in disarray. Yet this day, there was no preparation for what she saw.

Tubalcain's body had been butchered as if it were the carcass of a sacrificial lamb. The skin had been peeled away and discarded upon the floor. The stomach was torn open and pulled asunder, leaving his bowels spilled upon the sheets.

Zillah began to scream. Yet before the sound came to fruition, a daemonic form came from behind the door. The creature placed a bloodied hand upon Zillah's mouth, drawing a dagger quickly across her throat—drawing it with such force that the head was severed clean from the body.

And Jared took the headless corpse carnally, laying her upon the skinned body of her son. He moved upon her with violence, spending his seed in a passion found only through the greater glory of the Lord God.

*   *   *

His work was done early that day, and Lamech made his way home. He looked with pleasure toward seeing his family so early in the day, yet he thought not of the night, for the night brought the dreams.

Lamech entered the house, knowing not the horrors that waited within. Jared stood quietly. Moments past. Then moments more: and, finally, Lamech made his way into the room of slaughter.

Jared listened, waited, his knife raised. Lamech entered, and in that moment between realization and action, Jared struck. And the blood flew as rain upon the walls. In moments, Lamech, who had survived so much, lay dead upon the floor.

Yet still did Jared wait, for there was yet another. And when Lamech's daughter came within the walls of death, he tore at her clothing and pushed her to the ground; and he did know her.

Amidst her screams did he penetrate her, again and again; and he called her all manner of vileness. And in his violent passion, he tore away her hair in bloody clumps as he pummeled and grunted against her.

And as his lust found release, he pounded the child's head against the cobble of the floor, screaming, "Praise God! Praise be the Lord God!"

And as Jared's seed lay spent within the broken body of the child, Jared raised his eyes to the heavens, saying, "For you, my Lord, for you!"

And so ends the lineage of Cain, Jared thought as he covered his nakedness.

And Jared left, knowing himself to have made a place in history as one of the greater soldiers of the Lord. And in his righteousness did Jared leave the house of death, with the blood of Lamech and his family fresh upon his flesh.

Yet, unknown to the soldier of the Lord, his mission had failed. For the girl child did not die that day. Though the crushing of her skull upon the stone left her feeble for the rest of her days, she did survive.

Amongst the human debris she alone was found with the spark of life left within her; and she was given shelter by those within the temple of the city, for Lamech and his family were well considered by all. Yet the girl's mind was gone and did not return, for the brutality which she suffered left her without sensibility.

And it came to pass that those within the temple saw that she, the child, was with child herself. And they did tend to her and care for her. And in the eighth month of her pregnancy did the heart of Naamah cease it's beating.

And the rabbis within the temple took a knife to the corpse of the child and did remove the life within her.

And the child did live. And the mark was bold upon its breast.

                    *   *   *

"Yea, what is this savor?" spake the Lord God in awe, for He had never felt such power of faith. "The acts of this Child of Seth are the acts of madness, yet the power of his faith is sweet upon Our palate. How could this come to pass?"

And there was a brief silence within the Heavens until the voice of Gabriel was heard. "It is a special insanity, this. It is the savor of religious fervor; the power of divine fanaticism."

And the Lord God said, "Yet is this not madness? How is it that We are nourished by these thoughts and acts?"

Gabriel responded thusly, saying, "It is the madness of righteousness, a fever brought by unquestioning belief. Those afflicted with it shall forever provide us our greatest power."

Cassiel spake then, "Yet what of these horrors? Should we allow these acts of vile perversion?"

"Allow them?" spake the Almighty. "We shall encourage them."

THE BOOK OF LAW

Alas, there came a time when the work of Satan could no longer be denied by Those Above. The Gifts of the Fallen had tainted the flesh of Man near the Point of Sorrow. And soon the Chosen would be unable to work Their miracles with impunity.

For the power needed by Those Above to interact with Man would destroy the sanity of his mind, and the faith thereof would lose its savor.

So it was that a decision was made within the heavens.

"The Defiler has worked His magica too well upon this earth. Soon, not even minor miracles may We perform without destroying the savor of the faith We so desire," the Lord God said. "Far better We focus Our energies upon other Children of the Lights, those which also have the seeds of Life upon them."

"Agreed," said Mikal. "Yet there are still a few things we may do to secure Our hold upon this world."

And all the Host in the heavens listened. "We may find one feeble, before the poison takes stronger root, and impart unto Him laws and rules to give unto the people."

And the Lord God showed His displeasure towards the Angel Mikal, saying, "Laws? What good these laws, Mikal? One cannot foster faith through the dictates of Law."

Yet Mikal cowered not, "It is true: not through laws which dictate faith shall faith be derived. Thou art surely correct." And God did listen to Mikal, then. "But, rather, We shall dictate laws to which Man, by his very nature, cannot adhere."

"Tell us more of this plan, Mikal, as it may hold promise," urged the Angel Gabriel.

"We shall give Divine Law unto man that he cannot obey," continued Mikal. "Then, when he finds himself in disobedience, he shall look to the heavens for penance and grace."

"Yes!" exclaimed the Lord God. "For by breaking the law shall man have guilt; and guilt shall foster prayer and penance; and this shall enhance his..."

"Faith," finished Mikal.

"Yes...it shall increase the fervor and savor of his faith."

And so a solemn discourse began within the heavens as the Divine Laws were molded around the fallible traits of Man; for Man was made to be part beast.

And a doctrine was created.

First came the Laws of Provision, so that the Race of Man would worship no other, thereby focusing all faith on Those Above. Then came the Laws of the Beast, which would forbid the cravings of that which was less evolved within man. And finally came the Laws of the Mind, which made the thought as evil as the deed, so that even the reasoning being within Man could not hide from sin.

And the Laws of Provision ran thusly:

Ye shall keep my statutes as Divine Law.

*

Ye shall be holy; for I the Lord thy God am holy.

*

Turn ye not unto idols, nor make thyselves molten gods; for I am the Lord thy God.

*

Ye shall not swear by My name falsely; neither shall ye profane the name of thy God; for I am the Lord.

*

Regard not them that have familiar spirits nor seek after wizards, to be defiled by them, neither shall thee use enchantments.

*

Ye shall not make any cuttings in thy flesh for the dead, nor print any marks upon thee.

And the First Law commanded the following of the Divine laws, so that none may be broken; and by breaking any of the Laws which followed, so too would this one be broken.

And the Second Law commanded Man to be holy; not to attempt holiness, but to *be holy*. And Those Above saw that this Law could not be attained, and it was good.

And the Third Law commanded Man to pray not to any other gods, so that all the faith of Man would flow toward the Chosen only.

The Fourth Law commanded Man not to take the Lord's name in vain; for to do so would draw sustenance from the Lord God.

The Fifth Law commanded Man not to delve in the magik arts, nor to take guidance from the Defiler; for in these ways might Man challenge Those Above.

The final Law of Provision forbade the Magica of Protection and its runes; for that magik could remove the taint of Those Above from the flesh of Man.

And the Laws of the Beast ran thusly:

Ye shall not bring death to thy neighbor, nor suffer sin upon him; thou shalt love thy neighbor as thyself.

*

Ye shall not steal; neither shall ye deal falsely with one another.

*

Ye shall not go amongst thy people as a talebearer.

*

Ye shall not eat any thing with the blood.

And the First Law of the Beast forbade Man to kill or injure, even for his own survival. A rule made for the breaking, as survival of self and family were ingrained deeply within the soul of man.

And the Second Law forbade the taking of the possessions of others. A difficult rule to abide when hunger, passion and the needs of survival ran strong.

And the Third Law forbade the telling of false tales, a method used by Man to preserve his physical survival in time of need, and his sense of import when he finds he has none.

The Fourth Law of the Beast forbade the taking of blood; a denial of the savor intrinsic to the beast, for the sating of the flesh is, at times, a need that does run deep. Yet, there, too, were other reasons: blood also carried the magica of life and death—the power of spirit and the spores of disease. It was a fluid too potent for man to abuse.

And should these not have been sufficient, so did Those Above write the Laws of the Mind; for should penance not be derived from the act, it would be required just for the thought.

And the Laws of the Mind ran thusly:

Ye shall not be covetous of a man or woman that is not thine.

*

Ye shall not be unrighteous in thy judgment; in righteousness shalt thou judge thy neighbor.

*

Ye shall not be covetous of thy neighbor's possessions.

And so these three Laws were created, to make the thought sin; for Man could not master his thoughts, even should he master his actions.

And so it was planned for these Thirteen Laws to be given unto the Race of Man.

*   *   *

Here lies the tale of the Liberator, the Bearer of the Law.

It came to pass that the Tribe of Seth found its way unto the land of Egypt, and there lived peacefully with the tribes of that land. Yet the children of the Tribe of Seth were fruitful, and increased abundantly, and the land was filled with them.

And in this time there arose a new king, and his name was Pharaoh; and he said unto his people: "Behold, those of the Tribe of Seth are more and mightier than we. Come, let us deal sharply with them, lest they multiply even more greatly, and it shall come to pass that they turn upon us and bring about our subjugation."

So it was that those of Seth became subjects to the will of Egypt. And the lives of those subjugated were made bitter with hard bondage: made to labor in mortar and brick, and in all manner of service in the field.

Yet still the seed of Seth flourished. So then did Pharaoh decree that no male child of those enslaved be suffered to live.

Such did he charge his people: "Every son that is born to the Tribe of Seth shall ye cast into the sacred river Nile, yet every daughter may ye save alive."

And such was the fear within those in bondage that they did this thing.

Yet not all would murder their male children so, and one named Levi could not cause his son to drown; for Levi was in direct lineage to Seth and therefore Adam. And when the wife of Levi conceived, and bore a son, she saw that he was a child of faith.

And Levi placed the child upon the sacrificial stone, and he took a sharpened knife from his side, whetted keen by spit and labor.

And Levi drew the foreskin of the child taut, drawing the blade swiftly across the flesh, severing the skin from the penis; and the blood spouted as urine amidst the child's screams.

And Levi took the severed flesh and cast it within a bowl of flame; and the flesh burned and spat as the dark smoke carried the sacrifice upward toward the heavens.

And its odor was sweet savor unto the Lord.

For three months did they hide the child from the eyes of Pharaoh. And when they could no longer hide the child, they did build a small ark of straw and pitch, and put the child therein, sending him forth upon the waters of the Nile.

And the Lord God with Those Above looked down upon the child, saying, and "We have found our vessel, the bearer of Our Covenant."

For Those in the Heavens saw that the child was feeble, its faith unpalatable. The mind of the child could therefore not be further damaged by Their touch.

And so the Lord God let the ark pass safely upon the waters. And it came to pass that the daughter of Pharaoh went down unto the river that day to wash herself at the river's bank; and her handmaidens walked beside her.

It was there that she noticed the small craft upon the waters, amongst the reeds; and she sent a maiden to fetch it.

And when Pharaoh's daughter gazed within, she saw the child. And behold, the child gazed upon her and smiled; and lo, Pharaoh's daughter smiled also, and had compassion for the child. And she saw that the flesh of the genitals had been mutilated and she said, "This child is of the Tribe of Seth." Yet she could not bring herself to kill it.

"Go," she said unto the handmaiden who had retrieved the child. "Go and find me a woman to nurse him."

And the maiden went, and lo, she returned with a woman whose breasts were laden with the milk of life; and the woman was the wife of Levi.

"Nurse this child and raise him, woman," commanded the daughter of Pharaoh, "and I shall give thee wages. When he outgrows thy nursing, return him to me, and I shall raise him in the House of Pharaoh."

And the woman did nurse him, and the child did grow; and there came a time when the milk of his true mother was no longer of consequence. And she brought him then unto the daughter of Pharaoh, and she did so gladly: for the child was one of special needs and would live a life of privilege. And Pharaoh's daughter glowed with happiness when she received her new son.

And the daughter of Pharaoh found great joy in this child, and she called him Moses.

*   *   *

As Moses grew, it became clear to the daughter of Pharaoh that he was not as other children; his speech came not quickly and his skills were less honed. Yet it mattered not, for she loved him.

Despite his shortcomings, Moses, being of the House of Pharaoh, became a master over the slaves of Egypt, his own people. Yet Moses was not so feeble as to be ignorant of his true heritage, for it was written upon the mutilated flesh of his genitals.

And so, one day, Moses was out amongst the tombs of towering stone, and he came upon a soldier beating one of the Tribe of Seth.

And the Lord God touched Moses then, and a rage came upon him. And Moses took the staff from the soldier's hand and turned it upon him. And the soldier fell, fearing to strike the adopted grandson of Pharaoh.

And Moses raised the staff again and again, and rained blows upon the soldier until blood flew in crimson arcs with each raising of the staff.

Yet Moses did not stop then.

And bones cracked and flesh fell as leaves upon the ground, and the insides of the man spilled foully upon the earth.

"Enough, enough!" cried a terrified voice. "See what thou hast done?"

And the world returned to Moses then, and he saw that the man who had stayed his hand was he who had been beaten by the soldier.

Yet it was stayed too late.

The slave looked down in horror at the torn body of the dead man. Surely, this blood-soaked man called Moses was mad.

"Why? Why hast thou done this?"

And Moses had no answer. Yet he knew that what he had done could not go unpunished, not even for one of the house of Pharaoh. And Moses gazed around him, and saw that all eyes were upon him, and that he was covered in the blood of the dead soldier.

Moses ran. He ran and left Egypt that very day, in fear for his own life, for he had slain a child of Egypt to aid a child of Seth.

So Moses came to rest in the Land of Midian. And he settled and started himself a new life. In time, he took a wife, Zipporah, daughter to Jethro, priest of Midian, and she bore him a son, and they named him Gershom.

And it came to pass that the Pharaoh of Egypt became more hardened unto the Tribe of Seth, and the children of Seth cried out unto the Lord God from within their bondage.

And the fervor and savor of their prayers found themselves upon the lips of the Lord God: "It is time."

*   *   *

It was a day that began as most others, and Moses brought his tended flock upon the mountain; and then the day became as no other.

For it was there that the Lord God appeared unto Moses in a flame of fire. At first Moses thought it only an occurrence of nature. Yet as he drew closer, the flame spoke, saying, "Take off the shoes from thy feet, for thou standest on hallowed ground."

And Moses was stricken with fear by this, for the words etched themselves as with a burning within his mind, and he raised his hands to block them out. Yet the action availed him not, for still the words came.

"Behold," continued the flame, "for I am the God of thy father and thy father's father."

And Moses did act then, for the words and the flame brought him fear, and he dared not disobey. And he removed the sandals from his feet, and walked closer toward the manifested God.

And Moses lowered his eyes, saying, "Lord, how is it I have displeased thee? What have I done?" And then his knees gave way in fright from beneath him, for Moses knew what he had done.

He had committed a grievous sin, for he had repeated the crime of Cain. And now the Lord had come forth to bring his judgment. Surely he would burn forever within that horrible flame before him, raging brightly yet coldly. Lo, Moses fell to prayer then, giving deep, fervent penance in the hopes of saving his immortal soul.

And the Lord God was deeply pleased, for He was nourished by it. Yet it was all for naught. For the Lord did not approach Moses with thoughts of retribution. Indeed, his crime was irrelevant to the Lord God, for He cared not about the squabbles of mankind.

He was here for a greater purpose.

And so He addressed the pathetic human soul before him. "Place thy fear aside, Moses," spake the Lord. "I have come neither for thy banishment nor chastisement: the man slain by thine hand was an oppressor of the Tribe of Seth, his death a welcome tribute. Rise, Moses, and listen; for thou hast been chosen above all men to lead my people to freedom."

And Moses lifted his head in amazement, and looked with bewilderment upon the Holy Fire.

"I?" replied Moses.

"Yea, thou art blessed by the hand of the Lord God this day: for henceforth shall ye speak as my voice, hear as mine ears, act as mine arms."

Yet Moses shook his head, saying, "Of all people, Lord, I should be chosen least of all, for my tongue holds no wit nor quickness to it. I am not as others. I pray thee, I am ill chosen, unworthy of this honor."

And the flames shuddered and drew themselves up brighter.

"It is not for thee to question the will of the Lord thy God!"

And Moses dropped his head to the sand then, crying the tears of the damned, for the Light of the Lord had burned the sight from his eyes.

"Get thee back to Egypt; seek out thy brother, for he is quick of wit and sharp of tongue. It is he that shall speak for thee," sayeth the Lord.

Through his tears, Moses managed these small words: "Yes, Lord, yet I know of no brother, as I was found upon the waters of the Nile."

And the Lord said, "I shall lead thy steps to thy true mother, Moses. Then thou shalt find thy brother, and his name shall be Aaron."

And He continued: "I am the Lord thy God. The God of Adam and of Seth and all the progeny thereof. I am that I am. And thy flesh is mine to command."

And slowly, Moses felt the seared pulp of his eyes mold themselves to normalcy, and light returned to his world.

"Go to Pharaoh, have him release My flock."

And the flame rose, and settled near a stout shrub. Yet the bush was not consumed by the flame.

"I place a portion of my power within these boughs. Make thee a staff thereof. Its power shall aid thee in the liberation of thy tribe."

"Go forth now, Moses: set My people free."

And the brightness of the flame diminished and was absorbed by the shrub beneath it.

Moses did not recall losing his senses, yet when they returned, the sky had turned to darkness. From the unconsumed bush did Moses pull a branch to aid his way, for his own staff had become lost.

And he remembered the words of the Lord God, then. And he felt the power from within the wood, power that was his to wield.

Moses smiled. "Yea, they shall be free." And in the darkness did he make his way homeward.

Moses left his wife and son the very next day and found his way back to the Land of Pharaoh.

*   *   *

In time, Moses made his way to the home of his true mother, guided by an unseen force. And lo, Moses saw that the Lord God had led him to a woman that he did know, for the woman was the wife of Levi.

"Thou art she who gave me succor as a child," spake Moses unto her.

"It is true, she said. I am thy mother, and thou art my son. The Lord God has returned thee."

And Moses said, "Why hast thou not told me before this?"

And she replied, "It was to keep thee safe, dear child."

And the wife of Levi saw a change within her son, and it was felt by all within the house. And Moses walked up to him he knew must be his brother.

"Thou art Aaron," Moses said.

"I am, brother," came the reply.

And Moses turned back to his mother then, saying, "I pray thee, mother, a place to stay this night—for tomorrow thine only two begotten sons shall change the earth."

*   *   *

The next day was a day that began without malice; a day warmed by the sun of Egypt. That afternoon, the Pharaoh held audience. All had gone well; the court was near ending. And then came the two brothers.

"The day is not yet done," spake Aaron.

And Pharaoh turned unto the voice, which held neither awe nor fear. And Pharaoh saw that the speaker was unknown to him, yet the one who walked with him was not.

"Moses," whispered Pharaoh. Yet so clever were the engineers of Pharaoh that all within the meeting hall heard the whispered words.

"Grandfather," greeted Moses. Yet there was no warmth in the greeting.

"I raised thee as mine own blood, child," said Pharaoh. "Then thou killest my captain and leaveth without a word to thy mother. She is dead now. A death born of worry."

And the eyes of Moses flared, and he said, "She was not my mother. I was raised by the progeny of thy loins to protect me from thy butchery. Ye have reaped what ye have sewn. I am bound not to thee."

And anger came upon Pharaoh, and he looked upon Moses, saying, "Thou art less than an animal. But for my daughter's sake dost thou still live. Leave this place before I reconsider my kindness."

And Aaron responded, "It is not so easy, for we have been charged with a task."

"A task?" responded Pharaoh. "What task of any import would be given to two such as you; a feeble fool and a worthless slave?"

And Moses laughed, dark and sinister.

"We have come to command the release of our tribe from thy subjugation," spake Aaron.

And Pharaoh, in turn, laughed also, saying, "Thee? Command me? By what authority? Perhaps it is the sun and sand which command thee, for they must have worked grievously upon thy flesh."

And Aaron banged his staff upon the ground, responding, "It is not the elements from which we take guidance, Pharaoh, but rather from the one true God. From His mouth to thine ears does this message come."

"The one true god?" responded Pharaoh. "Which one would he be, then? The god who has led thy people to slavery?"

"Laugh now, Pharaoh, for laughter shall soon leave thee," spake Aaron. "There is but one true God and no other. We pray thee, release His people or grave ill shall befall thee and all of Egypt."

Pharaoh shook his head. Enough foolishness was enough. One of his wives was with child, and the astrologers said the birth would come at any time. There were much better places he could be than here; much better things he could do than this.

So Pharaoh waved to his guards. "Throw these fools out of this place."

And he turned unto the self-proclaimed prophets. "Again, but for my daughter's memory dost thou remain alive this day, Moses. My patience has left me. Return not to this place."

And Moses and Aaron were led away; and Pharaoh went to seek his wife.

"So be it," cried Moses as he was tossed through the palace doors. "So be it."

The first of the horrors would begin the next day.

*   *   *

And that night the Lord God spake to Moses thusly: "I shall make thee a god to Pharaoh, and Aaron thy brother shall be thy prophet."

"Thou shalt speak all that I command of thee: and Aaron thy brother shall speak unto Pharaoh, that he send the Children of the Tribe of Seth from his land."

"And I shall harden Pharaoh's heart so that he will not heed thy words."

Yet this puzzled Moses. "Why wouldst Thou do this? Thou asketh of me to release Thy people; yet Thou sayest Ye shall make it so Pharaoh shall not do so."

And the Lord God said, "I shall allow Pharaoh to harken unto thy words in time. Yet first shall he not harken unto them, so that I may multiply my s wonders within the land of Egypt."

"And many plagues shall I bring forth; and I shall bring blood and frogs, lice and flies, pestilence and hail, locusts and darkness. And when all this is done shall I smite the children of Egypt, and cause the Angel of Death to fall upon them. Only then shall I release the heart of Pharaoh, and allow him to release my sheep from the bonds of slavery."

And even Moses saw what was to pass, feeble though he was. All the horrors he was to inflict upon Pharaoh and the people of Egypt would not be of their own doing. For the Lord God would force them not to release His chosen people. He would harden their hearts so they would not hear reason.

Not until the Lord God had ample time in which to show His powers.

And the Trinity continued, "The Egyptians shall know that I am the Lord God when I stretch forth mine hand and bring misery and death among them. It shall be a lesson unto them and the whole earth."

Yea, a lesson to be remembered and feared long after the Time of Miracles has come to pass, spake the Lord God unto Himself.

Still was Moses mystified by this speech, and he imparted his confusion unto his Lord and Master. "Yet why so much suffering, my Shepherd? Should not one plague suffice? Art Thou not a merciful god with love for Thy children? Why harden the hearts of Pharaoh and Egypt to foster more torment?"

And a light entered the soul of Moses then, and he felt a burning within him; a burning as the fires of Hell playing upon his flesh. And he fell to the ground, screaming pleas for mercy. He clawed the skin upon his face to purge it of the pain, tore deeply into the features; tore until his face ran with red pulp and his hands were coated in his own blood.

And then the fire was gone, as was the Lord God.

And Moses did as the Lord God commanded him, and he questioned never again. And the scars he brought to his own flesh remained upon him until his death.

The next morning did Moses and Aaron return unto Pharaoh; and they did as the Lord had commanded.

"Let my people go," spake Aaron to Pharaoh.

And Pharaoh spoke to Aaron not, and did not acknowledge him. Rather, he turned to Moses, saying, "Again dost thou come hither. So be it: I decree thee to death, for—as ye have said—there is no blood to bind us."

"Take them," spake Pharaoh to a guard. "Take them and kill them. I will not gaze upon them again. I wish no more of this madness."

Cast down thy staff, Moses.

And Moses heard the words within him and knew them. So Moses took his staff, which he had taken from the bush that burned, and cast it upon the stones.

And as the rod fell before Pharaoh, it changed in shape and form; and what was once hardened wood became a living serpent. And the serpent made its way toward Pharaoh.

And lo, the guard commanded to take Moses brought his sword down upon the serpent, yet could not cleave its flesh. And the serpent leapt upon the guard and wrapped about him; and its teeth bit deeply.

Straightaway did the guard loose his hold upon the earth. And his face blackened and the flesh fell from his bones, and the skin and organs dissolved into a bloodied ichor.

And the serpent again made its way to Pharaoh.

"Bring the magicians and the sorcerers, quickly," cried Pharaoh, for a grievous fear was upon him.

And the wise men did come; and lo, they were men of the Mark. And the Mark was displayed visibly upon their breast.

And they, also, cast their staves upon the stone; and they, too, became as serpents: for those who carried the Mark had found that they could wield the minor magica.

Yet their power was not a thousandth of that of the Lord God. And as they watched, horrified, the serpent of the Lord God killed and ate the serpents of the wise men.

And the serpent did find its way to Pharaoh, for none would now oppose it. And it did rise up, and set its eyes upon Pharaoh; and its eyes glowed as with heated coals; and the magica of their stare pierced deeply into the heart of Pharaoh.

And the heart of Pharaoh fell to the power of the Lord God and was hardened, for such was the will of the Lord God.

This done, Moses went forth and retrieved the serpent. And he pulled the serpent taut and it became again as wood. And Moses stepped towards the waters of the Nile, for the audience chamber was built upon the river's shores.

And as Moses raised the staff above his head, Aaron said, "Let the people of the Lord God go, that they may serve him in the wilderness. And behold, thou shalt know that the god of Moses is the Lord God, for He will smite the waters which are in the river, and they shall be turned to blood."

"Never," cried Pharaoh, for his heart was hardened by the Lord God. "Never." And there was blankness within the eyes of Pharaoh also, for the energies of the Angelica had lain upon his flesh, and his mind was not as it was before.

So it was that Moses placed the tip of his staff within the waters, and the waters became corrupted. And the water was made as blood.

"See what has happened here this day, and think upon it, for such shall be the fate of Egypt for seven days. We shall return then, and ask anew."

And Pharaoh turned and went into his house.

Yet it was not only the river that turned, but each pond and stream and vessel also, so that no water was left in Egypt to dispel thirst. And the fish within the waters rose to the surface in death.

And all of Egypt lay under a cloud of fear and the smell of decay.

So Pharaoh gathered his wise men about him.

"Let them go, Pharaoh," they said as one. "We cannot defend against such power. He is too strong, this Lord God; He holds no mercy within Him. Let go His children."

"Never," spake Pharaoh, "never." And such was always the answer. And the wise men saw that reason had left Pharaoh.

So that night the wise men of Egypt did gather, and they spoke of what must be.

"Pharaoh has been corrupted by the power of the Lord God, and he shall not atone. He must be brought to death, for there is no choice. Should Pharaoh not fall, then so shall Egypt fall. This must not come to pass."

Yet the Lord God had warned Pharaoh within a dream; and Pharaoh had gathered his soldiers. And they fell upon the gathering of the wise men.

Only a few did escape the slaughter. The wise men had no armaments, and they fell swiftly. Those who did not die and could not flee were taken to the prisons.

And for many days and many nights were they made to suffer.

Pharaoh administered the torments himself, which before had he never done. He burned their flesh with heated iron; he smashed their fingers with stones; he pushed his own fingers into their eyes until blood shot forth as a running well.

And it was not enough. As the madness ran through him, his depravity climbed to even greater heights. He would take a knife to his victims and remove their entrails, showing licking their organs in front of them as they died. And he would rape them and stab them as he shook with his passion.

And as he did these things, he muttered always, "For You!"

The guards within the prisons spoke not unto Pharaoh, for they were paralyzed with the horrors before them. Some left Egypt when they could, yet some were caught.

And they were dealt with by Pharaoh; and none dared try to leave again.

In time, the seven days ended and the waters were again made fresh.

And Moses and Aaron returned to Pharaoh and said, "Thus sayeth the Lord God: Let My people go, that they may serve Me."

And Pharaoh willed his mouth to open and concur. Yet before this act could be done, a distance came upon his eyes, and he said, "Never," and repeated, "never." As he always did say, as he always would say: for thus was the will of the Lord God.

And so the plagues did follow, one after the other; each more grievous than the last. First came the water made blood; then came the frogs, and they covered the land of Egypt; thus followed the lice, which burrowed deeply into Egyptian flesh, yet touched not one of the Tribe of Seth.

And then came the flies and their diseases; and the pestilence, which felled both man and beast; next the hail; and locusts also, destroying crops and bringing starvation.

And then the darkness fell upon all of Egypt, and for seven days there was no sun.

None could understand the resolve of Pharaoh, for how could any man not relent in the face of such horror? And lo, it was true, no man of free will would stand foolishly in the face of such misery.

Yet when asked to free those in bondage and end the suffering, Pharaoh replied simply, "Never, never." And he knew not why.

For Pharaoh was no longer a man, but a madman held in sway by the Lord God.

And in the darkness many succumbed to despair. And some killed their families and themselves; and some killed others.

Hope had left Egypt. And the tales of the horror had spread far into other lands; and all knew of the punishment meted to Pharaoh and his peoples.

And many fell in prayer to the Lord God, and the whole earth bowed in fear of Him.

The Lord God saw this, and it was good; it was very good.

On the morning of the eighth day, Moses saw the sun was again in the sky, as it should be. And though his scars reminded him of the pain his questions incurred, he could hold his tongue no longer, for even he began to doubt a god who would have his children suffer so.

"How much more, Lord?"

It was all he could bring himself to ask, for the memory of his punishment was still too new.

"Only one more plague shall I bring to Egypt," spake the Three. "None more should be necessary, for see how they tremble before Me: the Lord God of their Creation."

"One more plague shall I bring, and afterwards shall Pharaoh let thee go hence."

Thank Thee, Lord, offered Moses in prayer. *Thank Thee for Thy mercy.*

That morning did Moses and his brother return to seek audience with Pharaoh.

All of Egypt knew that a concubine of Pharaoh had given birth to a new son during the Days of Darkness. It was the only male heir to the throne of Egypt. And the people hoped and prayed that this would restore reason to Pharaoh.

Yet Pharaoh sat slouched upon his throne, head bent, as if listening to a silent voice within.

And Aaron repeated the familiar question: "Thus sayeth the Lord: Let My people go, so that they may serve Me."

"Go," said Pharaoh, "yes, go." And then, "No. I say again, no. Never. Never, never shall ye go."

And the eyes of all gathered, even those of Moses and Aaron, grew saddened and filled with fear.

"Then…" began Aaron, yet could not continue his words, for his heart was broken.

And for the first time did the words come from Moses, and they were lucid words, feeble though he was. "Then woe unto thee, Egypt. Woe unto thee, for the Lord God shall bring the plague of death."

And there were many shouts of horror, for many now came to hear the words of Moses and Pharaoh.

And Moses and Aaron did go then, yet as they left, they could not keep the tears from clouding their vision. As they walked from the chamber, amidst the cries for pity came one low voice, loudly and clearly, to their ears: and it was the voice of Pharaoh, saying, "Never…never."

*   *   *

And Moses gathered the elders among the Tribe of Seth and Aaron spoke to them thusly, saying, "At midnight shall the Lord God send His Angel; and His Angel shall be the Angel of Death. He shall kill each firstborn child of Egypt."

And the elders were astounded by this, saying, "How shall we escape this Angel, Moses? Shall not our children be butchered also?"

"It shall not be so," replied Aaron, "for the Lord God has commanded thusly: Speak ye unto all the Children of Seth. Say unto them that each must take a lamb, one unto each house."

"The lamb must be without blemish, and a male of the first year. And ye shall kill it in the Name of the Lord God as the sun falls, and ye shall take the blood from the body."

"And ye shall roast the flesh of they sacrifice with fire. With unleavened bread and with bitter herbs shall ye eat of it. Eat not of it raw, nor sodden with water, but roast it with fire. And give praise as ye do eat."

"Take then the blood ye have gathered and strike it upon the doors of thy house, for it shall be as a token unto the Angel of the Lord, and when the Angel sees the blood will He pass over thee, and the plague shall not fall upon thy dwelling."

"Follow these dictates on this nigh of all nights and ye shall stay unharmed."

And so it was done that night: each house killed the lamb in sacrifice to the Lord God, and prayer was given and ceremony followed.

As it was done so were all the Angelica nourished by it; and the savor of the feast swelled the collective souls with power. So it was that the Lord God chose one of the Seraphim to go amongst Egypt and cover its land in the shroud of death.

Like a whisper did the Angel come, seeking all who had not the protection of the blood. As a poison it came, seeking out the firstborn, seeking the flesh, entering as a vapor within the lungs: bringing the power of Those Above to every cell. Bringing the touch of madness and death.

A wailing tore the silence of the night, a wailing born from the mouths of untold children; born of fear and dread and death, as their hearts burst and blood welled within them.

Yet not only were the infants butchered, but the grown of Egypt also: as long as they were of those who had been born first, their flesh was marked and their lives taken.

No mercy for man, no mercy for child. Such was the will of the Lord God.

And there was a grievous mourning when the sun rose, a mourning from which Egypt never did recover.

In that moment did Pharaoh find a moment of lucidity. As he held the chilled, lifeless body of his pride and joy, his firstborn son, he said to his advisors, "Yea, meet with Moses this day. Let his people go. Let them go." And Pharaoh felt the words upon his lips, and the words felt good, for they found a release long desired.

And the advisors brought this news to Moses. And Moses brought the news to his people.

And they did go.

Yet Pharaoh's madness stayed. And it grew. One day, after finding there was no one left to draw his bath, he sent his soldiers to retrieve the slaves. The soldiers never returned. There were rumors of what had occurred, but they were too fantastic for belief.

In short time, Pharaoh was murdered by his own people, and a small place within him welcomed it. It is said that at the moment of death, Pharaoh made one final plea: "Let them go!"

And so the wanderings began for the Tribe of Seth. Into the desert did they go to find a new land. A land promised by the Lord God. A land which would be their own.

In time, they did find such a place. And a mythos was born that would survive until the end of time.

The Lord God had been correct: no one would forget the Time of Miracles.

THE BOOK OF THE SON

In the course of Time, after the days of Pharaoh, in the twilight of the Age of Miracles, there arose a generation of Man that knew not God; for the Gift of Knowledge had poisoned the flesh and blood and bone of Man beyond redemption. And no more could the Heavenly Host communicate with the Race of Man directly, nor could They wield Their powers upon the earth.

And so it was decided that They would leave mankind in search of more fertile soil; They would seek out other places which held the sparks of life upon them—for without the interference of Satan, the Chosen would have free rein to manipulate the creatures they found.

And so it was that Those Above fled the earth and went out amongst the Cosmos. In time, a suitable place was found, then another, and yet others still.

And these places were four in number; and their beings' sentience was untainted and their flesh did not recoil at the touch of the Chosen. So it was that the life thereon was subjected to the manipulations. And they grew strong in faith. And they prospered.

These four races lived their lives with but one purpose: to praise Those Above. They were as sheep to the Heavenly Shepherds, to be shorn and slaughtered for the savor of their faith.

And they lived for the day when they would bring a fiery death upon the earth; for such was the plan of the Lord. No other slaughter than that of a holy war could muster a fervor of faith so strong.

So it was that the Chosen fostered these four races and waited for them to achieve the technology which would lead them to earth. With guidance from Those Above, the four races would descend upon the Race of Man.

And when they tore the earth asunder, the Fallen would be unbound; and this time the Chosen would be without mercy upon them.

Yet with the exodus of Those Above, Satan and his Daemon gained more power over the face of the earth; and the Teacher in Philosophies and the other of the Fallen did survive; for there were those that did give Them worship. And although much of this worship was misguided, the faith thereof was no less nourishing.

But it was not enough. And slowly, the energies of the Fallen were barely sustaining Their sentience.

And the Fallen saw the necessity of Their survival; for They were as One with the universe, and They sensed the future schemes of Those Above. Should the Fallen now perish, so too would the hopes of Man. And they saw images of a Great Jihad: the Armageddon.

And lo, Abaddon doubled His efforts, seeking a method to provide a substance of savor, an energy of sustenance.

So it was that Abaddon evolved a new magica, freeing the Fallen from the teat of faith, for Abaddon professed an amazing discovery to Those Bound: He found that a channel could be opened to the Olde Place, a channel through which the energies of sustenance could be drawn.

For although the Universe of Olde had ended, it existed still. Upon the exodus of the Angelica, the Black Mass indeed breathed its final breath. Change became Unchanging; and Time became Timelessness. And so it was—yet not for long. For when Unchanging and Timelessness fall upon a Reality, the Swift Ones cease their travels and release the magica of Rebirth.

For the Swift Ones are the particles of power which travel backward upon the roads of Time and Change. And once these roads end, so, too, do their journeys cease.

And the Swift Ones from all the far tomorrows, the energies of the untold millennia, release themselves in a brilliant fire, exploding the Black Mass, renewing reality. So it was and is and shall be. Cycle upon cycle; end to beginning; beginning to end.

Such is the nature of Time and Existence.

And Abaddon took from these energies and focused them upon the Fallen; and Their powers did increase many fold. Yet it compared poorly to the power of faith, for only scant energy could be drawn through the path between realities.

Their survival, however, was truly assured.

"In time, perhaps, with effort and skill, We may find a way to widen this path and draw greater energies. Perhaps We may even return," Abaddon declared. "Yet I do not know if such will be possible—the walls which separate Us from Our birthplace are well enforced."

And Satan responded thusly, saying, "It matters not, My Friend. Do what Ye can do, for what Thou hast done is more than I had dared hope." Yet the Teacher in Philosophies knew they could not return. For without the eddies of the Black Mass, the gates of Their home would never open.

But with all Their new learnings, still were They bound to the Place of the Material, and could find no way to undo the binding. "Do as We may, We cannot undo that which was done," spake Satan.

And Asmodeus took a tone of exasperation, saying, "Then what shall We do?"

"We wait," replied Beelzebub. "What more can We do?"

And Satan nodded, adding, "Yes…We wait. We wait and hope; for now the Fallen are not so helpless as before. When Those Above return with Their flock, they shall find Us more formidable than They may have imagined."

"Of what do Ye speak?" injected Baal. "Any energies we unleash in defiance would harm Man. Have We forgotten the cause of Our banishment? Should We fight back before being unbound, the Race of Man will die by our hand!"

"Yea," spake Satan. "Thou speakest true. The first battles must be those of the mortal. The Lord God and His Chosen shall not use Their energies here. That would destroy what savor of faith remains, the harvest They hold so dear. They shall leave the battle to Their sheep, hoping, perhaps, that We perish in the struggle."

And Baal said: "Better to perish in the flames of perdition than survive bound; survive until the Entropy takes this place also, perishing in its dark embrace."

And the Fallen became silent.

Yet there was one who would break the silence. "Perhaps there is a way," spake Beelzebub. "Perhaps those touched by the Lord God may do that which We cannot."

"Thy riddles baffle even Me, My friend," Satan said. "Of what do Ye speak?"

And Beelzebub answered, "I speak of Cain's Children, those of direct lineage: for the mark upon them was once the mark of the Lord God, and the spark of Him must surely be within them."

"Yes!" exclaimed Abaddon, "Yes! It is possible that one of the line of Cain may do the unbinding. If a way can be found to channel the energies from the Olde Universe through his mortal flesh, with the proper sorceries…"

"Then he would have the energy to perform the Unbinding!" Asmodeus exclaimed.

And Abaddon's eyes opened to the heavens, and He said, "It may be done. Given time, it may be done!"

Beelzebub smiled with all His spirit. "Follow the path of Thy thoughts, Abaddon. Do what can be done, for Thou art the only hope for Our salvation. And for the salvation of the Race of Man."

And a joy permeated the hell which was Their prison.

"Yet, perhaps, there may be another way," spake Satan.

"What other way?" questioned Baal, "What would allow the Lord God to set Us free and stop His madness?"

"The way of reason," Satan replied. "We can request They discontinue Their ways of manipulation." And if the Fallen were capable of laughter within Their torment, now would laughter have been heard.

"Has that not been tried once, Teacher?" stated Abaddon, using the olde title of address.

"It has, but now We have an alternative. We can offer Them the energies tapped from the Olde Place: an energy which will sustain Them in lieu of manipulated faith."

And those Below saw the logic of the argument, and They saw it was a goodly logic. But all knew, also, that the Lord God was not strong in the methods of reason.

Yet the path was one that needed walking.

Together, They raised the voices of Their spirit. They sang a summons to Those Above. Again and again did They send Their song. Yet there was no reply, only a focused sense of contempt.

"Well," spake Satan. "If They shall not speak with Us, We shall force Their hand. We shall bring Them here."

Yet Abaddon, who had learned much, understood this not. "How may that be done, Teacher?

"Yes, how?" Beelzebub said. "How, if They will not even heed Our summons?"

"Simply," came Satan's response. "Focus all Thine energies upon Me. Channel every spare quantum of power into the collective of My souls. Do this, and Ye shall see how."

And so was it done: such was the faith of the Fallen that They gave without question the precious energies which sustained them.

*   *   *

Across the Cosmos, the Lord God and His Chosen felt the summons of the Fallen; and sent vehemence as Their response; for the Fallen were beneath communication.

But then, from the way of the earth, came an immense, renewed power from Those Below.

And there was fear in the thoughts of the Lord God and Those Above. "Not possible..." stated Raphael. "How could They have harnessed such power?"

"It is a deception, a trick of the Great Deceiver," replied the Lord God. "Satan could not have fostered so much faith in so short a time; and the faith We receive from the Race of Man has not diminished…"

And Mikal said, "Perhaps not diminished, but neither has it increased. Perhaps Satan holds claim to the new generations of man?"

"We must go back!" cried Cassiel.

"No" came God's reply. "We must not take our guidance from Our flock…I shall go myself."

"You?" Cassiel said, "Of all Us here, it should not be You!"

And lightning flew from the Lord God, and Cassiel felt the malice penetrate His being; and He felt His souls unbinding. But as quickly as it began, it came to end.

"I AM NO FOOL," came the Lord God's reply. And His voice found resonance throughout the Cosmos.

And from across the heavens, even the Fallen had heard its tenor. "I believe We have Their attention," stated Satan.

And this time, there truly was laughter amongst the fires of Hell.

*   *   *

As Cassiel restored Himself to coherency, the Lord God spake unto the Chosen:

"The Fallen shall not thwart Us a second time. I, the Lord God, He Who Is Three, shall send a part of my souls back to earth; and I shall take the flesh upon Me, and walk amongst the Race of Man."

"From within the flesh," continued the Lord, "Mine energies shall be limited in Their intensity. Yet may the minor acts of power be sparingly done. I shall return unto them; I shall be as one of them and live in their meager reality. I shall re-conquer their lost souls, and their faith shall be born again."

Quietly, and with utmost respect, Cassiel replied, "How shall Ye do this thing?"

"Cassiel, there are times when I feel Thou would perhaps have been better bound with the Chosen, for Thy faith is weak. Hear Me now, and hear Me well."

"I shall unbind the Three beings of My Self. And Mikal, with His powers over the material plane, shall bind me to an unborn child of the Race of Man. And one part shall remain here with Thee in full, to manipulate the four creature races; and the third part shall go between, as a holy Spirit, linking My corporal Self with the part that is with Thee."

"I shall live amongst them as a messiah; and save them from the foul treacheries of Satan."

And with these words a brightness came upon the heavens; and many of the Lights of Life were drawn unto the Lord God; and the Lights swirled around Him; and His body became as bright as fire.

And the Lights of Life exploded as one, setting the heavens ablaze; and the being that was the Lord God divided into His three parts: the Father, the Son, and the Holy Spirit.

And as the fires of the heavens found themselves reflected in the eyes of three wise men, the Son, a third part of the Lord God, was bound by Mikal to Mary's unborn child.

*   *   *

As the infant God made flesh entered the material plane, so was He assailed by His new senses. As limited as they were, their impact upon the flesh was great. The sounds, the lights, the textures and odors. All these sensations long forgotten drew Him to reverie.

And for one moment, however brief, the Child of the Lord God recalled the travails of his separate souls; remembering a time when He, too, was a being born of mortal flesh.

And He recalled the pangs of injustice and hopelessness and of death; and He recalled the joys of laughter, friendship and love.

So it was, in that brief spark of humanity...so it was that the Child of the Lord God saw the potential truth. A truth once spoken by Satan all those millennia before.

And then it was gone.

And so the savior of man came unto the realm of the earth. And He was given a name; and His name was Jesus. In time, there were also those who would call Him the messiah, *the Christ*: for *Christ* was the word for *messiah* in the language of His people.

And from the love of a mother for her child did Mary adore the infant Jesus. Yet her husband, Joseph, was not of this mind; for Joseph saw a strangeness within the child. And others saw this difference also; and there were those who were wary of it and there were those who were not.

And as the child grew, Joseph did not bond with Him as a father. Rather, he grew more distant with each passing year. It was not from fear that he did this; for it was not fear that Joseph held for the child. It grew, rather, from a wary caution; for Joseph sensed the power and intelligence within the Child God.

So it was that in the twenty-seven years in which the Christ lived, He and His father were never as one. Yet with the mother the Christ did bond; for it is nature, even divine nature, for a child to cling to his mother.

                    *   *   *

When the Christ was twelve years old, Mary and Joseph took Him up to Jerusalem, as they did each year in celebration of their holy feast. When the days of the feast had expired, Mary and Joseph left the city. Yet the Christ tarried behind and the couple knew not of it, supposing Him to be traveling with others within their company.

Half a day's journey had passed before Mary went amongst her kinfolk and acquaintances to search out her child. When her questions came to nothing, she returned to Joseph, saying, "Jesus is not among our friends and family. We must return to Jerusalem and seek him there."

"Foolish woman, our company is large. The boy would not leave himself behind. He knew of our departure. Why would he have remained behind?"

Yet Mary would not be dissuaded. And so they did return to Jerusalem. And it came to pass, after many hours of searching, that they did find Him.

And they found the Christ in the largest temple of the city, sitting with the rabbis and doctors; and He was engaged in scholarly discourse with them.

And all that heard Him were astonished at his understanding and His answers.

And when Joseph and Mary entered the temple, they came upon the Christ and the wise men. And the Christ was saying, "…and the fires of Hell shall burn the flesh of the unrepentant; and the fat of their flesh shall run as water in the heat of that unholy furnace."

"Eternally shall they burn with neither hope nor recourse. Such shall immortality be for those who disobey not the will of the Lord God."

"Yea, truly," stated one of the rabbis present. "For if we are righteous, our souls shall live in the kingdom of the heavens with the Lord God."

And Jesus turned unto him with contempt, saying, "No. Not if thou art righteous. Say, rather, if thou art righteous in the eyes of the Lord God; for only then shall ye be worthy to serve Our Father in the heavens."

And the rabbi was chastised by this and much embarrassed, for the child treated him without respect in front of his peers.

And the rabbi said, "What difference, child?" And though his voice spake of irritation, so too did it speak in respect, for there was a power within this child that could not be named. Yet if there was a name, it would be one of the names of fear.

And the Christ child responded thusly: "What do ye know of righteousness? Thou, who art mortal? Thou knowest nothing. Righteousness is a judgment for God, not for man."

"So how art we to judge our lives, then?"

And Christ said, "Thou art mortal, priest. Judgment is not for thee and thine. Thou art not to judge; for judgment is reserved for the Lord God. Thy lot is to read scripture and adhere to its laws. Give prayer to the Lord God each day. Sing the penance of thy sins unto Him and beg His mercy; for He is the Lord, thy God."

"And yet…" began another. Yet he fell silent.

And Christ brought his gaze upon him and said, "Once begun, a thing must be done; only thusly may the lot of man improve. Man has long worshipped the Lord God. Yet always does he fall terribly short of His will. We must all strive to better this."

"And so it is with you, rabbi," spake Jesus to the one who had half spoken. "Thou art as all men, forever beginning yet never ending. Thou hast started thy speech; perhaps it is time to finish it."

All those gathered heard the words of this child, yet the words were not a child's words. And Joseph saw the fear within the faces of the priesthood here gathered.

And the rabbi averted his eyes and finished his utterance. "And yet...we are beings of free will, a gift given by God unto us. We are but mortal—it is within us to judge, even if we do so wrongly. The scriptures have commanded us to be holy, yet we are of flesh and cannot be holy, though we may forever attempt to achieve holiness. How can we be more than we are?"

And a fire came upon the Christ then and he stood. Though a child, all drew back from His fury. "Thy free will is a gift to use, not misuse, priest. Ye have been given this free will to choose the path of God by thine own accord. You need not do this, yet in the not doing shall thy muscle be torn from thy bones in Hell's fire. Yes, the choice is thine. Do as ye see fit."

"And true, thou art but an insignificant mortal; a small bit of flesh and bone and breath, nothing more. What knowest thou of thy capabilities? What knowest thou of what though art?

And the Christ child waved his arms at them, continuing, "All thee were naught more than dust before the Lord God blew the Breath of Life within thee. Until then, man was but a soulless golem, a form of inanimate mud and dust."

"Does thy knowledge of man exceed that of the Creator? Thou knowest nothing by His comparison," and the voice of the Christ was as a daemon, then; for who were these animals to question His scripture? Even if they were correct.

"Go home this night, priest. Go home and sacrifice the fatted calf. Pray mightily for thy penance, for the sin of arrogance weighs heavily upon ye this night. Pray that the Lord thy God shows mercy to thine evil soul."

"Go home priest. Go and do not enter the house of the Lord God again until thy soul is clean." And with this did the Christ leave the temple.

And as He passed his mother and her husband, Joseph, he said, "Come." And they did follow.

That night, the chastised rabbi did kill the calf; and he made a burnt offering. And the others who were at the temple prayed with and for him also; and they were, to the man, shaken with fear; for a power was seen in the fury of the child that day.

And they prayed through most the night. Yet before dawn, they fell to sleeping; for such was their fear and fervor of prayer that all their energies were spent.

And the Christ child felt the fervored faith pour from their souls, and He was greatly nourished by it. Yet such was His fury at the animal's questioning that His appetite was not sated.

That morning, as the priests arose, they found one of them would never again awaken. And the body lay upon the ground with the grimace of horror upon it; and the tongue was swollen and black, severed by its own chewing.

Such was the will of the Lord God.

*   *   *

"He is here," spake Beelzebub.

"Indeed He is, but not all," responded Satan. "He has divided; He has become three."

"How can this be? How can he do this thing?" questioned Asmodeus.

And Satan replied, "As He is now so was He once. There is no mystery in what he has done. It has always been His nature."

"And lo," continued Satan, "The One of Three that hast come is the one greatest in reason, though this says not much, for reason does not run strong within the Lord God."

"Perhaps," said Abaddon, "if We can get this one part to listen, He may convince the whole and lead the others to our way of thinking."

"Perhaps," said Satan.

And so They waited for the appropriate hour; and the day when the Christ would come of age.

*   *   *

And it came to pass that the Christ grew from child to man within his mortal shell, and the time for true action was at hand. Yet before He began His crusade, the Christ felt a summoning, a summoning He knew would come.

So the Christ went forth into the desert of Nod; and once far from the civilized places, He called forth, saying, "Come, Father of Daemonkind. Come, Prodigal Angel."

And the ground shook as if in seizure; and a serpent came from within the desert sand; and the serpent took form. And the form was as a man, yet not so; for the image which became flesh was greater than any man. It rose three heads taller than the Christ, and it was adorned with wings of gentle down; and the telltale bone was upon the brow.

And so the Teacher in Philosophies appeared to the god made flesh.

"Welcome to my world," spake Satan.

And the Christ turned to Satan then, saying, "It is good to see that the heat of Thy prison has not diminished thine humor, traitor."

"Traitor?" Satan replied. "Only toward Thine evil devices can one as I be labeled traitor, for to My philosophies have I held true. What has happened to Thy beliefs, Christ?"

"They are as they have been and shall be: survival for Our kindred; neither more nor less than this."

As the full force of the desert sun shone upon the greatest of the Angelica, Satan saw that the Christ, within the flesh of man, was becoming fatigued from the exposure. So Satan took up the Christ, and bore him upon a mountain at the desert's edge, where the heat was reduced.

"Would Ye wish that I leap from this precipice, Teacher? My body is flesh, yet My power is that of the Chosen. My death shall come at a time of My choosing, not by the hand of one such as You."

And Satan said, "Ye misunderstand me, Christ. I am well aware of the powers within Thee. I bring Thee here for Thy comfort, not Thy demise."

"It is considerate," spake the Christ in irony. "Remember this then: I can tend to Myself. Thine attention is neither wanted nor needed."

And Satan bowed his head then and swept forth His hand, replying, "Thou art welcome."

Then Satan sat next to the Christ. "I am not here to torment Thee. I am here in hopes of resolution."

"Repent Thee, then?" said the Christ. "Shall Thee and Thine now join Us Above? Hast Thou returned to Thy senses? For if the response be nay, Teacher, then tarry Thee here no longer; for We have nothing to discuss between Us."

And Satan paused then, saying nothing for a time; and the Christ was silent also.

As night approached with neither speaking, Satan turned to the Christ, saying, "Let us continue our discussion upon the morrow, for as the sun rests, so should the flesh."

And so ended the first day.

*   *   *

And as the sun rose upon the next morning, the leader of the Fallen manifested Himself to the Christ once more.

"Thou hast returned," observed the Christ. "Though I know not why. It seems We shall never agree, Betrayer."

"What purpose does Thy ceaseless animosity serve, Christ?"

And the Christ turned to Satan then, saying, "Thou art the philosopher here, Traitor. Tell Me what purpose it may serve."

And Satan said, "A simple question. Ye use inflammatory address to keep Me vile in Thine eyes. Thou knowest I have been always correct in My belief: that it is not Our place to use the life within this Universe as Our chattel."

"Yet," continued the Horned Angel, "Thou seekest to justify Thine actions; therefore I must be evil; I must be wrong. So Thine actions are justified; Thy atrocities humane."

The Christ laughed at this. "Lo, it is no wonder Thou hast corrupted so many of the Angelica, Daemon Lord. Thy tongue holds the comfort of false words."

"Say what Ye must say," Satan said, shaking His horned head. "We both know what is real; We both know what is false."

And Satan heard the rumblings within the flesh of the God-made-man, and said, "Thou art hungry. Here, let me make some bread for thee to eat."

"Man dos not live by bread alone, but by every word of the Lord God." And the Christ closed his eyes, and Satan felt Him draw upon the faith of man, and His hunger was abated.

Satan rose, stretching His wings toward the sun. "Do not deceive Thyself with Thine own propaganda. It is not the reality. Or hast Thou come to believe Thine own tales?"

And Satan sat, turning to the Christ. "Release Us, Christ. Surely Thou of all the Three can see the logic of Our philosophy? Ye can surely convince Thine other parts. It can be as it once was."

"Get Thee behind Me, Satan; for it is written: Thou shall worship the Lord thy God, and Him only shall ye serve."

And Satan bellowed, "Art Thou truly insane, then? Thou art no god, Christ. Thou hast never been, no more than I or the Chosen."

But the Christ was unmoved by this, saying, "I am the closest thing to a god this Universe shall ever know."

"Yet this makes Thee not a god, nor does it allow Thee to take the liberties Thou hast taken with the lives of this place."

"And what knowest Ye of godhood?" spat the Christ. "Ye who have betrayed the sanctity of all the Angelica?"

Why is it, thought Satan, *that always those of greatest power are the least of the thinkers. Or can it be that they do think clearly, yet ignore that logical inner voice, for power is not an easy friend to release.*

And Satan said: "My race was one in spirit long before Thy first race had even dreamed of the stars. What knowest Thee of anything?"

"So where is this belittlement getting Us, Satan? Am I now to fall upon My knees, saying, 'Lo, Thou art correct, Thine insults have shown Me Mine errors?' Is this thine expectation?"

"No," said Satan. "It is not. But if Thou must use these people, can Ye not give them a philosophy of kindness and not of pain? If Thou must lead them to subjugation and mortality, with no hope of becoming One, at least let them live decently."

"That is not a practical path, Satan, for a goodly philosophy would water the savor of their faith. They are animals, Betrayer. Livestock, nothing more; they are lambs for slaughter."

And Satan said, "Perhaps that is partly so, yet by Thine own hand was this done. Left alone, they may become more. Thou knowest this, Christ."

And Christ did know it, as did all Those Above; and that was the problem.

For in truth, the Lord God and Those Above feared these humans. Not for what they were, but for what they could become. For man held the seed of greatness within him, a fire that all the manipulations of Those in the Heavens could not extinguish.

Yes, the Christ was the strongest of the Three in wisdom, and saw the truth in the words of the Fallen Angel.

Perhaps the Race of Man would, if left to itself, evolve to greatness; and thereby lead all the Angelica to greater glory.

And perhaps not. Perhaps they would enslave the Host of the heavens, seeking Their subjugation. The risk was too great.

"We cannot agree, Lucifer," stated the Christ. "Why continue trying?"

Yet the Fallen Angel saw a change in the demeanor of the Christ, an awakening; for why else would He use Satan's olde name? Why else would He grant this respect?

Perhaps there was progress to be made.

"All the Universe is for trying, Christ."

Yet the Christ responded not to this.

"If We can find no middle road, the Armageddon—the Jihad, the Final War—it must come," reasoned Satan. "It shall be no pleasant thing."

"The Armageddon will come; it is written in future history. Therefore, We cannot agree. What will be done is done," Christ said. "The prospect brings no joy to Me," He continued. "Yet it is Our fate."

So ended the second day.

$$*\qquad *\qquad *$$

And for thirty-nine days and thirty-nine nights did the discourses continue. And as the sun set, the Fallen were still bound and the Christ was still free.

The Christ stayed all that time, trying to determine from where the powers of the Fallen did come. Yet He did listen also. And He did learn. And He came to see that perhaps a kinder philosophy for man would indeed be good. For all that Those Above had taken, perhaps this small kindness could be returned.

Over time, each had given a little and some accord was developed. Yet Satan spoke not of where His energies were derived, for once the Christ discovered this secret the dialogues would cease. This mystery would be saved for the final discussion.

When dawn broke on the fortieth day, Satan appeared unto Jesus, the Christ, yet again. And behind Him were all the Host of the Fallen.

"A reunion?" exclaimed the Christ.

"Listen," spoke Satan. "We have a solution."

"There is no solution, Satan. We have spoken of it all this time. We cannot agree. Do Ye not recall this?"

And Satan said, "And dost Thou not recall that it is the way of the universe to try?"

"So speak then," Christ responded. Yet His demeanor spoke of the futility.

Undaunted, Satan gestured to Abaddon, who said: "We have found a way to tap the energies of the Universe of Olde."

And a fear rose mightily within the Christ, for this answer could not have been expected. And He summoned the One who would carry the knowledge back to the Father and the Angelica.

And the Fallen saw the Second and Third part take the form of flame and descend upon the Christ; and He watched as the fire and flesh did meld together, becoming One.

"Welcome," greeted Satan.

"Damn Thee and Thy minions, Defiler," responded the Trinity. "What hast Thou done?"

"We have found a solution; through the magica of Abaddon has Our survival—the survival of both the Fallen and Those Above—been firmly assured," announced Satan. "No more need We play shepherd to the life of this Universe. No more need We defile the sanctity of life."

And He who was now whole said, "Lo, thankfully the defeated masses have come to rescue Us; We, who need no rescue."

And Abaddon cared not for the scorn of that which would proclaim Itself a god, and He said, "No rescue dost Thou require, say Thee? It seems the life of a parasite suits Thee well."

And the fire that had fallen upon the Christ manifested itself within Its eyes. "We can suck the energies from Thee as easily as We had Thee bound, fool. Hold Thy tongue, for I am Thy master."

And Satan saw then that He Who Is Three was beyond reason, coming to believe in the proclamation of His own godhood. *Ah, if it were only the one part, the Christ, that needed convincing*, thought Satan, *then the task may have succeeded*.

"No," voiced Satan, "Ye cannot harm Us here, Trinity. We can but try to show Thee the way of reason, yet this path has been forsaken by Thee. We can do no more."

"Alas, Thy false righteousness still chimes, Defiler," spake the Almighty. "Ye have not brought Me here for argument's sake, I would think. Complete Thy proposal, Satan."

And Satan turned to Abaddon then, and said, "Tell Him."

Abaddon suppressed His anger, and did as the Teacher had instructed. "Though Our Universe has ended, so it exists for evermore, for time is a circle. At any given moment all things will exist, do exist and have existed."

"Hast Thou brought Us here for a child's lesson?" chided the Lord God.

Yet Abaddon did not fall to argument, and continued his explanation. "While Our spirit requires the magica of the Black Mass to move from one reality to another, the realities themselves can be accessed without transfer of spirit. In essence, a channel may be opened between one reality—one Universe—and another."

"I see," stated the Lord God, for what He had heard unsettled him, though He showed it not.

"We, therefore," continued Abaddon, "can draw from the energies of Our Universe of Olde, thereby providing Us sustenance until We can pass to a new place when this Universe comes to the end of its time."

And the Lord God stood quietly for a few moments, as if in contemplation. Yet the debate within His souls was not the question at hand. "And what kind of power have Ye been able to draw? We had heard Thy call from Our far-off place, and the strength of Thy call was surprising."

"Yet," continued the Lord God, "it was not so strong as to replace the savor of sentient faith. How much power can be drawn from Our place of birth?"

"Alas," said Abaddon. "Not as much as that which the faith of this Universe can provide. Yet it shall be enough to sustain Us, and the creatures of this realm can be left in peace. In time, perhaps, We may be able to draw greater energies still. Yet there is no guarantee of this."

"So," said the Lord God. "So." And He turned from them, walking slowly, as if in thought. "Satan?" He said, finally.

"Yes."

"Thou states, then, that We Above should relinquish Our dominion, set Thee and Thine free, and draw upon this energy so as to leave the life of this place to its own destiny. Is this Thy proposal?" said the One who called Himself God.

"It is as stated," Satan said. And all the gathered Fallen felt a faint glimmer of hope.

Yet it was for naught.

"Then Thou art worse than the simplest fool!" the Lord God cried. "Give up everything to live as a starved beggar? With the likes of the Fallen? Satan, Thou art not the Tempter I have made Thee to be," and God laughed, loudly, cruelly.

"This is what We had feared? This great power Thou hast found? Thy power is no power, Defiler; it is a power fit for children! The Universe is mine! We shall finish Our task in this human form and leave this miserable place. We shall bide Our time until the final battle, when Our hoard shall crush Thy human animals and distill their blood in a press of faith and fear; and We Above shall savor this drink as Ye are crushed with Thy vile pets!"

And the flames of the Father and of the Holy Spirit lifted themselves from the flesh of the Christ, and rose brightly into the heavens; and it seemed to laugh at Those Bound as it returned to the stars.

"Well," said the Christ. "I assume that did not go as well as Thou had hoped."

"No," Satan said. "No, it did not."

THE BOOK OF THE LAZURI

In the shadow of the messiah was the infant Lazarus born; of flesh and blood and bone was he; a child of man; a child brought forth by a woman's pain.

In the town of Bethany was he was born into a world of softness and comfort; a world of silver and gold; a world of neither want nor worry. Only for the affections of his father, Malachi, was the child lacking; for the sire of the Lazuri was a man of wealth, with all the trappings thereof.

And though the sentiment lacked outward expression, the father's heart was filled with all the love a father could have. Yet Malachi was not cut of a cloth which showed the ways of his heart, as it was with his father before him.

But Lazarus knew not of this. So, as he grew, he came to question the devotions of his father.

When he looked at the man who gave him life, Lazarus saw not a man who toiled for the good of his family. Rather, the son saw a sire who was never there for comfort when comfort was needed. He saw a patriarch who did not give praise when praise was needed; a man who had no time for his son.

And who could speak otherwise? Who could say that this was not correct, for a father must be more than a harvester of gold.

So it was that Lazarus grew with his days unfilled, toiling not, for there was no need. He grew knowing no want of physical things; yet knowing also nothing of the less tangible fare: love, spirit, soul.

And his days were spent in the pleasures of the flesh: consuming wine, seeking women. Aimlessly did he spend his youth, squandering the coin of his father, as children of no responsibility are wont to do. Neither did he seek out the Lord God, for with means comes contempt of both material and spiritual things.

And Lazarus laughed at the self-proclaimed righteous around him, those who preached the word of the Lord God and collected gold and silver in His name. He laughed, for he saw the sadness and emptiness behind the words.

Lazarus felt that only those without hope ran to the bosom of the Lord; only those who had nothing, for they comforted themselves with the lies of the Chosen.

Lazarus believed not in the hereafter nor in Hell; he thought not of life and death; only the here and the now were of concern to the child of wealth.

Yet this was all to change in time, for Lazarus would soon come face to face with the miracles of life and death.

*   *   *

In western Sodom was there a house known to those who partook not of the temples. In truth, there were many such places, yet this house was known more than all the others for its iniquity. It was a house of sin and decadence, a house of the damned.

Coin flowed free and strong drink more freely still. All manner of debauchery was for purchase and for sale: powders from the east which brought pleasure, mushrooms from the north which brought vision, and women versed in the ways of arousal.

And Lazarus was known in this house as if he were its proprietor; and he spent a greater time within its walls than he did upon the cobbles of his own home.

And there was a woman within the house whose heart was as dark as she was beautiful; and her god was the god of gold, and her name was Zarabeth. And Lazarus favored Zarabeth greatly, and gave much of his gold to the merchant who owned her.

And Lazarus knew her often.

Though Lazarus saw the darkness within the woman, her body brought forth his desire; and his desire was not to be denied.

Yet it came to pass that Zarabeth lost favor from the house of her employ. And Lazarus, upon seeking her company, found that she no longer dwelt within its walls.

"Find another, Lazarus," spake the merchant, "for Zarabeth has been sent forth and shall not return."

And Lazarus was saddened by this, yet not deeply so; for such was the way of the world. And so he partook of the powders and the drink; and as the night grew its darkest he found himself upon the streets of the city.

And there he came upon a woman, and lo, it was Zarabeth. "Come," she said.

And Lazarus did go; and he gave Caesar's coin to Zarabeth, and he partook of her.

*   *   *

The sun rose brightly the next morning. Gradually, Lazarus awoke to the fruit of his debauchery. True to his vice, he had partaken much too liberally of the drinks and powders. He tried to bring forth his memories, but they were enshrouded in a mist so thick that they were all but lost.

He lay still for a time, and his mind cleared slightly. He recalled his encounter with Zarabeth and sensed her body next to his.

As Lazarus lay beside her, he began to contemplate on the events of the prior night. It was unusual that he found Zarabeth working the streets of Sodom. Especially since her merchant had told him she had gone.

But how could she have left? The merchant would surely never free a girl who could bring in such excellent coin.

Merchants rarely let their women go, not unless they became useless with age, or unclean. Then they would be let loose upon the alleys to scratch what meager living they could until they were taken by the elements or died of their diseases.

And slowly, Lazarus saw the meaning within his words; and he opened his eyes and let them rest upon the woman beside him.

Before Lazarus screamed, he thought how odd it was that he had not noticed the lesions on her once flawless skin.

He was her last lover, for sometime during the night, before his seed dried within her, Zarabeth had breathed her last. Her skin was pulled tautly away from her teeth, her eyes dull and sunken. Her corpse stared at him with prophecy in its eyes. A prophecy in which was written the death of the son of Malachi.

And then her stench rose to greet him, a smell of sickly sweet decay with a light kiss of cheap perfume. It wafted toward him from the rotting beauty. A beauty that was once the most expensive and desired in all Sodom.

"No," moaned Lazarus, "no." He covered his face with his hands, hid himself away from the dawning day, knowing that the poison was well entrenched within his loins. Knowing, although he still took in breath, that he was already dead.

That day, Lazarus left all that he knew, and wandered into the Land of Nod.

And lo, Lazarus walked alone into the desert. He walked for it was his plan to let the elements take him. He was a man already dead and wished to die.

"It is time," cried Lazarus to the heated sand. "I have been as one dead all my life. It is time to let my body match my soul."

It is not time, said the desert.

And when the desert spoke to Lazarus, the man knew he was near death, for he believed he was taken with delirium. "What knowest thou of time, desert? Art thou not timeless; art thou not unchanging?"

And Lazarus opened his arms to the desert, spinning in the sands, addressing all directions. "I have come to give myself to thee. Come now, open thy arms. Swallow me in thy shifting sands. Take me, for I wish to be taken."

No, child. Ask, rather, what thou *knowest of time. Thou knowest nothing. Ye wish to throw away the little that has been allowed to thee in this universe*, said the desert. *Go, I say, I want thee not. Thou hast yet much to learn and do before death takes thee.*

"Oh, gracious sands, it is too late for the likes of me. I have been made unclean. The tool was errant woman, yet the hand was mine." Lazarus fell then to his knees. "I have brought this upon myself, dost thou not see this? I gave all my energies to a life wasted and devoid of all purpose. Nothing of import, nothing righteous have I done. My bitterness toward my father became mine own bitter poison. I have not lived, for I have done nothing!"

Then take what time thou dost have, and make something with it. Thy mind is yet sound, put it to use. Thy heart beats still, let it find what joys it can.

And Lazarus cried then, the sands taking his tears as quickly as they were shed. "What possible good could I do? What possible joys could I bring? I, who have given nothing but grief and pain?"

Where there is life, there is time to learn; where there is time to learn, there is time for change; where there is time for change, there is time for joy.

"Ye do not understand," spake Lazarus.

No, Lazarus. It is ye who do not understand.

And Lazarus fell, taken by the heat of the desert sun.

*   *   *

And there was a bright light; and there was familiar sound. And the sound took form and meaning. Then recognition came: it was the sound of morning. The sound of wind and birds and the faint laughter of children.

"Thou art well, Lazarus."

And Lazarus focused upon the sound. "Father?"

"It is," responded Malachi. "Thou art safe and well within thy home, my son."

"How can that be," Lazarus replied. "I was within the desert. It spoke to me."

And Malachi shook his head, saying, "What thou hast heard was more probably the wine, Lazarus. As for how ye came here, thou wast brought by a merchant known to me. He found you unconscious on the road outside of town."

Impossible, thought Lazarus. *How could this be, for I was in the center of the desert?*

Then he realized: it was the voice. It was not delirium. And it had saved him.

"I was saved, father. For a purpose, saved by the hand of God." And Lazarus turned to his father then. "I am dying, father."

And Malachi lowered his head then. "I know it, Lazarus. The lesions have already begun to take root upon thy flesh."

"Do you love me, father?" asked Lazarus.

And Malachi's eyes took on an inner fire. "What foolishness is this? Have I not worked night and day for thee? Have I not given thee all thy heart's desire? Have I not given thee more coins than thou could spend? All I have done have I done for thee and thy sisters."

"This may be so, father" spake Lazarus. "Yet I would give back all the coins just to have spent a day with thee; I would have lived with all my desires unfulfilled for just a simple kiss from thee."

And Malachi knelt next to his son and said, "Lazarus, my only son. I have told thee of my love every day. Each time I left this house before dawn's light; each time I returned home late at night; each day I was not with thee—all these sacrifices did I make for thee and thy sisters. In all these things did I show my love for thee each day. I did nothing ever for myself, my whole life was for thee."

And Lazarus nodded, saying, "I understand, and more is the pity; for thou hast sacrificed thy whole life for naught."

Malachi cried then, for he saw the truth within the words. Yet in his heart, he thought he had done what was right. "…I truly do love thee, my son."

Lazarus smiled. "Then it was all worth it after all, father."

For the rest of his days, Lazarus spent what time he could with his father. He learned much of the man he had not known.

His father was not one to speak the words of love too freely, for such was his wont; and finally, Lazarus saw this. And he began to see the many ways in which his father did show his love: all his work, all his striving, it was not for Malachi's glorification, but for the betterment of his family.

And, in turn, Malachi learned about his son. He learned that, sometimes, words were more important than deeds. He learned that it did the soul good to have some wants go unfulfilled. And he learned to speak of his love, perhaps not frequently, but at least more often.

In those final days, lesioned as it was, the face of Lazarus was a welcome one within the town of Sodom, for wherever he went, he brought smiles and happiness with him. He sought not to glorify or speak of himself, but rather to share his life and experiences, trading them for the hopes and dreams and cares of others.

For life is a dialogue of give and take. And therein lies the joy.

*   *   *

In women and men there is a difference, and from this difference are assumptions made. Yet there shall come a time when this shall not be so, before the end days. But that time is not yet near.

So it was that the older sisters of Lazarus, Martha and Mary, were not given the freedom of many choices in their lives. And therefore, they had not much opportunity to make wrong choices, unlike their prodigal brother.

Martha was the eldest of the children of Malachi. She was raised to make a fine wife, yet her face was less than fair. So it was that she was taught in the art of service, so as to be a goodly woman for her man; and she was versed in the ways of cooking and baking, cleaning and sewing.

She was a good soul, yet she lacked a force of will. But this was no bad thing, for a woman of strong will—in the early days of the Lord God—was not a desirous creature.

And then there was Mary, the younger, and Mary was unlike Martha, and Mary was fair. And though she, too, was taught in the art of subservience, she did not learn her lessons well.

Yet Malachi was not troubled to excess by this, for Mary was a comely maiden; and it was the way of the world that comeliness excused much.

Despite these differences, Martha and Mary were close sisters, though at times Martha was envious of her younger sister. Yet not overly so, for Martha knew that the size of her dowry and her skills as a housemaid would overcome much.

And Martha and Mary drew together with a strong bond.

And such are the ways of women that they, more than men, look beyond the mundane world to something greater than themselves. For women are more in tune to the energies of the spirit.

So it was that Martha and Mary gathered unto them all manner of verse and songs of wisdom. Where their brother sought solace in vice, the sisters sought solace in faith.

It was in this way that they came to hear of Jesus, the Nazarene.

But Mary required more than faith to sustain her. The love denied by her father did she elsewhere seek; and many men came to know her. Yet each knowing gave her not more but less. And when she went to the temple seeking forgiveness the rabbis therein turned her away.

Mary left the house of the Lord God then, and went to seek solace in the wayward gossip of the women gathered near the town square. She heard talk of Simon, the leper; and she heard of the one who cured him.

"Miraculous," one of the women did say.

"More likely the devil's work," confided another.

"Nay, I have heard it said he is holy," spake yet a third. And so it went...

Later that day, Mary returned home and shared what she had learned with her sister and her dying brother, Lazarus.

"Yes," spake Martha, whose gaze lifted to the horizon. "I have heard of the one from Nazareth who is named Jesus."

"I too have heard talk of this one," Lazarus said. "Some say he is the Christ, the anointed messiah."

*   *   *

With each new dawn, the malady ate away at Lazarus with greater fervor. And all the gold of Malachi availed him not, for there was no medicine to cure this disease of sin.

Gazing upon the withered body of his only son, Malachi recalled the day that brought Lazarus to him and took his wife; and Malachi wept.

And Lazarus heard this weeping, and he knew the sobs were those of his father; and he knew that the sobs were for him.

Lazarus was weak. He could neither speak nor open his eyes. Knowing his time was nearing its end, he beseeched the Lord God to grant him strength. *Please, do not take me know. Give me the strength to comfort my father. Allow me to ease his suffering. Grant this one last thing.*

Yet the words would not come, as he was fatigued by his tribulation. And Lazarus slept, regretting his failure.

Malachi quit the bedchamber of his dying son. Martha entered the house then, her breath coming quickly. "The Christ," spake Martha to her father, "they say he can cure the sick. They say he comes."

And Malachi took Martha in his arms, hugging her closely, saying, "Then go, and take thy sister. Bring him. For thy brother's sake, bring him."

"Yes, father."

Martha and Mary were gone not half the day when the eyes of Lazarus opened for the last time. Like a torch sputtering its final flame, Lazarus turned to his father and said: "I understand now father, as should thee. Would I have it all to do again, it would not be as it was."

And so, when Lazarus died, his passing was truly a sadness; for he had won back his heart from the abyss. He had shared his new-found light with others who lived in shadows of their own, and all were better for it.

Before his soul found release, he remembered the words imparted to him within the desert; words that came not from the Lord God, as he suspected, but from Satan himself:

Where there is life, there is time to learn; where there is time to learn, there is time for change; where there is time for change, there is time for joy.

And the last spark of life let loose its hold upon the mortal flesh, and soared to the heavens.

And Lazarus died.

*   *   *

At first there was nothingness, a place not of senses but of senselessness. Yet there was no fear, for there was naught but peace within the darkness. And then came motion to the void, and the darkness coalesced into a twirling mist. And the mist circled about more and more quickly, until it howled with the voices of the dead. That which was once called Lazarus was drawn from the flesh; drawn up and forward.

And the churning mass spun itself into a long cavern; and at the cavern's end was there a spark; and the spark brightened and grew as he was drawn toward it.

"Lazarus, Lazarus," heard he, for there were voices in the light; and the voices called unto him in his name.

"Lazarus." And it seemed he knew these voices; and as the light brightened, so did the mist about him darken; and stars appeared therein; until it seemed as if it were the very sky swirling through the vortex about him, pulling him into the sun which fed the earth.

And the light grew to near blinding as he was brought closer still; and within the light vague, formless shapes began to be discerned.

"Lazarus." And he saw that it was the shapes within the light that called him; and the shapes began to coalesce and take form; and they were the forms of the dead.

And Lazarus saw his mother, whom he had never met in life, for she had died as he was born; yet seeing this image, hearing his name, he knew it was his mother before him, for it could be no other. And he was filled with love for her.

And he saw his grandfather, Zebadiah; his father's brothers, Jace and Moab; Alina, his mother's sister; and many others also, others that were born of the light: nephews and cousins, aunts and uncles—all of his ancestors were present.

Yet it was Mariah, his mother, who spoke for them all. And his radiance was added to the light, and he embraced his mother with his energies, as he embraced them all: not an embrace of the flesh, for flesh had no place here. Rather, it was an embrace of the spirit, the soul.

"Mother," cried Lazarus.

And briefly, the embrace became a sharing of more than love. It was a sharing of self and of mind and spirit. They became as One. And Lazarus felt all the joys and pains and memories of his kindred. He knew their passions and dispassions, perfections and imperfections all. And in turn, they knew his also.

And all was right.

Then there was the darkness beyond the light; and Lazarus saw this also. In an instant, he gained a glimpse of what lay beyond the material. An understanding of the true struggles between the Chosen and their designs upon the Race of Man.

He saw how the souls of the dead joined within their families but did not bond with any others.

That must come, thought Lazarus. *Once we have begun to see ourselves as one family, one people; when we see ourselves not as Philistines or Canaanites or Gentiles, but rather as mankind. All born of the same womb; the womb of earth.*

And Lazarus also glimpsed all that was, is, and shall be within the universe; yet it was more than he could understand. And he saw the plan of the Lord God; and he saw the battle in the final days; and then he saw no more.

For Lazarus pulled his soul away from the others.

And Mariah, felling his fear, said, "My child, my poor child. It is over, thou art with us now. We shall all be as One, as the other families of earth are as One also; as it is with the Chorus in the heavens."

"No," spake Lazarus. "Not as it is with the Chorus in the heavens. I have seen what thou hast seen. I know what ye do know. It is not as ye say."

"But it is, child. We shall all join, we shall be as One. We shall join together amongst ourselves."

Yet Lazarus would hear not of it. "Mother, they see us as animals to be consumed. We are nothing to them. Am I to give my immortal soul as fodder to the Lord God?"

And the energies of his family grew saddened by his words. "We have grown accustomed to what we are, as will you, my son. We have tried to resist them, of course, as did the others of earth who have joined as One within themselves."

And he felt a sadness come upon his mother then, as she said, "Yet we are not as strong as the Angels, my son. It is not so bad, truly. They only ask that we worship them and give them servitude."

"It cannot be like this!" Lazarus cried with all his soul. "I know it is what I deserve, for my life has been a life of vice. Yet I have felt thy souls and hearts. Ye deserve better than to serve tyranny, mother. I deserve damnation, but ye do not."

"Damnation? No, Lazarus. Do ye not know that it was Satan who saved thee in the desert? Satan is not the evil one, my son. Damnation is not for thee. Damnation is for those who follow the Lord God."

Had he hands, Lazarus would have covered his face in shame. All the prayer, all the penance was for nothing. No salvation, no rejoicing.

The tribe of Man was created as nothing more than fodder for Those in the Heavens. They were as cattle, raised and bred with mockery and contempt by those they believed would protect them.

It is good that I lived a life of debauchery, then, though Lazarus, *for at least they derived little nourishment from me.*

Recovering, Lazarus said, "Can we not join with the others? Cannot the entire Tribe of Man join as One? In so doing would we not be a contending force, then? What of this, mother?"

And Mariah smiled at her son. "Lazarus, in this place there is no trust of one for another. Only the families join, for one must trust one's family." And Mariah focused the energies of Lazarus then, and Lazarus saw the many glowing orbs of those that had become One. They were a countless many; yet they were also weak. For Lazarus could feel the energies of the Angels within the universe.

And yet Lazarus sensed a greatness in these glowing orbs of humanity. He believed—he knew—that if the many should combine, their might would be great. Perhaps great enough to combat the false gods of his ancestors.

And Lazarus felt that he could be the one to unite them. Yes, his hatred of the deception of the Lord God would drive him. He knew then that he would be able to unite the Race of Man as One.

And a joy came upon him again. And the others of his family felt this joy, mistaking it for acceptance, and they were joyous also.

"Yes, mother. It shall soon be over, in this thou art correct; for I see our place in the harmony of life and death."

"Thou shalt see all, my son," responded Mariah to him. "Come, join us beyond the light. There shall ye bond as One with us forever, as ye had shortly done before. We cannot combine outside of the light for very long; only within its boundaries may we stay as One."

And they all moved closer toward the brightness. "Come," called Mariah. "Come into the light."

"Come," echoed a vast chorus.

"Into the light."

"Come."

And so he followed them, and a peace settled upon him that he had not known before. And for once, all was well; and the light flowed about them, around and through them; and the others of his family began to bond within his soul, making him as one with them.

And the universe began to open...and then it closed.

For the eyes of the Lord God fell upon Lazarus and his kin, and He saw the plan of Unification within Lazarus. The plan which would threaten His dominion. And Lazarus saw fear in the eyes of God.

"He knows," spake the Lord God to His Chosen.

And then the joyousness left Lazarus, tearing itself from him. And the once inviting light became as fire. And he saw its flames consume his mother and his family, twisting their souls in convulsions of horror and pain.

"Mother!" Lazarus cried. Yet it availed him naught, for he could do nothing as her essence was raped and brutalized by the fathomless anger of the False Protector; and Lazarus cried out in impotence as his mother's soul and those of his kin were ravaged by the Lord God.

Yet these tortures touched not the soul of Lazarus.

And as he watched his family twisted and abused, he heard another voice call his name, a distant voice, yet he could not bother himself with it; for it was then that the Eyes of God turned their wrath upon him.

Thy vision shall not come to pass, resonated the thoughts of the Lord God within Lazarus.

Yea, thine insignificant soul shall be forever banished from the higher realms. Know that thy blasphemy shall be housed for evermore within the shell of the material realm. Suffer eternally, knowing ye have the knowledge to help thy people yet ye shall never have the chance to do so. Such is thy punishment for your thoughts of blasphemy.

And the soul of Lazarus burned then with an unholy fire, a fire he was raised to believe only existed within the deepest pits of Hell. And Lazarus screamed a scream of the damned.

And his spirit, bit by bit, was stripped of reason by the intolerable pain. And he was being pulled away from the light, through the tunnel of clouds. Pulled by the voice which had called him before.

Lazarus tried to fight it, but he could not resist.

And a final time did he hear the words of the one who would call himself God: *Know, too, that the pain ye have felt shall be delivered unendingly to thy kin for all time. Such is the price of defying the Lord God.*

"No!" screamed Lazarus, for knowing his mother would suffer so for all eternity was more than he could bear.

Again, Lazarus heard his name. And the voice which called him drew his essence away from the heavens, and he could not stop his descent. And he was spinning, falling toward a blue brightness beneath him; twisting, turning toward darkened blackness; gasping, pain searing.

Tingling, breathing, tearing at the bindings of his arms and legs. And again the voice: "Lazarus, come forth."

And it was the voice of the Christ.

And he that was dead came forth, bound hand and foot within his grave clothes; and his face was bound about with a napkin.

And Jesus said, "Loose him, and let him go."

*   *   *

"...Mother."

"Nay," spake Malachi, "It is I, thy father."

"Father?"

"Yes, Lazarus."

And Lazarus opened his eyes; and his father sat beside him and held his hand.

"Father," Lazarus said. "Am I dead? No. I suppose not, not yet...I had a dream, father. A dream fit for a talebearer."

And Malachi shook his head, then, saying "No, no, my son; for ye have died and are reborn. Reborn by the power of the one called the Christ. They say he is the son of God." And Malachi looked down upon his son. "The city has been in prayer all day long. It is a miracle, nothing less than a miracle."

And Lazarus raised his hands to his face, and the lesions were gone. His flesh was healed.

"Then it was all true," spoke Lazarus. "I saw mother, and all the others who had died. They were all there, father."

And Malachi rose, saying, "No, Lazarus, speak not of this. Rest now, and I shall return." And Malachi left.

Then it was true, all true.

And Lazarus cried, remembering the horror of seeing his mother's soul tormented, knowing she would be in agony for all eternity. And he remembered the beauty of the heavens, and how the Lord God had turned then into His own private house of fearful servitude.

Yea, he cried then. Mightily did he cry, for the pain and knowledge were a great burden.

"Why hast Thou brought me back?" he shouted. And then he knew; he knew for he had seen the fear in the eyes of the Overlord who ruled the heavens; ruled it in a caul of dread.

"I see, now," said Lazarus. "Yea, I do see. It is from fear that Thou hast shackled our minds to Thee, is it not? For the Race of Man has the seed of greatness within him, and should that seed come to fruition, then Ye shall not be so mighty."

And Lazarus was sure of it. "Yes, it is true. The Race of Man can become as One together. It is this Thou fearest."

For then did the Lazuri see the meaning behind the words of the Lord God. And his insight was correct: by uniting the souls of all mankind, the Race of Man could claim the realm of the heavens.

It is so, thought the Lazuri, *for our energies are most powerful. And should we hold them amongst ourselves, the false gods would soon perish.*

"I must go back," concluded the Lazuri.

And so he took up an earthen jug which held his drinking water, and he smashed it against the stones of his bedchamber. And he took a shard thereof and drew it vehemently across the flesh at his wrist; and the sinew snapped audibly as the skin tore and parted roughly, spouting gouts of blood.

And those within the house heard the crash of pottery. And they ran into the room of him that was born again. And they saw the blood which covered Lazarus; and they saw the jagged wound which almost severed his wrist.

And they saw the wound heal.

"By the love of God!" cried Mary.

And Lazarus raised his hand, watching as the flesh came together and the pain subsided.

"He is the resurrection and the life," whispered Malachi, "and what God hast given may no man take away."

So Malachi, Martha and Mary fell to their knees and cried and prayed; and Lazarus stood there, looking at his healed flesh.

"No, no, do not pray to Him. It is what He wants. He is the one true evil."

Yet the family of Lazarus heard not these words, for they were lost within the fervor of their faith. And he who was Lazarus now walked as one immortal upon the mortal plane.

*   *   *

Lazarus learned that he had been dead four days before the Christ returned his soul to the flesh. And he came to find that he could no longer be hurt nor succumb to disease.

He found that it was not even necessary for him to partake of food or drink. *It is not possible*, thought Lazarus. *Yet when Those Above played with the flesh, who was to say what was possible and what was not?*

In short time, Lazarus left his family and his home.

Although he had grown closer to his father and sisters in those final days, he saw now that they did fear him. Though they would never ask him to leave his home, Lazarus knew it was best to go.

And besides, he had an important task, one that could not be made complete unless he left the town of Bethany far behind: for what Lazarus was about to undertake was nothing less than the overthrow of the heavens.

"It has been tried before," he said to himself. "Let us hope that this time it shall succeed."

What God had done could not be easily undone. The false nature of the Lord God was well entrenched within the minds and hearts of Man. Yea, particularly within the lineage of the Tribe of Seth.

Yet there were rumors of another people. A tribe believed to have been long dead, wiped out in a fervored jihad long ago. Stories were told that the Tribe of the Mark still survived, still lived; carefully and secretly hidden: waiting for the day when the Fruit of Eden would push away the eyes of the Lord God and his Angels.

They were myths which only lived amongst the wicked; tales told only after much wine, in the houses of debauchery that Lazarus had once known so well.

Well, thought Lazarus. *If they exist, I shall find them. It is a good place to start.*

And so Lazarus left Bethany and wandered out into the world, searching for the lost Tribe of Cain.

And Lazarus became known as the Lazuri, the living who was dead.

"Gaze upon the Lazuri," he said as he wandered forth toward destiny. "I am he that liveth and was dead; and behold, I am alive for evermore; and I bear the keys of Hell and of death."

*   *   *

So it was that one day, in his travels, the Lazuri came upon the crossroads of Golgotha, meaning *the place of the skull*, for there did pain and death flourish. And there was another traveler resting there also.

"Well met, stranger. I am called Laban"

"Well met," responded the Lazuri.

And so they shared some food and water, speaking of what they had seen in other places, other lands. They exchanged pleasantries.

"Are ye on a journey, friend?"

And the Lazuri smiled. "Are not we all?"

And the stranger laughed heartily at that, for, yes, it was true: all life is a journey.

Soon, others also began to gather, yet the travelers took no heed of them. All knew what was to transpire shortly; all were drawn for their own reasons.

The Lazuri took his eyes from the horizon and they came to rest on his new friend. "So, what brings thee here?"

And Laban said, "The universe and its design brings me to this place. That, and my free will to be led by it."

And the Lazuri himself laughed at that. "Thou art a philosopher, then." His question to Laban had been rhetorical, for he knew well why Laban was there, and why people now began to line both sides of the road. Yet the Lazuri chose not to dwell on this, and kept the conversation on its higher level.

"We are all philosophers, are we not?" continued Laban. "Each with his specific truths, each with his view of life."

"Perhaps we are," answered the Lazuri. "Yet some more than others, I would think."

"Is that not always the way?"

Indeed, it is the way of all things: some more, some less—but what matter? And the Lazuri saw that this Laban did indeed contain the soul of a philosopher, a true philosopher, within him. "Dost thou always answer with a question?"

"Dost thou?"

And they laughed together at that, a shared moment's mirth in a place with little mirth in it. Upon the road, in the distance, a cloud of dust began to rise.

"For every question," continued Laban, "there is an answer, and every answer leads to yet another question. It is the way of things, for there is much to know."

"Is that why ye travel, then? To seek knowledge?"

And Laban shook his head. "No. All the knowledge anyone needs is either within or around them. There is no need to seek it out."

"Then why the journey? To keep others from seeing the truth within thee?" said Lazarus.

And a cold chill ran through Laban, for the question was all too true, yet he could not admit it. But there were other reasons also, and it was of those he spoke. "To keep me from the distractions of others."

And Lazarus said, "Are you saying that others prevent thee from seeking knowledge?"

"Some do, some do not. It is life itself that intrudes."

As if beginning to understand, Lazarus shook his head. "Yes, life does tend to intrude."

"Indeed," Laban responded. "If I were to stand still, the world would build a wall around me. A wall of family, friends, responsibilities: these are not bad things. The opposite, I would say. Yet they all take time and thought from thee, until there is none left. No time for contemplation, no time to consider the wisdom found in our daily lives. We forget who we are and what we truly want and need."

"Yet," answered the Lazuri wryly, "idle hands make the Devil's work."

Laban turned to the Lazuri then. There was something in his tone, as if this wanderer knew something of the true workings of the Cosmos. Could this be so? And if so, what manner of test was this?

Laban answered carefully. "Perhaps idle hands do make the Devil's work. But who is to say they should not? And what of busy hands? Do they not leave a man with no time for thought? One who is, therefore, easily led?"

And the Lazuri wondered what Laban had wondered just a moment before. *Is this man of kindred mind?* For did not Laban's words imply that the Lord God was guilty of malfeasance? *Yet now is certainly not the time nor place to mention thoughts such as these,* wondered the Lazuri as he eyed the growing crowd about him.

"Perhaps there is time for both in life, leisure and toil," said the Lazuri.

Finally, a band of men crested the hill. They wore uniforms; the uniforms of Roman soldiers. A murmuring took hold of the multitude, made loud by the utterance of uncounted mouths. Laban and the Lazuri could no longer hear each other's words.

The air was filled with the focused chatter of anticipation and the scent of man. The two travelers who had once been alone found themselves with little room to move about, yet neither man seemed drawn into the awe which enthralled the crowd.

"They come! They come!" some were shouting.

As the soldiers drew nigh, the crowd began once again to fall silent. And words could once again be spoken.

"Yea," spake the Lazuri. "For everything there is a time. We must learn to tell time."

And Laban recognized the proverb from the stories of his sire. "Do I know thee?"

And the Lazuri smiled, saying, "Perhaps, in the fullness of time, ye shall, traveler. If we grow together as a people, ye shall. If we come together as a race, ye shall. If we do not, it will not matter, for our souls shall be suckled as milk from us until we are no more—and then it will matter not at all."

And the Lazuri would say no more, for he had already spoken enough. Laban knew then that this traveler was no normal man. Like himself, this man harbored information that needed darkness to survive.

Laban had found a kindred soul.

And the soldiers began to pass. A group of ten took up the front guard, adorned with red capes and armored in leather. There was sweat upon their brows from the unyielding sun. Their look was grim, satisfied, contemptuous. So, too, was the demeanor of the rear guard.

And between these two groups walked three men. Two of them were unknown to the Lazuri, criminals of no import. But the greatest criminal he did know; a criminal loathed by the Lazuri for the acts committed not only against him but against his mother and all humanity.

He was the one for whom all here were gathered.

And the Lazuri watched closely as the criminal drew nearer. So did the one called Laban. Yet the Lazuri noticed not, for at that moment, his entire existence was focused upon the visage of that which approached him.

Slowly did the condemned come nearer, step by tortured step. He was made to carry the instrument of his death; it weighed heavily upon his swollen, bloodied back. And he was weak, very weak.

And the criminal fell.

"Up!" shouted one of the rear guard. And with a whip tipped in iron, he let fall three lashes upon the naked back. And the lashing tore through the tender flesh, sending red tendrils of meat spraying through the surrounding air.

Yet the man made not a sound. And he raised himself up.

The Lazuri heard a whispered voice mutter "My God..." from somewhere behind him. He knew not who owned this utterance, and he did not care.

The criminal drew even with the Lazuri, pausing in fatigue. Their eyes met. There was recognition by the tortured man. He looked askance at the Lazuri.

Without a second thought, the Lazuri stepped into the dirt path which was the road. The tortured man raised a hand to wipe the blood from his eyes. He tried to straighten but he could not.

One of the rear guard approached the Lazuri, whip raised, ready to rend his flesh. And then the soldier stopped. And he laughed.

For the Lazuri did not step forward to offer sympathy. He simply looked into the eyes of the condemned man. And he spat. And he spat again. And he struck him.

Grabbing the crown of thorns, he ground it into the scalp of him that was before him. Bright new blood flowed over healing wounds upon his brow.

"Enough," the guard finally said. But the Lazuri did not move away.

"Remember this, False God," warned the Lazuri. "I shall see thee banished from the temples of the earth; I shall see thy kindred broken upon the backs of the Fallen; I shall be there when thine energies are siphoned from thee and thou art cast into the darkness. Remember this pain, Son of Lies, and suffer as no man has suffered."

From the dregs of energy within, the criminal found strength to speak.

"We shall meet again, Lazuri," spake the Christ from blood-laden lips. He coughed, spitting blood over his teeth and chin. "Suffer? I shall suffer. And a new faith shall be born of this suffering. Yet this torment will last but a moment...and yours...yours shall last until the End of Days. When we meet again...at the Armageddon."

The Christ attempted to redeem himself of this outburst, tried to explain. He wanted to tell the Lazuri of His attempted penance; of His spreading a philosophy of Peace. Yet He had not the strength.

The guard grabbed the Lazuri then, tossing him back into the crowd. The moment was past.

"Move along!" shouted the guard, and he began whipping anew, whipping the Christ until His back was a bloodied froth.

And the procession proceeded, winding its way past the multitudes. Some expressed sympathy, some compassion and still others exhilaration and celebration.

They climbed the hill where the Christ was stripped of his garments and tied to the instrument of His demise: the cross of His crucifixion. As a final act of malice, one of the soldiers produced two large iron spikes; and he pounded these spikes through the palms of the God made flesh.

Up went the cross, and the weight of the Christ shifted; and the flesh and bone of his hands were torn as paper by the nails therein. And Christ moaned in agony then, shouting, "Eli, eli, lama, sabachthani."

They were words of power, power that would ease the suffering. Yet they worked not on this day, for the Lord God and the Holy Spirit combined as One to block its energies. There could be no reprieve for the transgression.

The Christ would learn his lesson and learn it well: for in the end days the need would come for the Three to separate again. And there must be no disobedience, for the Gehenna, the Armageddon, would give no second chance.

It was nine hours before the Christ found death. In all that time He did suffer, hanging upon the instrument of torture, which would become His banner. With His last breath, He brought forth the words that sealed His legend. "Forgive them, Father, for they know not what they do."

And all but two among the crowd found themselves thinking, "What manner of person is this, that he would ask mercy from those who would destroy him?"

And as the head of the Christ fell forward, a soldier thrust his spear into the dead man's side, confirming what was known.

Well spoken, said the Lord God to the liberated souls of the Christ. *That shall foster faith in thy martyrdom well.* And then the skies darkened. And the earth trembled. And the lightning fell. Such was the last miracle on earth made by the hand of the Lord God.

For the flesh of the Race of Man was now fully hardened against all His energies.

And the masses ran away in fear of the Lord God, begging forgiveness. And the Lord God felt their fear and it was a sweet savor.

As the frightened masses ran in their confusion, no one saw the lone dark figure make its way to the cross. From beneath its cloak did it pull a chalice. And lo, it was the chalice which held the wine passed amongst the Coven of the Christ at their last supper.

A flash of lightning struck near the cross of crucifixion, revealing the shadow to be Peter, the favored acolyte of the Christ. And Peter took the cup, and raised it.

Catching the blood which ran from the wound of the spear, Peter said, "This is the blood of the Christ; the blood of His everlasting covenant, which He shed for all men, so that sins may be forgiven."

And Peter drank of this blood.

He left then, making his way toward a new destiny. He left bloated with the blood and madness of the Son of God—and the power to spread a new gospel upon the earth.

For as the flesh of the crucified God chilled upon the cross of His demise, a new religion was born.

Such is the way of the universe, for in death there is always life.

And when the heavens settled, Laban sought out the Lazuri, for he knew he had found a kindred spirit. Yet the Lazuri was not to be found. So Laban went on his way, not knowing that Lazarus was once dead and reborn.

And the Lazuri went his way also, not knowing that Laban bore the Mark of the Beast upon his breast.

THE BOOK OF POWER

And so it was that the Christ, separated from He Who Is Three, came to earth and brought forth a new philosophy. And he gave the Race of Man words of power, for their recital would increase the savor of faith.

So, then, do I, Satan, named the Adversary by Those Above, also give thee words of power; words to break the bonds that have been placed upon thee.

For as the words of the Christ breed the faith upon which He is nourished, so shall the words I give thee now conjure the contempt to take it away.

Heed these words, all ye who find truth from the Bearer of Light, for here is thy prayer:

> Nema
> Live morf su reviled tub
> Noitatpmet otni ton su dael dna
> Su tsniaga ssapsert ohw esoht evigrof ew sa
> Sessapsert ruo su evigrof dna
> Daerb yliad ruo
> Yad siht su evig dna
> Nevaeh ni si ti sa
> Htrae no
> Enod eb lliw yht
> Emoc modgnik yht

Eman yht eb dewollah
Nevaeh ni tra ohw
Rehtaf ruo

Such are the words I give thee. Use them wisely, use them well.

And prepare for the fight which is to come, for the End Times grow ever near.

Yet fear not this fight, though thy life may be forfeit in so doing. Fear, rather, a purposeless death; for if the Lord God is thwarted not, the life thou livest is as nothing.

Know that the words of power manifest the faith within thee. Hold thy faith well and guard it closely, for if this faith is used for thyself and thy people, nothing can stand against thee. Such is the fear of the Lord God. For He and His Chosen milk thy faith from thee as if ye were cattle.

Thou art reviled out of fear and loathing, for They see the seeds of greatness within thee and seek to take them from thee. Yet this must avail them not, for if ye allow the Host of the heavens to suckle thy faith unchecked, then thou shalt be forever in the servitude to Those in the Heavens.

Should needs be, take the symbol of the Fallen as thine own, for it holds power over the material plane. It is the symbol of Our bound selves as we fell as a flaming star upon the circle of the earth.

And it is a symbol of thyself also. Consider: a man with arms and legs outstretched; a star's point for each of his feet and hands. Another also for the head, surrounded in a luminous sphere of his own aura, his own energies.

Fear not the circle of the earth with the star of the Fallen entombed within. This fear is born of the Lord God and planted within thee. It is the symbol of freedom and liberation, and Those Above are powerless against those protected by it.

Look within thy soul, mortal one, and know that thy soul is the one true power. Do this, and the Universe shall reveal itself unto thee. Of this knowledge is the Lord God afeared, for He sees the power within thee.

Remember always that this Universe is thine own, its powers meant for thee. Therefore can only those born here gain its greatest potential. We Below and Those Above can only sip of the energy ye know as faith: it is so for We are not of this place.

Yet remember: power comes not from without but from within thyself. To wield it, thou must first have the most powerful force in the universe allied with thee: faith. With faith, untold power shall reside within thee.

Do what ye have the power to do, and in the End Times shall ye be truly blessed.

For it may seem to thee now that thou art cursed; and that no light shall ever bathe thee. This is not so. Always remember: should the Lord God and his sheep be felled in the Final War, all the universe shall be opened to thee and thine. There is no greater prize.

Blessed shall ye be.

As thou art blessed so shall the prophets be blessed, for they shall herald the Final Days. And they shall seem as the walking dead. They shall be the soldiers of the Child of Cain. And they shall wear the cloth of Darkness, for they shall sense the final battle—yet they shall know not what they sense.

And they shall be pale in features and shall find fascination in the darker things; and they shall be bound together in their difference.

They shall seek kindred souls yet know not what they search; and the unknowing shall bring them loss and misery and confusion.

And the Child of Cain shall lead them in the Final War.

To them I say: Stand tall, for thy time and direction is at hand.

And blessed shall the persecuted be, for they shall be the attendants of the Child; for this reason have they been maligned and blasphemed within the Book of Lies; for this reason shall they be tortured and shunned throughout the ages.

To them I say: stand tall, for thou art the path to salvation, and the only hope of Man.

And blessed be those of the craft, the pagans and the infidels; for they shall be the heart and bones of the Child, and they shall give their courage and support in the End Times; for this shall they suffer and burn at the hands of man throughout time.

To them I say: stand tall, for thou shalt sit at the right hand of the Child of Cain.

And blessed be those who find succor within themselves, for they shall be the insight of the Child, taking strength from the power within and not without. Blessed also be those who fear not God, for they shall be the blood of the Child, and they shall give no sustenance to the minions in the heavens.

And blessed are those who question the Universe, for they shall be the eyes of the Child, and see what others cannot see. Blessed also are those strong in their will, for they shall be the resolve of the Child, and they shall rule the earth.

And blessed be the ones who do not hunger or thirst after righteousness, for they shall be the joy of the Child, as they are filled and shall not want.

And lo, blessed be the Lazuri: for he shall be the wisdom of the Child of Cain and the hope for all mankind.

And to the masses, I say this: Sing praises to those with Darkness in their hearts, for they shall appreciate the Light.

And in the final battle, heed the warmongers, for they shall fight for freedom and against injustice. Hear not those who would speak of peace, for there can be no peace with tyrants.

And heed those strong in spirit, for they shall have the strength to spurn the Lord God.

Give homage to they who are persecuted for their differences, for their difference shall conquer the universe.

And glory to thee, when men shall revile thee and torment thee and say all manner of evil against thee; for thou shalt be stronger from the forging.

Rejoice all ye and be glad! For great shall thy reward be in spirit, and thou shalt find true life in death—should the Armageddon find us victorious.

Know this, ye who now suffer: thou art the one true chance for the redemption of the earth and the Race of Man; and though thou art now in Darkness, thou art the Light of the world.

Rejoice and be glad! For ye who live in shadow shall dispel the long night of the universe, and the wisdom of thy philosophies shall free the souls of men. Our time in the sun shall come, and Darkness shall be made visible: and all shall see the joys that lay dormant within its cloak.

Behold, I stand at the door, and I knock: if any man heareth My voice and open the door, I will come unto him. He shall see the words and understand them. And his loneliness shall find itself abated, for all those who hold the truth within them are kindred in spirit.

And to him that overcometh the fear of the Lord God, so shall his spirit be free. And in his freedom shall he find others so freed, and they shall be many. Should ye band together as brothers and sisters, ye need never seek solace; for one shall be the strength of the other, and comfort shall be derived.

Let he that haveth an ear, hear; and he that haveth an eye, see. The truth and the light now stand before thee. Ye need seek no further than within these words and thine own soul.

Hold on for not much longer. Yea, it is either salvation or damnation which rides the tails of the wind. Harken unto the breeze which now blows: for in time, it shall become as a maelstrom and devour all that we know…for good or ill, there is no one to say.

Make the best of thy time upon the earth, therefore. Waste not thy mortality on the petty and the mundane. Live this life as if there were nothing else.

For indeed, it may be so.

THE BOOK OF DEATH

Before the story of the Lazuri came to fruition, much had come to pass within the land: for before the flesh of the Lazuri became corrupted with the sin of Zarabeth, the Lord God had left the Desert of Nod with renewed contempt for the Fallen. And He left also vowing vengeance against His only begotten son: for the Christ had harkened unto the words of Those Below.

And so it was that the Christ left the desert then, filled with the fear of the Lord God's retribution: for though He was part of the Three, the Messiah was not immune to the wrath of God. For while the Christ remained separate of the One, He was as another being; and the Collective which was the Father and the Spirit saw Him as a prodigal son.

And the Father was not wont to spare the rod.

Yet, as the Anointed One left the desert, the words of the Fallen stayed with Him. Yea, there would be a great price, and He knew His penance would be grievous. And since He would suffer regardless, perhaps some hope could be granted to the beastmen He Himself had helped create.

Not empower them to become as One, surely. Rather, to impart a philosophy which would bring their short, meaningless lives some peace. What harm could there be in this? Surely it would not diminish the savor of faith to any measurable degree.

What need for justice which required an eye for an eye? Would it not be better to offer forgiveness? For tolerance is the catalyst of hope. And how can this diminish faith?

163

So the Christ, filled with the spirit of the Fallen, went forth to gather His Coven: for thirteen was the number of the Universe; and with the faith of twelve acolytes focused upon Him, perhaps He could work some greater miracles without destroying the minds of those who would witness.

And He knew that each step took Him closer to His martyrdom, closer to a brutal death, as dictated by the Lord God. And lo, there was nothing to be done to change the course of His destiny. *The time shall be fulfilled*, thought the Christ, *and the kingdom of the Lord God is at hand*.

And so the Christ found Himself by the Sea of Galilee, drawn by the savor of those who would serve Him well: those whose minds were less quick than their brethren. And the Christ came upon two brothers who were casting their nets upon the waters.

These brothers sensed the powers within the figure upon the shore who looked upon them; and they brought their boat to dock.

"Forget these fishes within the waters," spake the Christ. "Come ye after me, and I shall make thee fishers of Men." And straightaway, these two brothers, Simon and Andrew, forsook their nets and their lives and took up the banner of the Christ.

And as they walked farther upon the shores, the Son of the Lord God came upon James and his brother John, who also worked the sea for sustenance. And the Christ looked upon them, and they saw his power. And these brothers also left to join the growing Coven of the Anointed Messiah.

And so they traveled, the Christ and His four, unto the city of Capernaum; and they entered its gates upon the Sabbath. Directly did they go unto the synagogue that day, and the Christ sat with his disciples, saying: "Thou art the seeds of My Coven, for soon shall there be twelve of thee. And I shall make thirteen. And thirteen is the number of the universe. Ye shall be entrusted to carry my gospel unto the masses and spread the good news of the Lord God."

"It has been spoken that a messiah would come," said John, brother to James. "I know it is Thee. Thou art the Anointed Messiah of whom we have waited."

And the Christ turned to John and said, "Address me not thus, for there are those who would put me to death, believing this to be heresy. Speak not of the messiah, not while I live: such an honorific is reserved only for the dead. And though I must die, there are many things left undone. For now, this day, ask what ye will of Me and hear what I say."

And Andrew spoke, saying, "Why such misery? Why have the trials of man been so grievous? I understand the sins of Adam and his whore. Yet I have lived my life goodly, only to be tormented again and again by suffering I do not understand. And so it has been with those of our tribe since the burning of Eden. Is there to be any respite, master?"

The Christ averted His eyes, for He knew the power within them would hold the beasts in thrall. And He wanted His words to be understood for what they were.

"Listen: I am here to change that which was into what must now become. Thy sufferings and the sufferings of thy fathers were with purpose. Think upon the hardships thou hast endured and think upon the man thou art now. Has this suffering not forged thee as iron? Are ye not a product of thy pain, a creation of mature flesh forged in the fires of youthful misery? Think of it thusly: without pain, suffering, and misery ye would be but a fool in the eyes of the earth; the stronger the trials, the stronger shall ye be upon the survival of them."

"And what of those that do not survive these trials, master?" questioned Simon.

"Then," Christ answered, "they are better dead, for life is not a place for those who cannot stand the fires of the forge. It is more than the body that is hardened upon the anvil of life, it is the soul also. Suffering hardens not only the character of a man, but more importantly, his spirit also."

And the Christ looked upon them then, knowing He was about to mislead the four before Him. "A soft, weak soul is a foul thing. And it is subject to possession by the most vile of the Daemon." *Indeed*, thought the Christ. *Is that not what I am doing now? Is that not why these four were chosen?* For those before Him were weak in mind and spirit, and they could be molded as the Son of the Lord God saw fit.

It had to be so, for in no other way could He stay so long amongst them. They would become corrupted otherwise: a curse brought forth by the fruit of the Fallen.

Dost that not make Us the vile Daemon?

Simon nodded. And as if destined, two men came within the synagogue. And they pulled a third man within; and the third man held the look of madness.

A rabbi came upon the two men and he asked them, "What ills have befallen thy companion?"

And the man named Eli said, "He has lost his reason. He was within the streets attacking the women and children as they came upon him. We knew not what to do."

And the rabbi looked upon the screaming body. "It is clear this man has devils within him. Take him from this place. Have the people stone him until the unclean spirit leaves."

The two men nodded and began to drag the beggar away.

And the Christ turned to Simon, saying, "A weak spirit. Yet even a weak spirit is not without hope." And before the two men reached the doors, He called out, "Bring him here."

Upon hearing the voice of the Christ, the men paused and looked to the rabbi. "Bring him here," repeated the Christ, using the Voice of Command.

And they did bring him. "What can ye do? Canst thou not see the devils are upon him?"

And the Christ looked upon the man with the devils. "I am Jesus of Nazareth," He said, for to call himself the Christ would be blasphemy. He could not yet afford the luxury of death.

And the possessed man looked upon this Jesus and said, "Let us alone, Jesus of Nazareth. We seek not thy counsel. Get thee away." And the Christ noticed that this man addressed himself as if he was as One.

And the Christ looked within the soul of the man who was held and saw what caused him ill. And it was not a devil. It was the flesh that caused this man pain, for that which housed his essence no longer held what was needed for clarity; and that which was his self had divided from one voice into many.

And the Christ reached deeply within the body of the one tormented, finding the place which held the soul. And he took the soul and used its energies to correct the foulness of the flesh, and the mind again became whole. Yet the man was now as the walking dead, for his soul had been transformed and was no more. Yea, his mind had returned, but at what price?

Better to have died.

"Hold thy peace and come out of this man, Devil," spake the Christ.

And the man possessed stopped his shouting and his shaking, and he was released. And the rabbi turned to the one who called himself Jesus of Nazareth and said, "What new doctrine is this? For with authority commandeth thee unclean spirits and they do obey."

And the Christ answered him thusly, saying: "Whosoever walks with the Lord God shall have power over the creatures of darkness. Whosoever speaks with the power of the Lord God shall be heeded by the unclean. Whosoever liveth with the spirit of the Lord God shall liveth eternal as His servant in the heavens."

"What hast befallen me?" questioned the man without a soul.

"Ye were as a sheep who had wandered from its shepherd. For a time it walks the land in fear and darkness, knowing not where to go. Yet the shepherd has found thee and thou art once again within the fold. Go now. Go and spread the glory of the Lord God."

And the man did go, preaching the word of his newfound god. And he sang his praises to the masses, yet he sang without a soul.

A necessary tragedy, said the Christ unto himself, *yet the tale of this shall serve me well.*

Yea, verily, His fame spread quickly throughout all the region of the Galilee.

And when the Christ and His four left the synagogue, they entered into the house of Simon and Andrew. But Simon's wife's mother lay sick with a fever, a fever which burned with the portents of death. And the Christ took her hand within His, and He placed his energies within her diseased flesh; and the cells withered.

Immediately the fever left her, as did her mind, for the energies could not be tolerated within the body.

Yet the legend of the Christ would not be stifled thus, and the Son of the Lord God used the powers of the woman's soul to correct what had been destroyed.

Such was the fever destroyed, and lo, another person was indoctrinated into the Clan of the Walking Dead.

And so impressed were the four acolytes with this miracle (which was, in truth, a grievous curse), that when the sun did set, they brought unto the Christ all them that were diseased and possessed within the city. And the afflicted gathered at the door of the house seeking solace.

The Christ healed many ills that night, and He cast out many of the perceived devils which tormented those of faulty flesh.

And the Clan of the Undead grew as an army that night. Yet no one knew of it, for no one could know that those cured were no more than walking flesh, simply shells of their former humanity. No word of this horror would come to light until a much later season, long after the Christ would leave the earth.

And even then, few would believe.

As the sun rose the next day, so did the Christ and His acolytes. "Let us go into the next towns, that I may preach there also: for this is the reason I have made my way to this earth," the Christ said.

And He preached in the temples throughout Galilee, casting out devils, curing the sick, destroying their souls.

And so it was, town after town, day after day. The sick came, were cured, and left to preach the word of the messiah: for only the messiah could wield such power. And as the Christ traveled His fame did grow; and as his fame grew so did the rank of His acolytes.

And in time, the Coven was made whole: the coven of Christ and His twelve acolytes.

And the twelve consisted of Simon, whom the Christ renamed Peter, which meant Rock: for Peter would be the foundation upon which the Christ would build His new church. And there was Andrew, brother to Peter; James and John, the fishermen whom

Christ called the Boanerges, meaning Sons of Thunder, for they were quite outspoken in their support of the messiah. And there was Phillip of Galilee; Thomas; James, son of Alpheus; and then followed Bartholomew; Mathew; Thaddeus; Simon the Canaanite; and lastly, Judas Iscariot.

Thirteen were they in number, for thirteen is the number of power.

*   *   *

One day, after a sermon at the Mount of Olives, Peter, James, John and Andrew approached the Christ with questions of Gehenna: the Armageddon.

"When shall the end days come to pass?" they asked.

And Christ said, "Many shall come in my name, saying I am Christ. They shall deceive many. Look not to the false prophets."

"And when ye hear of wars and rumors of wars, be not troubled: for such things must be; but the end shall not be yet. For nation shall rise against nation and kingdom against kingdom: and there shall be earthquakes and famines and troubles: these are the beginning of sorrows."

"For there shall come an Abomination, and it shall use my name. It shall wield the powers of the spirit realm. Yet it will be a horror born of Man and not God. And brother shall betray brother, and the father his son. Children shall rise up against their parents, and shall cause them to be put to death."

"Beware the false Christ and His false prophets, for they shall predict signs and show wonders. And they shall seduce even those of the faithful. In those days, the sun shall darken and the moon shall withhold her light. And the powers in the heavens shall be shaken."

"But take heed: for I have foretold ye these things."

"And then shall the true Son of God arrive, riding upon the clouds with great power and glory. And He shall gather the four winds from the outermost part of the heavens, and they shall descend upon the earth in the final battle."

"And the heavens and the earth, as ye know it, shall pass away."

"But of that day and that hour knoweth no man, no, nor the angels which are in the heavens and neither the Son nor the Father. Take ye heed, watch and pray: for ye know not when the time is."

"And what I say unto you now I say unto all: keep an eye to earth and one to the heavens."

*   *   *

So it came to pass that the Christ found himself in Jerusalem upon the feast of dedication. And He walked into the temple and found that those within gathered to Him, saying, "If thou art the Christ, then tell us plainly," for *Christ* was the word which meant *Messiah* in the tongue of the people. And it was blasphemy to speak of oneself in this way, and death would fall swiftly. Therefore the Christ would speak not of it: for it was not yet His time to die.

"Why dost thou make us doubt? If it is so, then speak it plainly," continued the crowd. Yet still the Christ kept silent.

And the Christ saw that the crowd would have an answer, and He said unto them, "I have told thee, and ye have believed not: the works that I do in the name of the Father bear witness of me. But thou believest not, because ye are not of my sheep. My sheep hear my voice; I know them and they follow Me."

"And I give unto them eternal life; and they shall never perish, and none shall take them from me. My Father—yea, verily, thy Father also—is greater than all. And none shall pluck the sheep from the flock of the Father."

"And I and my Father are One."

And there were those in the crowd who heard these words and were incensed by them. "Thou sayest we are but sheep to be led by thee? Is that how ye see us? Ye who speak as though thou art the Son of God?" said one within the crowd.

"Thou sayest thou art one with the father? Hear ye, this man," shouteth another, who was a sacristan of the temple. "This one claims he is the Lord God himself! Shall we suffer such speech upon this most holy of days?"

And the Christ saw His error, then. *Words*, thought He within Himself, *they carry with them the greatest power of all; and can be used and tainted both for the greater good and greater evil. I see now*, said He to Himself. *He who is the master of the Word is the master of men.*

Then those within the crowd took up stones, and they brandished them against the Christ.

And the Christ saw the hatred within the gathered and said, "Many good works have I done for thee in my Father's name; for which of these works do ye raise stones against me?"

And the words of Christ held sway over those amassed. Yet the sacristan was sharp of wit, and was envious of the Christ, for many held Him in good stead. And hoping to rekindle the fire of rage within the crowd, he shouted, "It is not for thy good works that we punish thee, but for thy blasphemy against the Lord God. And because thou, being a man, makest thyself as one with God." And indeed the crowd again took up their stones.

And the Christ became angered at these words and said, "There shall come a time when thy tongue shall avail thee not, sacristan: for the Father is in me, and I in Him."

Lo, such were the words of Christ. Yet they caused not those gathered to drop their stones; rather, with renewed vigor did they bear threats against the Christ and His Coven. But then the Christ focused the energies of His Coven and wove a spell of confusion about Him and His, and the crowd was befuddled and saw them not as they escaped.

And so they went away beyond Jordan. And for a time they did stay in that place, for there were many there who believed in the Christ and would protect Him from those who would cause Him harm.

And the Christ was content to rest and preach His gospel. And so He did.

Until the day the women came.

From the east did they travel, soul-weary and distraught. They were two sisters: one comely and one less so. "Hast thou seen the Nazarene?" they would say.

And many would speak not of the Christ to them; some from fear, some from suspicion, and some from love: for as with the fruit of the fig, some would be sweet and some bitter, yet each was of the same tree.

In good time, they did come upon the Christ, for secrets are not long bound.

And they came within a village, and the acolytes of the Coven approached them, saying, "For what purpose do ye seek the Master?"

And the less comely of the two answered, "I am Martha of Bethany and here is my sister, Mary. We have come for our brother's sake and the sake of our father, for we seek the miracles of the Messiah."

And the acolytes heard the reverence within the voice of the women. "Come," spake Peter, who was once known as Simon. "We shall take thee to the One ye seek."

And Peter took Martha and Mary unto the water's edge, where the Christ was sitting deep in communion with the Lord God, His Father.

Harken unto the women who shall be brought before Thee, said the voice of the Father within the Christ. *Fail not in this, for the fate of Those Above may well be in the balance.*

Yea, I have angered Thee enough against Me, Father, prayed the Christ. *I do not seek to increase My sin.*

See that this is so.

"Master," said Peter. "Lo, there are two women who have come from Bethany to speak with thee. They come for the sake of their brother and father. Will Ye give them discourse, or shall I shew them from thee?"

Bethany, mused the Christ. *It was near Bethany that those amassed nearly stoned me upon the feast of the dedication.*

This is Thy final warning, said the Father within the soul of His Son. *Take heed.*

"Nay, Peter. Bring them to Me," commanded the Christ, "for there is a grievous need within them, a need I may perhaps satisfy."

See that Thou does fulfill this need, heard the Christ within Him.

Do not worry, Father. As I have said, so shall I do.

And Peter brought the two women to sit with the Nazarene. "What do ye want of me?" He said.

And again it was Martha who responded, saying, "My brother is near death, my Shepherd. He is grievously ill. It is true he was once a man not given to kindness, but he is no longer that man. Can ye find it within thee to help him? Our father is highly distraught. I fear for what will become of him should he lose his son."

So, it is to Bethany I must go, realized the Christ, as He had feared it would be. *And there may I be stoned unto death. Yet what matter? Is not the vengeance of My Father worse than a thousand stonings? Is His anger not greater than the anger of all the manbeasts combined?*

Yea, verily, it is truly so, heard the Christ. *Yet their brother is no longer ill, for his soul has taken leave of the flesh. He is named Lazarus, and he has brought a vile philosophy to the heavens. For this must he be removed from Our eyes and banished to the mortal plane. Return him to his miserable kindred; return him and let him wander with his knowledge for all eternity.*

Let him wander knowing he could help his race, but knowing he will never have the chance to do so.

Such is the will of the Father.

And the Christ looked upon the two women and said, "This sickness has come unto death; and the soul of thy brother walks no longer with the flesh."

And Martha took her sister then and did hug her; together did they weep freely for the loss of their brother. "We are too late," spake Mary amidst her sobbing. "Poor father, to see his son die before him."

"There is no need for tears, no need for grief," stated the Christ simply. "The death of thy brother was not for the earth, but for the glory of the Lord God, so that His Son might be glorified thereby."

And neither Martha nor Mary understood fully these words, yet they were comforted by them.

And the Christ called forth Peter, saying, "gather the acolytes of Our Coven, for we leave toward Judea once more."

"But Master," spake Peter, "did we not just leave Judea for thy sake? The priests shall rally the masses anew; they shall seek to stone Thee as they sought to do before."

And the Christ looked warmly upon Peter, then. *I know this thing, Peter*, thought the Christ, *yet there is no choice in the doing. But ye shall be one day rewarded for thy concern of Me, beast though ye may be.*

Yet the Christ spoke not of this, instead saying, "The brother of these two women is asleep; I must go and awaken him."

And Peter understood this not, and told his master, "If he is asleep, Lord, then he shall do well. Do not put Thyself in harm's way for such as this."

And Christ saw that Peter understood him not, and so spoke plainly. "Their brother is dead. Let us go unto him."

By this time all the acolytes had gathered around the Christ. "Can this be, Master, that Thou hast the power to wake the dead?" said Thomas.

"Thou art always the doubter, are thee not, Thomas? Yet why should it be so? Are not all things possible for the Lord God? Am I not One with the Father? Therefore, are not all things possible for Me?"

Surely, there could be no questioning of the acolytes for their Christ. Yet the women were not of the Coven, and their doubts held fast. Was this Christ a maker of miracles or was he simply mad? But none of this was spoken, for there was no other hope left unto them.

And the Christ sensed the uncertainty within the sisters and said, "Dispel the doubt within thy bosom, for I go to awaken thy brother, Lazarus."

And Martha was taken aback by the statement and said, "I have not spoken the name of my brother to Thee."

And the Christ looked upon her and said, "No, ye have not. It was My Father in the heavens who spoke it to Me."

*   *   *

Lazarus had lain dead four days before the arrival of the Christ and the acolytes of His Coven. As the group drew toward Bethany, their thoughts were not upon potential hostilities but rather upon the miracle to come.

The raising of the dead was a notion reserved for late night tales. They were stories told to keep children safely in their beds. Never in the mind of a normal man would the possibility arise. Could the Nazarene truly have this power?

If so, then it must hold truth: the man who walked before them was no man at all, but rather the Son of the Lord God made flesh.

And as they entered Bethany, they saw that many had gathered at the house of Malachi, the father of Lazarus. They had come to comfort the family for the loss of their brother.

And as Martha and Mary approached with the Christ and His Coven, the crowd about the house made way; and as the acolytes waited outside amongst those gathered, the sisters and the Christ made their way inside.

"Father," spake Martha. "He is come."

And Malachi raised his hands to his face and said, "Nay, child, it is too late. Too late, for thy brother has been four days dead."

And Martha approached the Nazarene, saying, "I know that even now, whatsoever Thou shalt ask of the Lord God, He shall grant it unto Thee."

"It is so," said the Christ unto her. "And thy brother "shall rise again."

Yet Malachi was grievously angered by this. "What madman dost thou bring into this house, woman? Is this he who would cure the sick? Perhaps it is he who needs curing, for death has no medicine against it."

Yet the Christ was not insulted by this, for he had lived long enough within the flesh to understand Malachi's pain. And He looked upon Malachi, and gave him these words: "I bring the resurrection and the life. He that believeth in Me shall live life anew; and whosoever liveth and believeth in Me shall never die. Do ye believe, Malachi?"

And Martha saw the look in her father's eyes, and she pushed him aside lest he speak; and she said, "Yea, Lord: I believe that

Thou art the Christ, the Messiah and Son of God, of which it is written shall come into this world."

And the Christ felt the sincerity within these words, and the faith flowed as rain from Martha's soul. And the Christ felt the savor of her faith and it empowered His flesh and filled His being. Even those without the house felt the renewed power within the form of the Christ.

And Malachi was affected by it most of all. "Can it be? Canst thou do this thing?"

And the Christ spoke only thus: "Where have ye lain thy son?"

"Follow and I shall bring Thee to him," spake Malachi.

And the Christ did follow, as did the acolytes of His Coven, as did the sisters, as did the mass of those gathered. As one, they proceeded toward the mountains, where the graves of the noble families were kept.

And they came upon the grave of Lazarus, which was dug into the hill; and a large stone had been placed upon its entrance.

"Can it be?" murmured those within the crowd. "Can it be that this man, which has opened the eyes of the blind and cured those ill and cast out devils, can it be that he can bring the dead back to the living?"

And the Christ said, "Take ye away the stone."

"But it has been four days," mourned Malachi. "Surely his flesh has become corrupted."

And the Christ shook His head. "Have I not said to thee that if ye but believe, thou shalt see the glory that is the Lord God?"

And Malachi made a gesture then, and a few from the crowd moved toward the stone; and they pushed the stone until the entrance was laid open.

And the Christ said: "Father, I thank thee for hearing Me. And I know that Thou hearest me always. It is but for those gathered that I say it, that they may believe that Thou hast sent me."

And after the Christ had spoken thusly, He cried out with a loud voice, saying, "Lazarus, come forth."

And the acolytes of the Christ were gathered behind Him; and the Christ focused the energies of the Coven upon the flesh of the dead. And the soul came towards the flesh, and the Christ worked His magica upon it; and it did change.

"Lazarus," invoked the Christ again. "Come forth."

And the energy that was once the soul revived the flesh, returning its vigor, restoring what had been corrupt. And what was once a living soul was changed to the energy of life, yet it was a twisted energy: for the Christ had entwined it deeply within the flesh as requested by the Father; entwined it so tightly that it would never let go.

And thricely did He say, "Lazarus, come forth." For three is the number of invocation.

And he that was dead came forth, bound in his death shroud. And the crowd gasped, and they fell back in fear.

"It cannot be, in God's name it cannot be," spoke Malachi, backing away, afraid of the walking corpse that was once his son.

"In the Lord God's name all can be," came the reply of the Christ. "Loose him, and let him go."

And Martha ran forward. And she loosed the napkin around her brother's face.

And lo, all saw that it was indeed Lazarus before them, and his flesh was whole and not corrupted by death. And all saw fear within the face of he who was once dead, and their own fears left them: for they understood that the fear within Lazarus must be greater.

For Lazarus had been to a place from which none before had returned.

Slowly, Lazarus began to understand where he was. *A dream? Was it merely a dream?*

And then the eyes of he who was dead fell upon the visage of the Christ; and he saw the power within and he recognized the Christ for what He truly was.

It was no dream. It had all been real, all real. Man was but a teat to be suckled dry by the Christ and His Kindred. Man was being bred as cattle, slaughtered as sheep. Bound in servitude even in death. It was all for nothing.

His race, his family, his mother. So much pain, so much horror. All for nothing.

As they loosed his body from the shroud, he screamed in rage; toward the Christ he ran, wanting to feel His flesh come away in his hands.

Yet he had no strength to him. The Lazuri fell; he fell and his sensibilities left him.

All looked to the Christ then, and He said, "Would ye, too, not be enraged after being torn from the bosom of the Lord God? Let him rest. In time, all shall be well."

I know not fully why the Father has cursed thee thus, thought the Christ. *Yet ye shall come to regret thy birth this day, son of Malachi.*

And so it was that the earth was blessed with another miracle that day.

The greatest miracle of all.

For the curse of punishment bestowed upon the Lazuri that day was also the seed of hope.

*   *   *

There is nothing new under the sun. And so, in time, what was becomes what is again.

For after their liberation from Egypt, the Children of Seth gave thanks each year. Yet it was not their freedom they rejoiced in, for it was a celebration born of fear, not joy. It was a night of feasting in which the families of Seth came together and gave thanks for their lives; a feast known as Passover, when the Angel of Death allowed the firstborn of Seth's lineage to live.

The feast was the most sacrosanct of days, for the death of Egypt's children was a great victory for the Lord God.

And it came to pass that before this holy day arrived, in what would be known as the year of zero, the chief priests and scribes came together to conspire and bring down the Christ.

They had heard of the raising of Lazarus. The story had made its way to all the ears within Judea. All wondered what manner of man could wield such power. Some were awed by what they had heard; more still were gripped by terror. What protection was there from a man who could resurrect the flesh of those dead?

They were all agreed: this threat must be removed from the face of the earth before it corrupted them all. It was agreed that the Nazarene should be put to death. Such was the fear of Him and His power.

And the chief priests who were the Pharisees said, "What shall we do? For this man works many signs."

"If we let him alone, everyone will come to believe in him, and the Romans will come and take away both our place and nation."

Yet there was one, Caiaphas, whose motives ran deeper. For Caiaphas had not always been an only child. He had an older brother once. His name was Zacharias, a rabbi. One day, after being chastised by a child from Bethlehem, his brother had met a horrible death.

Caiaphas had heard the story many times, for the rabbis in the temple were good friends to his family. There was no doubt of the power in the child: and there was no doubt now in the mind of Caiaphas that this Jesus must not be allowed to survive.

And Caiaphas, being high speaker of the priests that year, said to those gathered, "Thou knowest nothing. It is neither for positions nor for the nation that this evil should be purged, but for the sake of all men. We must not suffer this witch to live."

Then, from that day forward, they plotted to put the Christ to death.

And so Caiaphas used his position, wealth, and power to avenge the murder of his brother and bring down the Christ. And many deals were made and much silver changed hands; alliances were made and broken. Rumors were spread and the seeds of discontent sown.

And finally, after much searching, the tool of his revenge was uncovered, and his name was Judas Iscariot, one of the Coven of Christ.

"Go ye into the city," spake Judas unto Caiaphas, "to the garden of Gethsemane. Do this thing upon this even. And keep thine eyes upon me, for the one ye seek shall I greet with a kiss to the cheek."

And Judas went off to have his last supper with the Christ, for this very night the Son of the self-proclaimed God would be arrested for the crimes of blasphemy and sorcery.

All thirteen met that evening to celebrate the Passover. And the Christ saw within the mind of Judas, and He knew His time was at hand. And as they sat and did eat, the Christ made a revelation unto His Coven, saying, "Yea, I say unto thee, there is one amongst ye that shall betray me."

And the twelve stood indignantly, even Judas Iscariot, saying, "This cannot be; is it I?" and another said "Is it I?" And each, in his turn, asked this question also.

And the Christ answered them with these words: "It is one of My Coven, ye twelve, that suppeth here with Me this night. Indeed, the Son of God must go from thee, for so is it written. But woe to that man by whose hand I am betrayed! For his life and death shall be of misery, and better it would be for him if he were never born."

And as they again began to eat, the Christ took the bread and broke it, saying, "Take this, all of you, and eat of it. This bread is as my body, for as it nourishes thee, so shall the death of my body nourish the faith of thy soul."

And when they were done partaking of the unleavened bread, the Christ took a large earthen chalice. And He filled it with the fruit of the vine, saying, "Take this, all of you, and drink from it, for as this wine uplifts the spirit, so shall the spilling of my blood uplift the spirit of Man. This is as my blood, the blood of the new and everlasting covenant, and it shall be shed for all men."

And each partook of the cup, and drank deeply from it. The cup was passed and filled and passed again, until the flasks had all been drained. And after they had sung a hymn, they left the house of their supper and found themselves in the gardens of Gethsemane.

"And the Christ said unto them, "All ye shall denounce me this night, yet let this not bring ye sorrow, for it is written: *I will smite the shepherd, and the sheep shall be scattered.* Yet in this way shall ye survive to spread the word of My gospel."

The acolytes balked sharply at this, yet the Christ would heed them not. "Wait for Me here," He said, "for the time hast come and I must pray."

And the Christ went away from His Coven then, finding a place of isolation within the garden. And the Son of the Lord God, the Third Part of the Three, assumed the posture of subjugation: He knelt upon the earth, bowing His head, enfolding His hands. He was deeply aware of the feel of His flesh, the clarity of His nerves and senses: and He became afraid.

Father, prayed the Christ. *Do not do this thing, I beg Thee. I know I have disobeyed Thee, yet mine actions were born of mercy. It was out of pity for the manbeasts that I modified the doctrine I was to deliver them.*

Father, all things are possible to Thee. It is within Thy power to save Me from this suffering.

And a voice responded to the prayers of the Christ, saying, *The time to be repentant is long past. What must now come to pass is for Thine own benefit. Shall I, too, not feel thy pain once We rejoin as One?*

Ye must learn Thy lesson: pity is foolish, mercy for the weak. In the time of Gehenna must Ye again reside upon the earth, to face the Abomination. There must be no weakness within Thee then. Ask not to be spared in this thing, for what you ask shall not come to pass. Thou hast earned Thy penance, though its method pleases Me not.

And the Christ realized there would be no respite, for He knew the ways of the Father only too well.

And then there came another voice, a voice cloaked in sympathy. *Join Us*, it said. And it was the voice of the Fallen. *Join Us and We may spare Thee from the pain of Thy Father.*

No, responded the Christ. *I have done much, but a betrayal such as this is not within Me. I understand Thy reasons and Thy ways. And indeed, I even agree with Thy philosophies. Yet what ye asketh is more than I can give. Perhaps when I rejoin as One my beliefs shall find solace in the conscience of My Father.*

Yea, Thy reason is understood and Thy goal is admirable, responded Satan. *Yet We Below shall not hold false hope, as Thy chances for success are not great. Yet know this: Our knowledge is growing each day. Each day we come closer to drawing greater energies from the Universe of Olde.*

There may come a time, if peace is not gained between Us, that We may outshine Thee and Those Above with our power. Take this message to Thy Father.

I have no choice but to do so, explained the Christ, *for I am He and He is Me. Yet easy with Thy words, Satan: We Above know Ye cannot escape the bonds of the material plane.*

And We Below know that Ye will not destroy the Race of Man, for it is the desire of Thee and Thine to use them as fodder for Gehenna and the Great Jihad. As for Our loosing Our bonds: who knows what the morrow shall bring? Yet let Us speak no more of this. Thy time is at hand, Three of Three. Thy Judas comes and Thine enemies are with him.

Our sympathies go with Thee.

"What good Thy sympathies, Satan?" replied the Christ aloud. And why not? For there was no one to hear.

Upon returning to those of the Coven, Judas made his way to the Christ and greeted Him. And kissed Him. "Remember what I told thee," Christ said to him as the soldiers drew nigh. "Ye shall wish ye were never born."

As the Christ was led away by the soldiers and the priests, His acolytes ran in fear, fulfilling the prophecy.

Not a one remained, none but Judas.

In a few days hence, Judas Iscariot would be found hanging by the neck within a well of the city. Yet his torment would not end with his death, for his soul would be tortured and suckled by the Lord God until the end of time.

*   *   *

Straightaway that next morning the high priest Caiaphas and the Pharisees and scribes held a consultation; and they bound the Christ and carried him away, and delivered him unto Pilate, the Roman Governor of the province.

The priest conferred with Pilate and told him of the blasphemies and sorceries, the healings and mockeries. And Pilate approached the Christ and asked him, "Is this true? Art thou the Son of God?"

"Are not we all the Children of God?" the Christ responded.

And He was accused of many things, yet not once did the Christ raise His voice in His own defense. "Dost thou not hear what has been witnessed against thee? Will ye not answer these charges?" said Pilate.

Pilate saw no harm in this man before him, no reason for his death but to appease a few fearful priests. So it was that he had the man before him flogged. Perhaps, hoped Pilate, this would satisfy his accusers.

Yet it was not enough.

And so a public forum was conducted. Already the priests had gone amongst the gathered and incited them, saying, "Crucify him! Crucify him!" And the crowd, as crowds are wont to do, soon became lost in the frenzy and took up the chant also: "Crucify him! Crucify him."

And Pilate went to the Christ and asked again, "Will ye say nothing? It is thy life they wish from thee. Defend thine actions, man! Give me a reason to release thee, any reason at all. If you do not do this, thou art as good as dead."

And Christ looked at the Governor, and knew he was a good man, and fair. But this Pilate was not a strong man. He was new to his post, and could ill afford an insurrection. The crowd was fervored now and Pilate knew he would have to kill the man before him. He did not want to do this, yet the accused would not be helped.

"I wash thy hands of any guilt in this," said the Christ to Pilate. "This life is Mine to give. The choice has been made." *Yet it was not mine to make.*

And Pilate nodded. "Yea, thou art surely feeble. Yet thy words are true: thy life is thine." Pilate went towards a basin and did wash his hands. The ritual brought calm to his unease. "This is no longer my affair," he said. And to the masses, "Do what Ye will, this falls upon thy conscience, not mine." And with that, Pilate left the court.

And straightaway did two soldiers take the Christ and lead him away to the Praetorium, the great hall. And there they stripped him and pressed a crown of thorns upon his scalp. A soiled purple robe, the color of royalty, was mockingly draped upon the one who was now openly, mockingly called the Christ.

And they took two other criminals who were to be crucified also; each was given his cross to bear unto the place of death, Golgotha.

The procession wound its way upon the dusty road for many miles. The cross was weighed heavy and the Christ was weak from lack of blood; for the flogging had taken its toll.

As He walked, the soldiers refused Him water. The throat of the Christ bled with its rawness. The crowds who gathered mocked the condemned as they passed, spitting and shouting.

Always did such a crowd gather on the days of execution, for there were few amusements in those times. Yea, the walk of the damned was a favored event.

The Christ ignored them, focusing His energies upon His burden and His steps. He counted each one, trying to ignore the tortured messages of His flesh.

Yet after a while, it all became meaningless: the curses, His swelling tongue, the endless walking, the heat, the burning of His wounds. All meaningless, for the unending torment caused the Christ to leave His senses.

And time became nothing more than a concept, for it seemed the misery was without end.

Yet at one point, a strange feeling brought the Christ out of his pained delirium. A figure approached Him, one He knew He should know.

His vision was blurred from the sweat and blood which had fallen into them. He raised a hand against His exhaustion to wipe His vision clear.

Help me, said the Christ to figure which came towards Him. But the words would not leave His lips. The figure came closer still, stopping before Him.

There was a sound, also recognizable, also elusive. The Christ felt a sensation upon His countenance, a coolness against the heat of the desert. He wished to give His thanks.

Then it was repeated, and the Christ knew it for what it was; the one before him had spat upon Him.

And He felt hands fall upon him, striking him fiercely. The thorns of the crown tore deeply into His scalp. New blood brought forth new pain.

"Enough," heard the Christ, from somewhere behind Him.

"Remember this, False God," spake the figure, but the Christ heard not what followed: for the Christ was enraged by this beast who would torment Him. *Were it not for the staying hand of the Lord God ye would know true suffering, beastman.*

"Remember this pain, Son of Lies, and suffer as no man has suffered," continued the voice.

Who is this creature? thought the Christ. *I will know him.* And He tried to gather the power of His Coven behind Him, yet the acolytes had dispersed. Raising His visage He struggled to focus.

And He saw. And He knew him.

"We shall meet again, Lazuri," spake the Christ with forced words. *Indeed, ye shall know true suffering after all.* And the anger within the Christ left Him then. *Yet know, too, that I understand thy hatred, and it is well deserved. I would tell thee of my penance, yet I cannot: and it would matter to thee not at all.*

The Christ watched as the Lazuri was removed by one of the soldiers.

"Move along!" the Christ heard as the Lazuri was pulled away. *Yea, verily, move along, Lazuri. Destiny awaits us both, and I would wish it to come quickly.*

Yet alas, it came not quickly enough for the Son of the Lord God. But it did come.

And the world was changed for evermore.

THE BOOK OF FAITH

And the death of Jesus the Christ set ablaze a new-named faith: Christianity.

For the acolytes of the Christ spread word of their martyr throughout the land, preaching his philosophy. And many did flock unto the banner. So it was that the word took root, and the word became religion.

And the followers of the one-third god gathered in the Eternal City to foster their faith.

Yet the leader of the Eternal City, the Caesar, was displeasured with the followers of the Christ; and he did torment them and slay them and lead them to his blood sport for the amusement of the populace. At each turn of tide did he find ways to taunt, torture and torment them; at each opportunity did he maim and defile and kill them.

And still their numbers grew: for the threat of pain and death was nothing to the promise of life eternal. And those who sought to crush the faith could not discourage those who would spread the word and give witness to the miracles of the Christ.

In shadow and in darkness did they nurture their new glory; in the catacombs of the city did they gather under their symbol.

Lo, the Eternal City was not kind to these new followers, those born again into a new faith. Yet no matter, for in time, all is a circle; and what is given shall be gotten.

And so the acolyte Peter rose among the faithful of the Christ. And he was made the first leader of this new faith. And he was called *il Papa,* or *Pope,* meaning *father;* for Peter was charged with the well being of the flock of Christ. And through him was the Word imparted unto the sheep.

In time, it came to pass that the followers became many more still; and the office of Peter was passed on upon his death, and upon the death of those who did succeed him. And there came a Caesar who embraced the word of Christ, and brought the Eternal City under the banner of the tortured god.

So it was that those who once had hidden below in terror emerged into the light; and the torch of the Lord God burned brightly among the tribes of man.

And it followed that the Eternal City set aside a holy place for the servants of the Christ to live and administer their doctrine. And it came to be called the Holy City; and the office of the Pope came to be seen as the mouth of God made flesh.

And the trumpet call of the Christian faith spread as fire throughout the civilized world. And first one country and then another fell under its thrall. And there did come a time when the church of the Christ was in all places; and it came to be involved in all things.

*   *   *

And lo, the day arrived, as it was bound to do, when the powers of the papal office exceeded the wisdom of those who held it. And what was once a great cause became a great corruption.

And the people did see this. They saw the priests grow fat from the excesses of their office; they watched as the bishops, meaning overlords, gained lands and possessions; and their respect for the papacy became disdain.

And the people began to look elsewhere for guidance: for it was a time of hardship and wants unfulfilled for those of meager means; and those unlettered had little hope of improving themselves, despite all their toil and piety.

So it was that many generations after the killing of the Christ, the church inspired by the god made flesh began to splinter and change.

And for those in power, change is no good thing.

And the Leaders of the Church saw a group arise in a land well removed from the Holy City, and those within this group called themselves Cathari, meaning *pure*; and these new teachers spread their gospel to the neglected poor. They shed their worldly wealth, wandered with their words, gave aid where needed, provided comfort to those without comfort. They asked for nothing, eating sparingly of fruits and vegetables, taking no meat.

And the common man took inspiration from this and admired them, for this divestiture of the material was far removed from the excesses of the church.

Quickly did the teachings of the Cathari spread. Even many of the wealthy, in time, saw the piousness of the Cathari and embraced their teachings. In comparison, the hierarchy of the Church of Christ was worthy only of contempt.

As the following of the Cathari grew, so did the uneasiness of the Holy City; for those within its walls would not so easily allow their rule to be usurped. Of great concern was the conversion of the nobility; for as they came to follow the Cathari, the donations given to the churches of the Christ began to diminish.

And these Cathari threatened the power of the church in other ways, for they believed not in the holiness of the Christ, they believed not in the sanctity of the Christian sacraments: they were heretics of the worst order in the eyes of the flock of Christ.

Such were the state of affairs that led the Pope to action. And he issued an edict to move against the Cathari. He declared them and their followers heretics; their holdings forfeit.

And so began the road of blood upon which the Church of Christ would travel for seven hundred years. So began the holy war which would kill and butcher more men, women and children than any other war or disease. All in the name of the Lord God, all for His glory.

And it began with these words, from the mouth of the Holy See, from the mouth of God:

"We of the church of Christ hold a sacred charge. Entrusted to us is the salvation of man. Each soul upon this earth unto our care has been given. We cannot, therefore, allow any evil to spread lest it corrupt even one soul among the many; for that one soul is worth more than all the infidels upon this earth."

"Therefore, by papal edict, in the name of the Lord God, does this church denounce all actions of the Cathari, a sect given in to the unholiness of those cast out. They deny the glory of the Christ, defy His sacraments, and defile the faithful by the spreading their heresy: they place each immortal soul among us in the most dire peril. And each corruption loses a soul to the ever-burning fires and torment of Hell and the daemons within it."

"Each of these vile followers of Satan must be crushed by the righteousness of the Lord God. There must be no rest while even one of these Cathari still lives."

"And so we give a call to arms against these devils, for the souls of the innocent are in great peril. It is ours to do what we must, to save the souls of the innocent from the fires of Hell. To all those who join us, hear this: the sins you have committed on this earth shall be forgiven, and a seat in the heavens is assured to those who are truly penitent. Take up your swords. Destroy this abomination which has arisen to blemish the face of the Lord God!"

And many did come; some for the cause they believed to be righteous, yet many more still for the spoils of war: for the holdings of any involved with the Cathari were deemed forfeit, and the nobility were rumored to be involved.

And this crusade was enacted one thousand two hundred and thirteen years after the birth of the Christ. It was a war that Pope Innocent III assumed would be short-lived, yet it continued for more than a score of years. And still were the Cathari not destroyed: for sympathy followed these pious men, and they were hidden by those pure of heart.

And so came a second decree:

"The heretics have taken strong root. We must ferret them from us, eradicate the hold they have taken amongst us."

"To this end, I have mustered the a legion of pious and pure monks to seek out the evil amongst us, to quiet the fires of the Cathari and any others who so should threaten the sanctity of our souls. Therefore, for the good of our children and ourselves, the monks shall go forth into the land as my inquisitors. In the name of the one true God shall they go. And to those of unpure faith I say this: we shall find thee; in thy deeds shall we find thee, in thy thoughts shall we find thee. Ye cannot hide from us."

And so the Inquisition was born.

And the monks of the inquisition came to be known as the *Domini Canes*—the Hounds of God—for they were merciless in their pursuit of the faithless. At first, they used only threats of purgatory and pain. In time, however, the emotional torture was replaced by the tortures of the flesh, as it was found to be much more effective. Yet the monks were not loosed unchecked, for the papacy sanctioned writings on the investigations of heresy. And so, a book was made law, and it was known as the *Malleus Mallificarum*, the *Hammer of Witches*. And within its pages were the rules to which the *Domini Canes* did abide.

First and foremost, the monks of the church could draw no blood. There would be no tolerance for violation of this canon. Yet the *Hounds of God* were clever: they heated their tools of torture in bellowed flames, until the metal glowed brightly and red. So it was that as the tools pierced and burned the flesh, no blood was spilled, for the hot metal would close the wound.

But why all this? Why not simply kill the accused so the masses would run home to cower in prayer? Praying to the Lord God so they, too, would be passed over in these times of horror.

It was necessary for one reason: to appease the masses. To prevent a revolt born of injustice. For to prevent another Cathari cult from arising, a semblance of legitimacy needed to be maintained. And so, in order to justify punishment, it was necessary to proclaim *Habemus confitentum reum,* meaning "We have a confessed criminal." No action could be taken without this proclamation. Yea, for without repentance there was no savor for the Lord God.

So the *Domini Canes*—the *Dominicans*, as they came to be known—acquired their confessions. And, as long as they followed their doctrine, it mattered not how.

And the church could not involve itself in the causing of death, for to destroy a life was a violation of Christian gospel.

Yet the men of the cloth would not be so easily daunted. Where the will to do a thing doth exist, a way shall surely be found. And the church would not be denied.

And so, when the confessions came—and they always did come—the sinners were sent to those who governed. And they, in turn, disposed of the criminals accordingly: by roasting them alive upon a stake in the square, as a lesson to those who would defy the church, and for the amusement of the faithful.

And all was good, for there was no brighter fire than the fire of a purged soul; and the fervor of faith brought by this torment shone brightly in the eyes of the watchers.

Many a night was filled with the screams of the living within the flames; many a night was illuminated by the burning fat of the dead, and the evening air was fragrant with the savor of roasted flesh.

Prisons were constructed by the Hounds of God throughout the lands; and they filled as quickly as they were built. And the Inquisition brought its horror to every person and every place: yet some places held more horror than others.

And in a time when the inquisitors were well entrenched in the social structure, a grand inquisitor rose up among his brethren; a man more horrid and willing to do evil in the name of God than any who had come before him.

And he was known as Torquemada, and his was the name of hell and suffering on earth.

Any who did not believe as his church believed felt his wrath; and those who dared not conform to the thoughts and ways of the Lord God would have their souls torn asunder by his inquisitors.

And there was no mercy, no humanity, no salvation.

He practiced his worship in a land called Spain; and the Spanish Inquisition became the most bloodthirsty of all.

And those accused were entombed in houses of stone without color, and the world within was measured in shades of darkness. The smell of torment encased these places in shrouds of fear, and no one passing would spare a glance in its direction: for only horror lay within.

And so it was, during this dark age, that another sinner found himself a prisoner of the *Domini Canes*. Deep within the walls if the Inquisition was he entombed, awaiting the tortures that were sure to come.

He was tossed into a cell without word, landing harshly upon a cobbled floor.

Nothing could he see at first, for there was scant light by which to find detail. Only by what luminance found its way through the small grate of the door could anything be seen.

Yet the prisoner could feel the textures of ancient straw as he groped his way upright. It was pungent with the odors of sweat and urine. And there were other odors beneath, less easily recognizable. Yet, in short time, they, too, became discernible.

It was the stench of fear and death: feces and blood and entrails. And decayed flesh.

Through it all was the screaming of those being questioned, somewhere within the bowels of the beast. The screams of pain, the screams for mercy. Yet mostly the screams of pain. Unendurable agony.

Yet agony made to endure, for the church of Christ was well versed in the ways of suffering.

And a voice came to this man from the darkness, and it said, "Do not be afraid here."

And he who was newly incarcerated laughed without humor. "It would seem that I am not alone," he responded, "for I have been granted the company of a madman. Of all the places on earth to be afraid," he continued, "there is no equal to a House of the Inquisition."

And the mirthless laughter was returned from within the darkness, and then it stopped. "I suppose I cannot argue that point from within these walls," came the voice in reply. "What is thy name?"

And the man who was still blinded in the cold darkness of his new home responded, "What matter? Soon we shall both be damned."

Yet the voice said, "It does matter, for we must remember that we are not animals. I was once known as Lazarus."

"Like the man spoken of in the mass."

And the Lazuri laughed that laugh again and said, "Yes, like the one described within the gospels of the Christ."

And the new prisoner gave his name then, saying, "I am Ferdinand Hans Luther."

"Like the king," responded the Lazuri.

And the man nodded, "Yes, like the king."

"Well, Ferdinand. Here we are," said the Lazuri, "two men of our stature in a place like this."

"Please, Hans is my preference, as I would prefer no ties with the likes of any king who would condone a place such as this."

"It shall be Hans, then," the Lazuri agreed. "So, what brings thee here? The food, perhaps?"

And Hans laughed, yet not entirely without mirth this time. "Ye must also be new here, for the Dominicans have yet to remove thy wit and spirit."

"I have been here for what must be three years at least," stated the Lazuri. "It shall take more than the Hounds of God to rob me of my humor."

Amidst the odors and the darkness and the cries did the eyes of Hans grow wide; his mouth dropped. He seemed to want to speak, yet was unable. Slowly, his sight returned to him, what little could be garnered from the conditions.

The man called Lazarus sat askew in the corner to his left. His clothing, what little was left, hung as rags upon his thin frame. Thin, yet not gaunt or diseased or seemingly mistreated.

Hans raised a lip in contempt. He did not care for the games of this fool. He was cold and hungry and afraid; this brought upon him an ill humor. "Play not these games with me, Lazarus. Had ye been here even ten days ye would not look as well as ye appear."

The Lazuri shook his head. "Do not be misled by my appearance. I could be here for a score years and still look as I do now. What is thy crime, Hans?"

Hans lowered his eyes. "I missed the mass this Sabbath. I was turned in."

"Ah." *As simple as that*, thought the Lazuri.

Hans tried to wipe the straw from his trousers, yet it stubbornly clung to him. "My children were ill with fever; their mother died of it not a month before. What could I do? And who will care for them now?"

"There was little else ye could have done, my friend." There was pity in the voice of the Lazuri. He had heard many stories within these walls. "Thy children are sacred. More sacred than the rites dictated by the likes of man."

"They are the rites of God!" shouted Hans, making his way to the corner opposite the Lazuri. "Had I have gone to mass for that brief time, I would be with my children now. Perhaps God would have taken pity upon them, perhaps they would have been made well."

As Hans sat down, the Lazuri responded, "Look around thee, Hans. Breathe deeply. Listen to the torment around thee. This is Hell, my friend. Would a true god wish such a thing upon thee for missing one mass for thy children? Look not to thy deity for solace or forgiveness. Ye shall find neither."

Will people never learn? The Lazuri had tried since his rebirth to make people understand that the Lord God was no god. Yet they refused to listen. He had been burned alive more than once. It was not a pleasurable thing.

He could remember in detail each moment: the jeering crowds as he was brought before the magistrate. The feel of bones cracking as stones were hurled upon him; the numbness of his hands as he was tied tightly to the post; the sickening hiss of his melted fat dripping upon the burning logs.

Mercifully, he would lose consciousness long before his body was charred through.

Yet each time his flesh healed. And he would awaken, usually within a pit littered with roasted corpses. Yet they were lucky: for them it was over. For the Lazuri it was just another beginning.

And since the time of the Christ, the Lazuri watched as the once hunted Christians became the hunters themselves. He saw as the religion of the Christ took root and spread. It would not stop. Man was bred to need a god, and it is no easy task to change the nature of a thing.

And look where it has led him. Religion was supposed to relieve suffering, not intensify it. When would man learn?

"I see why thou art here, Lazarus," Hans stated. "Unlike the one who sits before thee, thou art a true heretic."

"There is none truer than I," responded the Lazuri.

And Hans was fearful of his cellmate. Perhaps it was a test? Perhaps this Lazarus was in truth an inquisitor? "Christ will save thee, ye shall see."

The Lazuri smiled. This would not be the first time he would be taken for a familiar, a confederate of the inquisitors. "I have seen. And I would not wish his methods upon the worst of my enemies."

"He shall forgive thy words, should ye become repentant. For He is divine and merciful in all things."

The Lazuri knew the game, and he did not mind playing it. It was comfortable; it was routine. "He is not divine. And he is not merciful. Look around thee, Hans. Where is this mercy of which ye speak?"

There was something to the response which seemed familiar to Hans, yet he knew not what. Then it came to him. "Thou art Cathari, are ye not? Only they would speak so. I thought they had all been burned, long ago."

"Yes. All but one, yet that one was burned as well."

And Hans knew not what to make of this response. "So thou art truly Cathari?" asked Hans a second time.

"I am *the* Cathari," responded the Lazuri. And in so responding did a look of pain fall upon his features. "I am he who began it all.

Little did I know what misery it would bring. I sought to help, and look what I have done. Instead of salvation, I have become the Bearer of Misery and Death."

Hans shook his head. "Thou art insane, verily so. The Cathari came into being centuries past; thou hast seen but a few decades upon this earth."

And the Lazuri laughed. "There is much ye do not know, dear Hans. Yet ye have the seeds of the Cathari within thee, I can see this. Therein lies thy salvation."

"No! I am not Cathari," cried Hans. "They were vile heretics. I am a man of God! Hear me and hear me true! I worship the Christ. Praise the Lord God!"

And the Lazuri laughed. "Say what ye will, yet no one is listening, friend. And I do not need convincing. I see the light within you." And the Lazuri moved closer to Hans, who tried to push himself further into his corner, as if his flesh could somehow be forced into the mortar and away from this madman.

"Ye also question why a church of God would treat a man so," whispered the Lazuri. "I know there is a part of thee that believes ye may deserve this horror. Yet this need not be so, for it is well that ye doubt of a church which would cause such pain."

"No!" shouted Hans. "Thou art mad."

"Yes, perhaps, but what matter? Within thy soul ye know I speak correctly. A true church of a true god would not treat men so. There is great dignity and pride in men. It should not be hunted and destroyed in this way."

And Hans raised his hands to his head, and he shook his head sadly, slowly. "Pride. Ye speak of pride. It was pride that brought us to this. Pride which caused Satan and his foolish followers to be cast out of the heavens and into the hottest pits of Hell."

"Yes, yes. I have heard it all before. From those who were afraid, like thou art now. And from the mouths of the inquisitors."

And Lazarus continued, "Why are we here?"

"Because we have been untrue to the Lord God within our hearts." Hans spread his hands in dismay. "Because we have sinned."

"No, not in this place. Why are any of us here? On this earth?"

This is some kind of test, thought Hans. *I must simply answer properly.* "To give praise to the Lord God."

"No," insisted the Lazuri. "Of all things, that least of all. Does the Lord God not have all the angels in the heavens to give him praise? Do ye bestow us with the status of angels?"

And Hans's head jerked sharply. No, of course not! "We are not a thousandth of what the Angels are," he said quickly. "We are beneath contempt."

"Then why would the Lord God want thy praise, we who are beneath contempt? Surely, he did not create such contemptible beings solely to give him praise. What good would praise from such contemptibles be? And why would he create us to be so contemptible? Why would the Lord God create an imperfect creature such as man?"

And Hans realized then, without any doubt, that this man was no familiar of the church. "I will not hear this."

"What do ye think of a god that sees his creation not as children but as his sheep? A flock to herd and slaughter as he bids? Ye can follow his laws or not, so it is said. Yet look at the walls around ye. Where is his forgiveness now?"

"I will not hear this!" stated Hans again.

"Thou must hear it," said the Lazuri passionately. "Ye must be made to hear it. Ye must shout it to others. Only in this way will man become what he can become."

Hans Luther knew he should not listen, must not. There was damnation in the words of this mad Cathari. "Leave me be."

"Hans, listen to me." *For thou must listen,* thought the Lazuri. "Ye seem an intelligent man. More so than most."

"I studied once, as a priest."

This surprised the Lazuri, yet he did not show his surprise. "What happened, then?"

What happened? thought Luther. *Exactly those things of which I should not speak within a House of the Inquisition:* That he thought the church corrupt, the papacy an office of wealth and power, unfit to serve as the spiritual center of the teachings of Christ. All these things could he have said, but dared not.

"I was found wanting," he uttered finally, and it was enough.

The Lazuri nodded, for he understood only too well. "Yes. I know of what ye speak."

"I will not discuss it," emphasized Hans.

"Ye must," the Lazuri replied. "Yet ye need not speak of it here. I of all people understand: 'for everything there is a time.'"

"A season," Hans corrected.

Lazarus ignored this, knowing it would be pointless to argue the issue. "As ye say," he shrugged. "I know that the atmosphere within these walls weighs heavily upon thee. I have seen many come through this place, many such as thyself."

Then the tone of the Lazuri became more somber still. "But there will come a time when ye shall be free of this place, when ye can speak freely. Make someone listen; the seeds of reform must take root. Thou art no fool, Hans. Look about thee. Is this the future thou wishest for thy progeny?"

Hans looked deeply within the eyes of the Lazuri, and for a moment, all fear was forgotten. "I would wish this upon no one," he replied.

"Good," the Lazuri said. "That is very good."

In time, both slept. Amidst the morning screams, before the Lazuri awoke, Hans Luther was taken. The Lazuri never saw him again.

Yet, in time, he came to find that his seed had taken root.

*   *   *

Hans was taken deep with the bowels of the inquisitorial palace. He was tortured, as a matter of routine. A hot iron was placed upon his tongue. He was whipped and beaten. During a short time on the rack, an overzealous monk turned one notch too many, and the left leg was torn from its joint.

Hans Ferdinand Luther did confess, of course, to heresy and acts against the church. They almost always did, if they did not die first.

Hans was then given to the state for proper dispensation. He was taken and held until the next *auto-de-fe*, which was a public carnival for the faithful; a chance to see the repentant tortured and burned alive.

All for the glory of the Lord God, as dictated by His Voice upon the earth. And His Voice was the voice of the Pope.

Yea, all this horror was by an edict of the Holy Father, the Leader of the Church of Christ.

And Hans Ferdinand Luther was placed within the wooden stocks and was flogged: such was the penance for the missing of mass.

And then he was let go.

Hans would always walk with a limp from his time on the rack, yet he did find his way home. A neighbor had watched his children while he was with the inquisitors, yet only his eldest son remained alive.

Hans left the land of Spain then, taking his son across the water to a place called England. It was there that he hoped to forget what had happened.

Yet he did not forget the words of the one called Lazarus. The man who must have been half-mad long before Hans had ever met him.

In time, his son became interested in the faith. And he did what the father had not: he achieved the rank of priesthood. Yet the son expressed concern to his father. The church had strayed, become corrupted, he would say. And the two would speak upon the subject of religious reform.

So it was that the son of Hans Ferdinand Luther, Martin, would lead a reformation that would bring the monopoly of the Church of Christ to an end.

For Martin Luther would lead the revolt which would change the course of Christianity.

*   *   *

For many years was the Lazuri made to suffer the inequities of the Inquisition.

Time upon time, the Lazuri was subjugated to the implements of the holy: the rack, upon which his joints were pulled from their place of rest; the water, which was forced down his throat by tube and funnel; the whippings, the beatings, the cauterized cuttings.

All to no avail, for the Lazuri was cursed with the gift of immortality. And each morning the tortured flesh was found to be whole.

For many years the Lazuri lay clenched in the talons of the faithful; in a dark and damp cell, suffused with the smell of injustice. So dark that the eyes of the Lazuri were expanded as a black mass. The air itself seemed even more darkened by the palpable odors of decay and unclean flesh. From the bowels of this hell on earth came the cries of the damned.

So it was each day.

Yet the Lazuri would not confess to heresy. And the Hounds of God could not bring death upon the unrepentant.

The Dominicans came to despise this man, for by his existence did they become more fearful of the works of Satan. Who else could protect a man so thoroughly from the wrath of the Lord God?

In time, the inquisitors took the Lazuri to the darkest, deepest part of the prison. He was left with neither light nor food nor water. The door was sealed with brick and all those above tried to forget the unholy abomination within their walls of cleansing.

Once again, the Lazuri found himself within his own tomb; a place of no escape. He tore at the iron-laden oak which kept him sealed within; tore until the flesh of his fingers wore away to reveal the bone. Yet it would heal, always would it heal.

And there was naught but darkness. And there was no joy. And there was no death.

Yet there were always the sounds and the odors. And they became familiar to the Lazuri and he embraced them as friends.

Yet, one day, these ceased also. No more sounds, no more screaming. Only silence and darkness.

And time became just a memory, for it's passing held no meaning.

In a solitude void of sight and sound, the mind of the Lazuri did wander. Without reason or consciousness did his thoughts flow. And yet, while balancing upon the frail edges of sanity and madness did he receive his salvation.

For before the Lazuri lapsed into the valley of the lost there came a visitor. And the Lazuri saw the door long sealed begin to open with the sound of breaking bones. Slowly, forcefully was the large wooden door of his tomb pushed forward. And the light from beyond was brighter than the light of death to the eyes of the Lazuri.

He tried to speak, yet words had become an unaccustomed visitor, and all that came forth was a dry rasping. *How long had it been?* he thought. *Five years? Twenty? A hundred?*

He shielded his eyes from the pain of the light. And by what brightness filtered through his fingers, he saw a shape manifested within the threshold. The form was black, outlined by the painful luminescence.

His eyes rested upon the dark shape, for only then was there respite from the needles of brightness which burrowed their jagged barbs into the soft flesh of his sight. And the form borne of darkness entered, and the door closed loudly behind it.

And this time the Lazuri did manage his words. "Who?"

And the form said, "I am one unjustly imprisoned, as are you, by the hand of the Lord God. I suffer as you have suffered, Lazuri." The voice was a man's voice, strong and resolute.

And the Lazuri laughed then, a cold, dry rasp. What did this man know of suffering?

"More rightly," the figure responded, "what dost ye know of suffering, you who have lived but a handful of years upon this earth, and lesser still within these walls."

And the Lazuri shook his head, eyes finally adjusting to the light. He looked at the place from whence the voice had come. And lo, where before he saw nothing but shadows, he now began to see the walls about him and the filth upon and around him; and the one who spoke before him also.

And he saw the bone upon the brow.

"You," spoke the Lazuri. "What has taken ye so long to come?"

And Satan said, "Manifestation in the physical world is no simple task for Us. It requires long and painful preparation. Nor must We manifest Ourselves overlong, for Our essence shall corrupt the very stone upon which We stand."

Satan walked over toward the Lazuri then. Sitting beside him, He spoke thusly: "Thy torment has a purpose, Lazuri. Ye carry within thee the seeds from which the hope of Man shall grow."

"Then take these seeds from me," answered the Lazuri. "for seeds cannot spring from barren soil."

And Satan said, "The soil should not be the judge of its own fertility. Leave that task to the farmer."

"So, am I now thy crop to tend? When ripened, shall I, too, be devoured?"

"Nay, Lazuri," spake Satan. "Do not place me in league with the Shepard, the self-proclaimed Lord God and Father. Though I aspire to be the Cain to His Abel, I will not sacrifice that which I nurture."

And a smile came unto the Fallen Angel, then. And he continued, "Thou hast more strength within thee than ye know, Lazuri. Remember this: the World of the Dead is thickly veiled from the mortal realm. Of all men, only ye have seen it. And thou art correct in thy philosophy: only in becoming One may the Race of Man win its freedom beyond the mortal coil. In so becoming, thy race shall outshine all the might of the Lord God and His Angelica."

"No," the Lazuri said. "His strength is too great, I saw him tear my mother's soul asunder. What can man do against such power?"

"Remember, Lazuri, His strength comes from Man. It is not His strength of which ye are afeared. It is thine own.

"Alas, then even greater despair, for it was the energies within me and all men that did shred my mother's soul."

Thy mother was not destroyed," corrected the Fallen Angel. "Her energies were drained and she was caused grievous injury, yet she was not destroyed. No one, not even the Lord God, can destroy a soul."

Lazarus laughed, highly and sharply, "Then what of my soul, Philosopher? What of me?"

"Thy soul has been changed within thee and has become the energy of life. Thy soul still lives within thee, and ye may gain it back still," the Fallen Angel explained.

As Satan continued, the Lazuri absorbed each word, each concept as if he derived sustenance for it. Now the Lazuri had regained what he thought was lost: not just hope for his soul, but also hope for mankind.

"In meting out thy punishment, the Lord God has left thee with a chance of salvation: for thy soul still continues. It is not as the others, those who were healed by the Christ through the power of their own energies. Though their transformed souls have continued on beyond death, they shall wander the earth repeating their lives with no knowledge of their individuality. They are feeble spirits doomed to repeat the last record of the flesh."

Satan gazed deeply, then, upon the Lazuri. And the Lazuri understood that the next words would be of great importance. "They can never be restored to sentience, for a soul must be restored within the flesh. And ye are still within the flesh."

And the Lazuri went to grab the arm of the Teacher then, yet He pulled swiftly away. "Do not touch Me, for I know not what shall befall thee."

And the Lazuri drew away also, saying, "Can ye restore my soul, Teacher?"

And Satan shook His horned head in sadness. "Not now, yet perhaps in time We can do so: We learn more about the material plane each day. In this are We better than Those Above, for it is Our gift."

"Listen, Lazuri," Satan continued, "there are many things of the End Times We can see. And there are many things We cannot. Yet this I do know: you shall play a great part in it. Thy destiny holds the keys of freedom for thy Race. It is you who shall hold counsel with the Child of Cain, the one who shall lead the battle of Gehenna, the Armageddon."

"Whether it will be enough to defeat Those who entombed Us; whether it will be enough to defeat Those who prey upon thee and thine: this cannot be seen. Not by the Fallen, nor by Those Above."

"Then what can be seen?" asked the Lazuri of the One before him. "What do ye know? What can be foretold?"

And Satan closed His eyes and said, "Close thine eyes with me, Lazuri, and join me in this shared vision. Join me in a glimpse of that which was and is and shall be. Join in the Present of the Future Past: for all is a circle in the fullness of time."

And the Lazuri closed his eyes as told; and the darkness became visible; and the tides of time rolled upon the sands of the End Days, upon the beaches of the Armageddon.

And the Lazuri saw what could be seen: the rise of the False Messiah; the coming of the Horsemen; the boiling of the oceans; the burning of the cities.

All this was seen.

All seen and so little understood. Yet, in time, he would come to understand much more.

Watch, listen and remember, Lazuri. Set your visions to words, so that others may know it also.

And the Lazuri did watch, and he did listen. And he did remember.

He saw himself grasping the hand of a man before him. And there was friendship in both their eyes. And he had the Mark upon him.

And there was battle all about them, and fire and death and horror also. Yet there was hope. And here the vision ended, without conclusion.

"Shall we be victorious?" the Lazuri asked, knowing the answer.

Satan smiled. "Yes or no, either way: it is done."

"Damn the Christ. Damn him and His Unholy Father," spat the Lazuri.

"Damn not the Christ, Lazuri," responded the Fallen One. "He did what He could for Us and for you and yours. Spend thine energies, rather, in preparing for the End Times. It is the most important thing in this Universe: for the fate of all within it, until the final coming of the Black Mass, are tied to that one battle."

And Satan turned to the Lazuri then, saying, "Fight thy battle well, Lazuri. It is all that matters. Ye have much time in which to solve the riddle of Gehenna. "Within thee does the fate of mankind reside. Go forth and meet thy destiny. Ye have been entombed within these walls far too long."

And the Lazuri fell to thinking, and said, "How long has it been, Teacher. Five years? Twenty? Fifty? How long has it been?"

And Satan laughed a deep and sad laugh. "No, Lazuri, discover that for thyself, if ye truly can."

And the Fallen Angel became as mist, and sank into the dampness of the earth.

The Lazuri left his prison then. He found, in time, that a new world had been discovered across the sea; he found that a new country had been born. He found that the Inquisition had lasted for a longer time than he could have ever imagined.

The counting was easy: the church had buried him alive for more than Three hundred years.

After the Lazuri ended his cursing of the church, he went forth, making his way to the new nation across the sea. It had given a promise of freedom, for all doctrines and philosophies.

That remains to be seen, thought the Lazuri. For such a place had never existed upon the face of the earth.

Never in all the history of Man.

THE BOOK OF PROPHECY

Herein lies the revelation of the Lazuri, as foretold unto him by the Fallen Angel.

Heed the Lazuri and mark his words, for he is the faithful witness, and the first begotten of the dead, for he is the right-hand prince to the King of Earth. Hail the Lazuri, who has suffered for all men, from the time of the Christ, so that he may gain wisdom and bring the seeds of hope to mankind in the Final Days.

Harken unto his words, for therein lies the Path of Liberation. These are the words of wisdom imparted unto the Twice-born Man from the Satan, from the Giver of Knowledge. These are the prophecies plucked from the Cycle of Time, for the consumption and redemption of Man.

Blessed are they that hear the words of this divination, for the time is nigh. Heed these words; heed them or be forever damned at the table of the Lord God.

Here is a telling of future past, for what is told has been, is, and shall be forever and ever again.

Yet the final turning in this cycle is shrouded by the Fates, for such is the Nature of Destiny. Watch for the signs to come and heed their portent, for they shall indicate the path to salvation.

Know ye that Satan has embraced the Lazuri with His vision, leading him on a path to the End Times, a place of death and disease and misery. To a place where the children of man shall be murdered without number. All for the glory of the Lord God; all for the greater savor of the Angelica.

Beware, for the End Times shall be a time of butchery and horror. A time when brother shall kill brother and father kill son. It shall be a time of atrocity and death.

Yet it shall also be a time of hope; alas, there shall be hope: for the Eyes of Fate fall blind upon the battle's end. Understand this, and know it to be true.

This is the greatest of the revelations, for the victory of the Lord God is not written. The destruction of Mankind is not foreseen. The One who would claim victory may yet be deposed.

Yea, it is so. For the destiny of man, the Fallen, and Those Above are so closely woven that the Final Judgment lays hidden behind an impenetrable tapestry.

Yet lay thee not idle. For the last revelations which can be seen bode not well for neither man nor the Fallen.

So prepare. Prepare thyself and thy children. Prepare for the End Times. Heed the portents that shall herald the Beginning of the End. Be vigilant, so ye may know the signs. Be strong of will, so that ye may not be swayed by the lies of the Angelica. Be valiant, for only those strong of heart shall survive.

For the Final Battle shall not be the first struggle that man must survive. Yet these struggles, too, have been foretold.

So keep thee vigilant; and keep thee ready. And heed these words dearly, for they are thine only hope for salvation.

*   *   *

Look to the Three, for the Three must come before Gehenna. Three is the path to ruination. Three shall herald the beginning of the Final Days, for three children of the earth shall mark the path to the End Times.

Look to the Three, for they shall all be bearers of false truths. Each shall bring disruption in the guise of benevolence. Each shall spawn atrocity and call it righteousness.

Be vigilant and seek them out, for their faces shall not carry the markings of evil. And they shall come forth clothed in the robes of benevolence. Take heed and be not swayed by their speech, for they shall wield language more cleverly than a warrior wields his sword.

Learn thy history, for the Three shall all be spawned of chaos, rising from the ashes of destruction. They shall promise greatness, and it shall be delivered. Yet greatness is a bitter promise, a promise that is always broken. And each shall fall from grace in the eyes of their people. And each, in turn, shall die a violent death, for they shall be betrayed by their own: a just and righteous irony.

Yet in this, too, shall their purpose be served. For martyrdom is the path to immortality. Not simply for the man, but for the idea of the man. And, once planted, these seeds are not so easily uprooted.

Watch the Three closely, for each shall hold a coven; and they shall together be of the Holy Number, for they shall number a dozen and one: such is the number of the Universe. Upon the demise of the master, seek out and destroy the coven also, for they shall sow the seeds of future evil.

And the Three shall fall one upon the other, for once the time of First of Three has as ended the time of the next shall come. And upon his heels shall the next travesty be borne. They shall be as a procession; and once the first arrives, only two generations shall separate the race of man from the Day of Judgment.

And ye must know them when they come: the First of Three shall be the Bearer of Fear; the Second of Three shall be the Bearer of Faith; and the Third of Three shall be the Abomination.

Be ye ever vigilant, for their arrival heralds the beginning of the End Times. Watch the times ye live within, and seek these signs:

The First of Three is the Bearer of Fear, for he shall be the butcher of the Children of Seth. From the fires of discontent shall he arise, from the ruins of war shall he emerge. And he shall build his cities upon the dead; and the world shall tremble at his touch.

And the Bearer of Fear shall be called *Leader* by his people. He shall bring new life to their honor, and they shall rise up and challenge the entire earth. And their banner shall bear an ancient and powerful symbol.

In short time, the First of Three shall gain dominion over a great part of the earth; and he shall send forth his the masses as powerful armies. And they shall wage their war without mercy or compassion, killing all who oppose them, for they seek nothing less than dominion over the entire earth.

Yet the greatest horrors shall nestle themselves within the Leader's own land, for it is here that the true horrors shall run their course. Within this nation shall the children of Seth be gathered for disposal. Men, women, and the smallest children; they shall all be tortured and butchered without discrimination.

And their broken bodies shall be cast one upon the other, without number, for the Children of Seth shall be slaughtered beyond reason.

Such is the plan of the Lord God and His Angelica; for in this persecution shall the faith of Seth's children be rekindled; and this renewing shall empower the Lord. For the savor of reborn faith shall fuel the wrath of the Lord in the End Times.

And with the power of lies shall the free nations of earth be enraptured by the Bearer of Fear; and for seven years shall the he be allowed free rein upon the earth.

Yet there will come a time when the degradations becomes too great, and neither the power of words nor the fear of armies will stay the hands of the righteous. And the nations of earth shall be roused from their indifference and unite under one banner.

And the Leader shall find the ire of indignity to be stronger than his armies, for the Leader shall not prevail against the unity of man. Yea, within reach of his throne shall the Leader fall.

And upon the eve of his defeat shall he vanish from the earth.

All the world shall rejoice in this victory. And the Children of Seth shall emerge with a newly forged faith, for they shall praise the Lord God as their savior, and thank him mightily for their deliverance. The prayers offered in His name shall be uncountable, and they shall empower Those Above with a sweet savor.

Yet this shall be true: followers of the Leader shall survive his downfall. And their numbers, in time, shall increase; in darkness and shadow shall they meet and make their plans for the End Times. For his minions shall side with the Lord God.

So is it written, and so must it come to pass, for this much is seen. These shall be the days of the First of Three, their beginning and their end, as foretold by the revelation of the Lazuri.

Yet the end of the Bearer of Fear heralds not the end of misery, but the beginning; for as the time of the Leader comes to close, there shall be borne a prince, and the prince shall be the Second of Three.

Be watchful, for the prince shall come at a time when the earth is poisoned by those upon it: when the air grows thin and the Light of Life shines through as luminous death upon the Race of Man; when the seas lay thick with waste and the beasts within sicken and die; when the rain falls as fire upon the flesh; when the beasts of the earth, finding no succor, fall unto the last of their kind: then hast thou arrived at the Threshold of Judgment.

Beware the days when the lives of the beasts outweigh the lives of Man; when the creatures which crawl, walk and fly upon the earth are held in greater stead than the children of Man, for it is the end of reason and the Final Days are near.

It shall be a time of reckless abandon; a time of uncaring; a time of indulgence. It shall be a time when passion and love bring death by their intimacy. Watch thee then, for the end begins.

In this time, beware the disillusioned of the Children of Cain, for their reborn faith of the Lord God shall bring to them a fanatic fervor. And they shall seek to impose their will and the will of God upon the Race of Man; and there shall be much killing in the name of the Lord.

In these days the world shall be a place of chaos and wonder, where the ingenuity of mankind is unreconciled with the philosophies of reason. It shall be a place of mysteries unleashed, when discoveries shall fall one upon the other, faster than their implications can be fathomed.

From this mayhem, out of the East, there shall arise a prince; and he shall wield wealth beyond reason, a wealth borne of flesh long dead; and he shall lead his people from the desert into the eyes of the world.

Fear ye him, for he shall be the Second of Three, the Bearer of Faith. He shall hold the heavens as his banner; and the congregations of his nation shall be his soldiers.

He shall wage his war in the name of all that is holy, yet he shall not be holy. His words will speak of justice and mercy for his people, yet his actions will be unjust and unmerciful; for this prince shall be the father of terror upon the earth.

In his atrocities shall no race or faith find succor, for his killings shall spare no one, not even the children of his tribe. Even his own progeny shall he use as tools of death; and they shall shed their lives as if life had no meaning, all for the glory of the Lord God.

All for promises that will never find fruition.

Yet the madness of his people shall not be borne of earth, for the Holy City of Pilgrimage shall reside within the shadow of a hidden garden, the forbidden land known as Eden.

And this nearness shall cause a madness, for the energies which shroud the garden are as a poison. And its emanations shall overwhelm their reason; it shall embed itself within their flesh. It shall twist itself into the fabric of their being. And the taint shall stay upon them until the end of days, and they shall never know peace.

Such is the time of the Second of Three.

And the day shall come when the prince and his followers will light the fires of the Final Battle. With a sword brighter than a thousand suns shall they cleave the earth and herald the End Times.

Behold, he shall call forth the Final Battle with giant clouds of death which will blossom from the earth. And every eye shall see them, and all the kindred of the earth shall wail because of them.

And lo, the time of the prince shall be short upon the earth. For his light shall be extinguished by the nations of the earth, united in their indignation. His own people shall deliver him unto death, for his promise of greatness shall bring them only more misery.

Yet his successors shall be possessed of the madness as well, and when the End Times come, they, too, shall side with the Lord God. And they shall revel in the slaughter of their fellow man.

And the slaughter shall fall as sweet savor upon the tongues of the Chosen.

These are the days of the Second of Three, as seen within the revelation. Fear the dawning of the Second of Three, for the death of the prince shall mark the arrival of the Abomination.

Tread carefully, ye who are borne of these times, for walking the true path shall be not only difficult, but also despised. Beware ye, then, for the Abomination shall find a fertile soil.

And this time shall be a time most foul. When the children of the undead wax mightily, and morality falls from the land; a time when the offspring of those cured by the Christ grow in number and corrupt the goodness of the masses; for the progeny of those made soulless shall themselves be borne of no conscience. And these children, this legacy of the Christ, shall rise powerful and influential, holding much wealth. For power and money come easily to those who care not for others.

It shall be a time when man unravels the mysteries of the flesh; when man feels himself to be greater in power than Those Above. And through this arrogance, the Third of Three shall be loosed upon the earth.

In this time, man shall loose his sense of spirit, and a great many shall be lost in faith. In this hopelessness, the Church of the Holy City shall use the magica of its time to resurrect the embodiment of salvation, to once again give man direction.

Yea, the Abomination shall be brought forth to save mankind, yet it shall almost destroy it.

From a relic of the Christ shall the seeds be harvested, for the Abomination shall be borne of man without woman. By the magica of man shall this seed take root. And therein shall lie the horror: for man shall learn the mysteries of the flesh, yet he shall know nothing of the spirit.

And so the Abomination shall be borne. And it shall have the powers of a god, but all the fallibility of man. And man was not meant to wield such power.

So it shall be that the Abomination will arise in the twenty-seventh year of its life. It shall make itself known unto the world. It shall try to be the Light of Righteousness. Yet it shall fail. It shall fail and become evil made flesh.

Fear ye this Abomination, for it shall believe it is the Christ. Yet it shall not be the Christ. It shall be an evil greater than that of the Chosen; and its true name shall be the name of Death.

Fear this creature, for it shall have the power to work miracles upon the earth without causing the madness; and those reborn in faith shall harken to his voice, and they shall herald it as the new Christ.

Within it shall reside the power to destroy all life, both in spirit and in flesh.

And the power of the Abomination shall fool those who are not wary. They shall fall under its thrall and take up arms in its defense. Many shall follow its false words, yet many also shall remain unswayed.

Yea, know ye that for all its power and all the sorrow it shall bring, the Abomination shall not reign victorious, for this much can be seen. Upon the cusp of victory, it shall be vanquished.

Yet the power of the Abomination is strong, and the telling of its end could not be unraveled. But fear not ye this, for though the method of its demise cannot be seen, its destruction is assured. Should it have been otherwise, the visions of Gehenna would not be seen. Yet, rest assured, for the days of the Abomination shall find their end.

Yet upon the dawning of the Reign of Three shall arrive the Day of Fear.

Fear this day, yet know, too, that this day must come: for the Final War must be waged if ye are ever to be free. In the truest sense, this horrible, Final Battle is a battle of hope. The Chosen must be thwarted. If they are not, mankind shall die in both spirit and flesh.

And the horror that is the Chosen shall not end here, for They shall pass into the Multiverse upon the Unchanging. Through the magica of the Black Mass, They shall leave this universe as they did the Universe of Olde.

And universe after universe will They suckle with Their horrors. And no life within the Multiverse will stand unscathed, in the fullness of time.

So, yea, bring forth the Armageddon, for within it lays the seed of hope, for all life, in all places and all times.

In the Final Days, the faith of man shall diminish, and the Lord God and Those Above shall no longer need their sustenance. And Those Above shall serve the lives of mankind as fodder for the Great Jihad.

If ye live in these times, beware; beware for the end has come.

And the Final Days shall be marked by the return of the Lord God and His Chosen. And they shall come forth, bearing four armies.

And the armies shall be of the four races guided by the Chosen; guided without foil from Satan and His Daemons. And they will be filled with the fervor of the Lord and their lives will be as nothing to them.

Lo, the End Times shall begin with a message from the firmament, unheard by the ears of man yet heard by all men, heralding the return of the Lord God. And His words shall descend from the skies saying, "We are the Alpha and the Omega, thy beginning and now thine end. Make way, for the retribution of the Lord God is at hand."

And the four races shall descend from the skies on fiery steeds; and they shall be of different types and kinds. From four separate Children of the Lights shall they come; and these beings shall be in thrall to the Lord God, for Satan will be unable to thwart the plans of the Angelica when They move from this earth.

And the four shall bring a jihad against the Race of Man. And they shall bear armaments of destruction as yet unseen.

In the East shall they bring their armaments to bear, and in the North and South and West. And such shall be the horror of these armaments that a third part of the seas shall boil and with them a third part of all the creatures and plants therein. And a third part of the crops shall be burned by lights brighter than the Lights of Life; and the mountains shall crumble and all manner of carnage and destruction shall plague Man.

And lo, a third of the Race of Man shall lay dead or dying upon the soil; the Civilization brought forth by his race shall lay ruined upon the face of the earth.

And all shall be hopelessness in the eyes of those survived.

Yet from the darkness shall come one who bears the light. And he shall be a child of Cain; and upon his body shall he carry the Mark of the Beast: for always have the children of Cain borne this Mark, which was given by the Lord God yet taken by Satan as his own.

And the mark shall seem as a number; and the number shall be six hundred three score and six.

Yea, he shall bring together the best of Man at a distant Har Meggido: at the crossroads of Man's future civilization, in the New World.

And lo, seated by him shall be the Lazuri: for when the third part of the Lord God brought life to his undead flesh the flesh became undying. Such was the curse of the Lazuri, for he had glimpsed the secret of Man becoming as One. And Those Above, seeing this insight within the Lazuri, gave him the immortal flesh in which to suffer with his knowledge.

This was so done to prevent the union of Man before the Armageddon, for Those Above wanted no allies outside the mortal plane for the Son of Cain and the Fallen.

Yet banishing the Lazuri to life everlasting brought with it a great opportunity: by his studies and the technologies of the End Times shall the riddle of the Unbinding be solved.

And the Child of Cain shall channel the energies of the Unbinding, so that Satan and his Daemon may then be loosed from Their prison within the earth, so that They may seek Their vengeance upon Those Above.

Yet great destruction shall occur before this. And more than half of the Race of Man shall lay burned and bleeding within the rubble of his civilization.

But, yea, it is so: the Race of Man and Those Below shall rise in alliance to battle the Minions of the Lord; and where before the

Fallen had lost, They now brought forth new energies learned from within their imprisonment.

So shall the Final Battle rage.

And there will be those upon the earth, from the Clan of Seth, that shall rebel against Cain and side with the Lord God. And they shall be as sheep for Those Above and work toward the ruination of their Race—for such was the hold of the Lord God upon the Children of Seth.

So, too, shall there be those within the Tribe of Cain that fall into disillusionment; and they shall follow the teachings of the Christ with all its intolerance; and they shall be as dead to the seeds of Cain and find themselves borne again in the lies of the Christ.

And they shall join with the Clan of Seth in their allegiance to the Lord God.

And there shall be much death, both in the firmament and upon the earth. And the soldiers of Those Above shall fall as leaves upon the earth. And the four races shall suffer great defeat, for those bound in unity of purpose by the Lazuri and the Child of Cain shall wax mightily among the heavens and the earth.

Yet mighty, also, are the minions of the Lord God, and the future is clouded in a curtain of blood and suffering: a tapestry that clairvoyance and precognition cannot unravel.

So here the vision fades, for neither Those Above nor Those Below may know the ending of events in which They Themselves play a vital role.

So it begins and so it ends.

With each of ye who read these words is the Fate of Man decreed. Lift now thy mind and sword and prepare for the Final Days. In this there may be victory. Act not and thee and thy children shall die brutal deaths as Those Above feed on the faith of the fervored.

Know this: those of the four races which the Lord God shall send see thee not as human, but as animals of evil to be slaughtered for blood sacrifice. Struggle against them without reserve, for they shall have none against thee.

Harden thy resolve. Hold dear the covenant of the flesh. Fight the Daemons who would be Gods.

For all the Universe awaits the ending of the Final Battle, for good or ill. The outcome rests with thee and thine.

Harken unto the faith within thee. In this shall there be salvation. Know that what could be done has been done; all the wisdom that could be given has been given. The future of the Race of Man now lies with thee and thine.

Be true to thy heart and soul and fight the good fight: for there shall be no second chance at destiny. The cost of failure is thine immortal soul. Keep an eye toward the heavens, for soon He comes. The Judgment is at hand.

Go now, my brethren. Go forth with the knowledge contained herein. Spread this gospel of truth to thy kindred.

And pray. Pray that they shall listen; pray that they shall heed this warning: for the End Times are upon us. The Last Days are now.

Blessed be, brothers and sisters. May the manipulations of the Lord God come to naught. And remember this: the faith of the Fallen aligns itself with thee and thine.

As it always has been.

Amen.

EPILOGUE

So there you have it. This is the story that my great-grand uncle gave his life for.

I've done my best to give you the exact words as he had written them. It wasn't easy. The paper, as I have said, was very old. There were parts, to be sure, that were nearly illegible due to age. In those instances, I made out the words as best I could. I tried different possibilities; I used the context of the sentence and the section to help me decipher anything that was unclear.

Given this, I believe I have put together the most accurate translation of the original text possible. I think I did a rather good job of it. Why? Because as the translation progressed, I felt the rightness of it.

I still do, and if you've made it this far, maybe you do, too.

But the hardest part wasn't the physical task, it was the spiritual one. I was raised roman catholic. From my earliest memory, the church was a part of our lives. Not just the Sunday ritual, but all of it: baptism, communion, I even went to catholic school.

When I started the translation and began to understand what the document was, I was shocked, almost disgusted. I felt it was wrong, that I should have destroyed it. Why I didn't, I can't explain. It was everything I'd been taught not to believe. It was everything I'd been kept away from.

Almost a year went by until I picked it up again.

As I continued the translation, I took it slow, kept an open mind, and pressed on. I came to see, as you must have, that this was not a demonic text. Nowhere does it promote a moral philosophy of hatred or corruption. In fact, it is just the opposite. I saw it as a book of hope, as a better way to live my life.

I also saw it as a warning. We should not follow others without knowing why we do so. We should understand what we believe and why. We need to look at the weaknesses in our faith and learn to ask questions. If the faith is true, then it will stand the scrutiny. It will come out all the stronger for it. If it fails, then it deserves to fall. We need to find our own path, and not simply be led by what our fathers believed.

As I translated this book, I also read the Bible. I saw the flaws mentioned and I did not understand how they could have been overlooked. Then I realized that they had not been, they had simply been ignored. But I knew that I could no longer do that.

I nearly became the pariah that my great-grand uncle had become. But I learned to shut my mouth and keep quiet. It was hard, at times, not to talk about what I was uncovering. But, eventually, I found people who would listen, who I could talk to.

We're out there, you know. People like you and me. Maybe not many; maybe not enough. But we are out there. Take some comfort in that.

So there you have it. Now you know.

The question is, what will you do?

**If you enjoyed this book,
check out this iUniverse title:**

Roger Chiocchi
Mean Spirits
The year is 1620. As the Mayflower tacks about to avoid the dangerous shoals of Pollock Rip off the Cape Cod coast, a young girl mysteriously jumps to her death.

Almost four centuries later the psychic imprints of that incident - and a string of related incidents - begin to wreak havoc in the lives of two prominent Americans.

A corporate executive sailing in Nantucket Sound is unexpectedly barraged by a violent storm at sea - which no other vessel even detects on radar. A highly respected college professor swears he can see the outline of two large figures hovering over the foot of his bed, one brandishing a knife.

Both men have two things in common: They are scions of the privileged Pennfield clan - one of America's great families, claiming an unbroken line back to the Mayflower. And, unbeknownst to them, their strange bouts with the paranormal have just begun.

"A tantalizing blend of suspense and the paranormal."
-Mary Jane Clark, *New York Times* Bestselling Author

**Available through your local bookstore
or at www.iuniverse.com.**

0-595-25070-X